Seducing
ABBY RHODES

ALSO BY J. D. MASON

And on the Eighth Day She Rested
One Day I Saw a Black King
Don't Want No Sugar
This Fire Down in My Soul
You Gotta Sin to Get Saved
That Devil's No Friend of Mine
Take Your Pleasure Where You Find It
Somebody Pick Up My Pieces
Beautiful, Dirty, Rich
Drop Dead, Gorgeous
Crazy, Sexy, Revenge
The Real Mrs. Price

SEDUCING
ABBY RHODES

J. D. MASON

St. Martin's Griffin
New York

SEDUCING ABBY RHODES. Copyright © 2017 by J. D. Mason. All rights reserved. Printed in the United States of America. For information, address St. Martin's Press, 175 Fifth Avenue, New York, N.Y. 10010.

www.stmartins.com

Designed by Steven Seighman

Library of Congress Cataloging-in-Publication Data

Names: Mason, J. D., author.
Title: Seducing Abby Rhodes / J. D. Mason.
Description: First edition. | New York : St. Martin's Griffin, 2017.
Identifiers: LCCN 2017010840| ISBN 9781250052261 (trade paperback) |
    ISBN 9781466853768 (ebook)
Subjects: LCSH: Triangles (Interpersonal relations)—Fiction. | African
    American women—Fiction. | BISAC: FICTION / African American /
    Contemporary Women. | FICTION / Contemporary Women. | GSAFD:
    Romantic suspense fiction.
Classification: LCC PS3613.A817 S43 2017 | DDC 813/.6—dc23
LC record available at https://lccn.loc.gov/2017010840

Our books may be purchased in bulk for promotional, educational, or business use. Please contact your local bookseller or the Macmillan Corporate and Premium Sales Department at 1-800-221-7945, extension 5442, or by email at MacmillanSpecialMarkets@macmillan.com.

First Edition: July 2017

10 9 8 7 6 5 4 3 2 1

To Ida and Julian,
finally

Acknowledgments

When writing stories, sometimes as you go along, you believe that you have it all figured out. You think you know how characters are going to be, how they're going to behave, and live. In some cases you may even know how the story's going to end. I believed that one character was gone from my life for forever, but I should've known better because I fell in love with him. It's funny because he and I have had a roller-coaster relationship that has often left me angry and in tears, but just when I thought I'd washed my hands of him for good, he comes back and does or says something to win me over again. He's been emotionally abusive to me for years, but I stay because he's in my heart and soul.

Thank you, Jordan Gatewood, for being the person you are, even when you were at your worst. And thank you, Abby Rhodes, for being magical.

I've been obsessed with these two for nearly two years and I'm not sure that's a good thing. I'm hoping that readers will be pulled in to their relationship the way that I have been and that they'll never want to see it end. Personally, I'm really not all that romantic.

Never have been and I never thought I wanted to be until I realized that, like most women, I get butterflies in my stomach when reading stories with romantic encounters, hoping that everything will work out despite the pitfalls and setbacks. I have had that hope for these two from the moment that I knew they had a story to tell, but watching their relationship unfold as I wrote it, I realized that there is never a guarantee that love can conquer all, no matter how much you hope that it can. Things don't always turn out the way you want them to. That's a hard lesson. One that makes life interesting.

Thank you to those readers who have been on this journey with me for so many years. When I first started writing, I believed that over time the job would get easier. The truth is that it's harder to write now more than ever, but I wouldn't have it any other way. I still get nervous before every release wondering if people are going to like my story, which isn't always the case, but so many of you have stayed on this train with me and for that, I am so very appreciative. Reading, like writing, is a labor of love, and as far as I'm concerned, we're all in this together. It's lovely being reminded of that.

As always, much gratitude goes out to my editor, Monique Patterson, her assistant, Alexandra Sehulster, my publisher, Macmillan, and my agent, Sara Camilli. I'm still here because of all of you, and I thank you so much for all your support and encouragement.

To my family, thank you for your patience. It's been a busy couple of writing years and I couldn't have done it without you all leaving me alone, ignoring me, letting me ignore you, and not going off on me when I was irritable, overworked, and overwrought. And most important, for still wanting to be around me when I finally popped my head up from my Hobbit hole to rejoin the living.

Blink, Texas

Trouble Me

"FIRST OF ALL, I'm not a medium, Abby," Marlowe Brown said, walking up the steps to the house before she'd even said hello.

"You're not, but you've got a good sense about things like this."

Marlowe showed up today wearing at least a thousand golden braids that hung down to her waist, looking every bit the regal goddess that she was.

"Second of all," she said, stopping in front of Abby on the porch. "You already know it's haunted. You don't need me to tell you that."

"I need you to tell me how haunted," Abby countered. In the few days since she'd closed on the place, she'd felt weird in this house and had heard what sounded like whispers and floors creaking. Shadows moved in her peripheral vision, but she'd never seen any definitive evidence that there were ghosts here. Like everyone else, she'd heard the rumors, so her imagination could very well have been working overtime, making her think that the house was more haunted than it actually was.

"I need to know if it's a little haunted or majorly haunted and if the spirits here are dangerous. You know. Evil. Did I make a mistake buying this house?"

Abby wasn't a huge fan of sharing her home with ghosts, but this house was an investment, a flip that she hoped to renovate and turn around in a few months. She'd paid a good amount of money for it, so ghosts or no ghosts, Abby had to see this through to the end.

"I tried burning sage like you told me," Abby said, following Marlowe inside. "I don't think it worked, though. How would I know if it did?"

Marlowe stopped after taking three steps inside, turned in a slow circle, and had a strange look on her face that set off a silent alarm in Abby.

"What?" Abby probed cautiously. "What is it?"

Marlowe might claim that she wasn't psychic, but she was definitely sensitive to things that scared the shit out of everybody else.

"There are definitely spirits in this house," she said, intensely studying the room.

Goose bumps erupted on Abby's arms. "I knew it," she murmured fearfully.

Yeah, she was scared, but she was also out a hell of a lot of money on this place. So, Abby willed her fear aside and grabbed hold of her practicality. "But are they good or bad, Marlowe?"

Marlowe held up a hand. "Give me a minute," she snapped. "Discerning spirits ain't easy, Abby."

She took another couple of steps inside the living room, stopped again, and stared down at a particular spot on the floor.

Abby came over, stood beside her, and stared at the floor, too. "Do you see something?" she asked.

Marlowe shook her head. "I feel something," she said introspectively. "Pain. Sadness. Anger." Marlowe finally looked at Abby. "Love? Yes," she quickly added. "Regret?"

Abby shrugged as if Marlowe had asked her a question. "I don't know."

Marlowe nodded. "Yes. It's all of that. Passionate and desperate. Dangerous."

That revelation sent a shiver up Abby's spine, and her imagination started to run off into all kinds of directions. Rumor had it that some man had been murdered in this house by the daughter of his lover. But then other people said that his wife had shot him and blamed the other woman or her daughter or something like that.

"There's a pattern, Abby," Marlowe stated, concerned, making her way down the narrow hallway leading to the main bedroom at the end of it. She stopped along the way and looked into the only bathroom in the house and then into the other bedroom. "Something keeps repeating," she continued. "Happening over and over again."

"Like what?" Abby probed.

Marlowe shook her head in frustration. "I can't . . . I don't know. But something ain't finished here."

"What ain't finished?" Abby whispered in awe. "Maybe if I know what it is, I can help to finish it."

Now she really was starting to get scared. These dangerous and passionate spirits were living in her house. She'd seen enough horror movies to wonder if there were bodies, actual bodies, hidden in this place, maybe under the floors, or even in the walls. What the hell had she gotten herself into?

Marlowe walked into the main bedroom. An old, dirty mattress lay on the floor, left behind from the most recent residents. In all the years the house had been vacant, people had come and gone, some in the middle of the night, in such a hurry to get out of this place that they didn't even bother taking their belongings. Graffiti dirtied the walls. There were strange stains on the carpet that could've been anything. Holes had been punched through the drywall. Windows had been broken.

"Why the hell did you buy this place, Abby?" Marlowe asked, incredulous.

"It's an investment," Abby said, almost too terrified to speak but feeling like a fool as soon as she said it.

Marlowe tilted her head to one side as if she didn't believe Abby's explanation. That accusatory look of hers pressed down heavily on Abby.

"I liked the house," she reluctantly admitted as if she were ashamed to say it out loud. "I don't know. It's a nice lot, and the house is quaint." It was extremely small and quaint, swallowed up by the massive yard it sat on. "I don't know, Marlowe. I just felt drawn to it. I have for a long time."

Hearing herself say that out loud, Abby began to wonder if somehow the ghosts in this house had tricked her into buying it.

Marlowe studied Abby for a good, long time, so long that it made Abby even more nervous.

"You're welcome here," Marlowe finally said with a sigh. "No one else has been welcome here before you, so consider yourself fortunate."

Abby's eyes darted around the room. "So, they like me?"

Marlowe nodded. "I think they do."

"Well, at least that's something," Abby said, relieved.

"I sense male and female energy. But mostly male."

"But not evil?"

Marlowe shook her head. "No, I don't think so," she murmured. "Frustration. Angst. Desperation. I think all these things are coming mostly from him. But it could be her, too."

Abby thought about it. "So, they're trapped?"

Trapped ghosts. That couldn't be good.

"They want something, Abby. They need it. They're desperate for it—something or someone."

Again, their eyes locked onto each other.

"Me?" Abby raised a pensive hand to her chest.

Marlowe took a deep breath. "I can't be sure. It might not be a person at all. All I know about you is that they don't mind you being here. They want you here."

Marlowe walked past Abby and went back to the living room. "They both died here, but not together. I think it must be her sadness that I'm feeling and it's his rage. He's the angry one," she said, sounding more definitive in her assumption.

"Did she kill him?"

"I can't tell if she did or not. But the love is powerful. It's thick and almost oppressive."

"His or hers?"

"His, I think. Like he wasn't ready to let go. To let her go."

Passionate, angry lovers, trapped in her house, waiting on something—maybe Abby—maybe not.

"So, do you think they'd be all right with me renovating the place?"

Again, Abby had to be practical with all this, supernatural or not. After all, that's why she'd bought it, and the sooner she could get busy working on it, the sooner she could be done and leave these ghosts to do whatever ghosts did. Abby had considered keeping the house and eventually moving in, but the thought of sharing this place with angry, passionate, sad, and obsessive ghost lovers was just not sitting well with her right now. Not that it would be fair to sell a haunted house to somebody else, either. But if she fixed it up, made the place nice again, maybe the ghosts would decide to leave or at least not scare people. It was just a theory on her part. One that she hoped could end up being true.

"I don't think they'd mind," Marlowe said with uncertainty. "I mean, if they like you, then I don't see why not. Maybe you could come in and knock down a few walls and then see what happens." She shrugged.

Abby nodded. That sounded reasonable. She'd start with something small like widening the passageway between the living room and main hall.

"But they want something," Marlowe continued.

"You can't tell what that is, though."

Marlowe thought long and hard before finally responding. "If I had to guess, I'd say that maybe they're still here because their story didn't end the way it was meant to, the way they wanted it to. That's how it is sometimes for ghosts. Spirits linger because their lives were cut short before they were ready."

Okay, so having Marlowe come here was helpful to a point. At least Abby knew that she wasn't crazy and that the house was haunted, but the ghosts liked her. Hopefully, they liked her enough to let her open up the space, maybe add a bay window, and put in some new flooring.

Neither of them heard the car pull up in front of the house. They didn't even realize that someone else was in the yard at first.

"Fine." Abby sighed. "So, I guess this is good and that maybe I didn't waste my money after all. I might even be able to turn a profit on this place if I . . ."

"Oh, my damn goodness," Marlowe muttered under her breath, staring at the screen door.

"What?" Abby asked, turning to see what Marlowe was looking at, or in this case, who. He was a god! Tall, swaggering, handsome. "Who's that?" Abby asked, mesmerized. Her heart pounded like a drum beating in her chest.

"I have no idea—but the spirits in this house just exhaled, Abby."

Some Kind of Madness

---

*"EVERYBODY'S ALWAYS GOT A gotdamn opinion about me
and what I do. I don't give a damn about their opinions. I make
my life. I live it how I want. I do what I want to do."*

Jordan walked up to that small, beige brick bungalow, hearing
echoes of his father's voice and half expecting to see Julian Gatewood coming out of that front door to the porch, greeting Jordan
with that proud and defiant expression of his. Growing up, Jordan
had both admired it and loathed it, but somehow, he knew that
he'd inherited it. He and Julian had never been close, but the old
man had always had a profound effect on Jordan whether he had
intended to or not and whether Jordan wanted him to or not. Julian had died nearly thirty years ago, and Jordan had always
thought that his father's influence, the impact he'd made in Jordan's life, had died with him. Lately, that didn't seem to be the
case. Something felt unresolved between them.

He'd been on his way to his ranch located just outside of Fort

Worth, but instead of taking the exit to get to it, for some un-known reason, Jordan kept driving until he ended up here. In all the years since his father had been killed here, Jordan never once set foot in this house. He'd never even seen it in person. But lately, he'd been staring at it online. It had been on the market for months, maybe longer. Jordan's fascination with the place didn't start until after he was released from the hospital. His renewed interest in his father's death didn't start until then either, when it struck him how the shootings practically mirrored each other. Two women arguing, one man, and a bullet—or in his case, two.

The Julian Gatewood that Jordan had grown up with would never come to a place like this. This town, this house were insig-nificant for his father, and Julian never bothered with small things. The only version of him that Jordan had ever known was the version he'd grown up with in that Dallas mansion. There was another as-pect of his father, one that he kept separate from his family and had stored away in this house. Without understanding why, Jordan was curious as to what would compel his father to spend so much time here away from that grand life he'd built for himself in Dallas. Could the reason have been as simple as a woman? Jordan shook his head slightly at the thought. He'd seen Ida Green, the woman his father had been having the affair with before his death. This was her house. And she had been as insignificant as her property.

A car and a pickup truck were parked in the narrow driveway. Near the sidewalk was a "For Sale" sign, planted in the ground. The front door was open, and Jordan heard voices coming from inside. Just as he started to make his way up the stairs to the porch, a woman pushed open the screen door and stepped outside.

"May I help you?" she asked in an exaggerated Texas drawl, wrapping her mesmerizing lips around every syllable in dramatic fashion.

The two of them stared at each other. He'd never seen this woman before in his life, but for some reason, he couldn't take his eyes off hers. Had he walked past her on the street, he probably wouldn't have noticed her, and it would've been his loss. Pretty, dark skin. Exaggerated, dramatic, up-slanting eyes. Heart-shaped face. Those lips. Jesus! She wore loose-fitted jeans, low and beltless on her hips. Tiny waist. She was petite and, in her own way, curvy and flawless. Loose, natural curls framed her face, and a fitted white tank top filled with perfect breasts that dreams were made of.

He quickly attempted to compose himself.

"Are you lost?" she asked, interrupting his train of thought that had been uncharacteristically derailed.

"I saw the sign," he said, quickly glancing at it. "I'd like to take a look at the property."

There was something about that nervous look in her eyes, the shifting she did from one foot to the other—she was putting out a vibe, compelling and telling, without realizing it. She wanted him gone, which most certainly made him all the more curious about her and this place. Jordan had always relied heavily on his intuition when it came to people, and right now, he was able to read her like a book.

"I'm the owner," she volunteered. "Closed on the place yesterday, Mr. . . . . ?"

"Tunson," he said without hesitation, but unexpectedly. "Jordan Tunson."

It felt right to use that last name, and it wasn't a complete lie. Gatewood had adopted Jordan when he was two. Tunson was his birth name. If she knew the history of this house, then the name *Gatewood* would certainly draw more attention to him than he was interested in having at the moment.

She looked as if she were going to ask him to leave, and leaving was the last thing he wanted to do.

"I've been driving for more than two hours, all the way from Dallas," he said quickly. "If nothing else, I'd just like to look around."

He wasn't asking, because Jordan wasn't accustomed to asking for permission to do anything, but it was as close as he could bring himself to begging.

Another woman appeared at the door. She was lovely, too. Taller, full figured, lighter skin, with breathtaking light brown eyes and long hair. The woman outside glanced uneasily over her shoulder at her friend, who ignored her in silent protest. "Might as well come on in," the one inside the door said, smiling at him.

Jordan trailed behind the darker woman as she followed her friend inside. As soon as he stepped into the living room, a wave of nausea hit him like a fist to the gut. Jordan resisted the urge to show how uncomfortable he actually was. He swallowed. How in the world could a larger-than-life man like Julian Gatewood ever fit inside a place so small? Jordan was six three, and if he'd been a few inches taller, his head would've scraped the ceiling. The whole house had a claustrophobic feel, stifling and dark. The entire living room wasn't much bigger than the shower in his penthouse.

He turned in a slow circle, examining dated wallpaper, broken windows, stained carpet, and yellowed, peeling linoleum floors in the kitchen just off to the side. Jordan stopped when he faced the woman who'd met him outside and again caught her gaze and held it for a few moments before she managed to peel hers away from him.

"It's not much to look at now," the woman with the braids

offered. "But Abby here could build a house from the ground up with a nail file and some rubber bands." She laughed.

Abby. The other woman's name was Abby. And she built houses. Interesting.

He continued surveying the space, recalling an old memory that he'd forgotten he'd had of a photo, a crime scene photo he'd seen of Julian lying facedown on brown carpet. Jordan focused to get his bearings until he'd pinpointed the location on the living room floor where Julian's body lay. Jordan stared at it, realizing that in that spot where his father lay dying was precisely the moment when the baton of their lives exchanged hands between Julian and Jordan. He looked up at the narrow hallway leading to the rest of the house. Floors creaked with every step he took down the narrow corridor, and he stopped briefly at what was probably a bedroom. Across from that was a bathroom. Jordan walked the rest of the way to the end of the hallway and pushed open the door.

"Did you close that door?" he heard one of the women whisper.

"No. I thought you did."

This room was slightly larger than the other one that he'd just passed down the hall. Instinctively, he knew that Julian had slept in this room with Ida. Jordan doubted that it could fit anything bigger than a full-size bed in here, which again left him wondering how his father could've been remotely comfortable in this house. Jordan was just about to turn away when a piercing and dizzying pain shot through his temple.

Don't. A woman's voice. He glanced back at the two women, standing there, staring at him. *Stop.* A woman was speaking. At least he thought . . .

Jordan faced the bedroom again.

The hairs on his forearms stood up. Jordan didn't understand. He didn't like this feeling. Jordan looked down the hallway at the two women huddled together, talking to each other, and for a moment, he felt a sense of familiarity, like he'd been here before or he'd seen this before. A foreboding feeling washed over him. All of a sudden, he felt uncomfortable being here, and it was time for him to leave.

You Will See

"WHY IN THE WORLD DID you invite him inside?" Abby whispered to Marlowe as that Tunson guy walked through her house.

"Better to face your destiny than run from it," Marlowe said, sounding crazy.

"What?"

"He's beautiful, isn't he?" Marlowe gazed admiringly at him.

There was no word for what he was. He towered at least a foot over Abby, who stood five two.

"Yeah, well . . . beautiful or not, I think he's possessed by one of these ghosts." Abby folded her arms across her chest and shuddered as he stopped at the smaller of the two bedrooms and stared into it.

"Why would you think that?" Marlowe asked.

"Shouldn't you be the one telling me that?" Abby shot back indignantly. "You're the psychic."

"The spirits here are all kinds of happy, Abby." Marlowe's eyes lit up like it was Christmas morning.

"Why?" Abby whispered back.

Marlowe shrugged. "Don't know, but he's welcome here, too. Maybe even more than you are."

Abby thought about that for a minute, watching him stop and study the other two rooms. She doubted seriously that he'd wanted to buy this place. It just didn't seem like someone like him would be interested in a house like this, unless he was a flipper, which could've been the case, but he didn't look like the type.

Physically, there was absolutely nothing wrong with the man. He was the inspiration behind the words *tall*, *dark*, and *handsome*. He was a lot lighter than Abby, but he was a brooding kind of handsome, like if you told him that he was good looking, he'd probably just look at you like he already knew that. His shoulders were so wide that he had to turn sort of sideways to walk down the hall to keep them from rubbing up against the walls. She didn't like the way he looked at her, though. His eyes were so dark that they looked black, and piercing, too piercing. He stared too hard at her, like he was looking for something.

If these ghosts liked him better than her, then Abby needed to consider her options. She leaned in close to Marlowe. "Maybe I should see if he wants to buy it from me," she suggested.

Marlowe immediately shook her head. "Not going to help."

"What do you mean by that?" Abby was starting to panic.

"I don't even know," was all Marlowe would say about it.

Abby had been feeling sick to her stomach ever since he'd walked into the place. Then all of a sudden, her head started pounding as soon as he turned around and looked at her.

"He needs to go," she muttered to Marlowe.

"You gonna tell him?" Marlowe asked, smirking.

Abby rolled her eyes and shook her head. Why'd he have to look like that? And why'd she have to like looking at him so much that it embarrassed the hell out of her? It had to have been those ghosts. Marlowe had said that there was male and female energy in this house, and since Abby and Jordan Tunson were welcome, she could only surmise that somehow those ghosts were using both of them to maybe manifest themselves. That had to be it.

He sauntered, not walked, but sauntered back down the hall toward them. Every smooth step he took mesmerized Abby. Her knees weakened and palms started sweating. When he stopped and stared at her again, she licked her lips, but didn't realize that she was doing it until it was too late, and she caught the expression of amusement on his face. Abby looked away.

"Thank you for indulging me," he said graciously, more at her than at Marlowe, even though Marlowe had been the one who'd invited him inside.

Who talked like that? He was big city all over.

Abby cleared her throat, shifted her weight from one foot to the other, and nodded. "Sure," she forced herself to say. "No problem."

This house was too damn small, forcing him to stand too close. She could feel him, smell him, and he smelled so good.

He just stood there. *Leave already!* she wanted to tell him. "In case you're interested, there's an old farmhouse for sale off Paris Road," she offered for some asinine reason, daring to make eye contact. "It's, um, been on the market for a while. Got about twenty acres. Needs work, though. More than this."

"Thank you," he said. "I'll have to consider taking a look at it."

His voice was deep, resonating, seeping through her pores down to the nuclei of her blood cells. She hadn't even noticed the beard before. How'd she miss that? It was cut close, but it was a beard all right, framing some nice lips, hugging a strong, square jaw. How'd she miss all that? And he looked expensive. Casual, but like he'd never set foot inside of Target.

Abby looked around expecting to see Marlowe and to have her say something to rescue Abby from this awkward experience, only to find that the woman was standing outside on the porch. Abby rushed out to her.

"What are you doing?" she whispered. "Why'd you leave?"

Of course, he was right on her heels. "Thank you again, ladies."

Abby stepped aside to let him pass.

"It was no problem," Marlowe offered, nudging Abby in the arm with her elbow. "Was it, Abby?"

"Not at all," she awkwardly responded, "and you're welcome."

"Have a good afternoon," he said, finally leaving.

Abby took a much-needed deep breath as she and Marlowe watched him climb his big, handsome self into that old pickup truck, start the engine, and finally drive away.

"What was that?" Abby hastily asked, turning to Marlowe. "What just happened?"

"How should I know?" Marlowe said, frowning.

"You're the psychic."

"How many times do I have to tell you that's not what I am, Abby?" Marlowe argued.

"You said that this house exhaled when he came here. What'd you mean by that?"

"I said the spirits in this house exhaled. It seemed like they felt at ease when he walked in."

"Why'd he make them feel like that?" Abby was nearly hysterical.

"Look, it was a feeling, Abby. I can't explain it any other way."

"Did you feel what I felt?"

"What'd you feel?"

Abby froze. How could she put into words what she felt when she didn't even know?

Marlowe must've seen the confusion on Abby's face. "What do you *think* you felt?"

She searched inside herself for answers. "Weird." It was the first word to come to mind.

Marlowe waited. "In a bad way?"

Abby nodded, and then she shrugged. "I guess. I didn't like the way he looked at me," she hurriedly added.

"And how'd he look at you?"

She thought for a moment. "Hard. Too hard. And too intense."

Obviously, from the look on her face, Marlowe didn't get it.

"I think he was possessed," Abby continued. "Can that happen like that? Can a person walk into a haunted house and get possessed as soon as he does?"

"I don't know, Abby. He didn't seem possessed to me."

"How would you know, though?" Abby challenged.

"How'd *you* know?"

"I don't. I'm just guessing."

"Because he looked at you too hard and too intense?" Her sarcasm wasn't wasted on Abby.

Abby paused and thought about it. "Yes."

"He smelled good."

Abby shrugged. "I guess."

"Great body."

"It was, but none of that matters if he was possessed."

"I see," Marlowe said introspectively.

"Do you think he'll be back? I mean, you said this house wanted him. Do you think it's enough to compel him to come back to it?"

"Didn't it compel you?" she asked. "You said you bought it because you were drawn to it."

She shook her head. "Nah."

How many times had Abby driven past this place through the years? How many times had she imagined how she'd renovate it if she had the chance? She'd stood out in the front yard numerous times, staring at it, feeling like she belonged in it, and every time she'd walked away from it, she'd missed it.

"Nah, that wasn't it," she lied. "Not really compelled. It was a business decision."

Marlowe gave her the side eye, curled her lips, and nodded her head. "That's your story and you're sticking to it?"

Abby sighed. "That's it. And yes."

*Love is a fire. But whether it is going to warm your
hearth or burn down your house, you can never tell.*

—Joan Crawford

Every Story Has Its Scars

FIGHTING WAS WHAT HE DID. Being a fighter was what he was. A black man with balls big enough to jump into a white man's game, and they hated him for it. But he was a fighter. Dammit to hell to anybody who tried to tell him what he could or couldn't be, what he could or couldn't have.

How long had he been marching? That cold, slate-gray sky pressed down on him the same way it always did. The road under his feet, muddied and thick, tried to pull him under like quicksand, but he wasn't having it. He'd taken a wrong turn somewhere, which sometimes happened, but never enough to derail him for good. Nah. Up ahead. There it was. Home. Small and unimpressive on the outside, but inside was his life. He kept coming back only to find it empty, but it didn't matter. Everything he needed was inside that place. His next breath was inside that tiny house, and he'd keep on coming back until he caught it.

All he could ever remember was reaching for the handle on the door, but he could never recall pushing it open. He just appeared, like magic inside that house. Everything about it was familiar, but the contradiction that this was his first time here was never far away from his thoughts. Those damn voices floated around him like clouds, distracting voices and shadows that brushed past him like smoke frustrated him.

Don't turn away, he ordered himself, staring down the narrow hallway to the open doorway at the end of it. That's where she'd be, waiting for him. But if he moved too soon, he'd lose her. If he blinked, she'd disappear as quickly as she'd appeared.

". . . *something ain't finished here*."

"Hush!" he said to those voices. "Shut the hell up!"

He took a step toward the hallway. An anxious feeling ballooned in his gut. What if she . . . what if she didn't come back? What if she was gone for good this time?

"I'm here, baby," he called out. "Ida?"

The dark-skinned beauty slowly emerged from the back room and stood just inside the doorway. She hadn't left him. His love was still here.

"I-I'm home, baby," he said, filled with so much relief at finally seeing her. "I'm here."

She greeted him with a soft smile, and that was everything. He sighed and took a pensive step toward her. He had to be careful, so careful, because the space between them was fragile, weak. He didn't know how else to explain it, but Ida was like a dream that he never wanted to wake up from, but if he stirred too much, if he moved the wrong way, she'd fade away.

He held out his hand to her. "Meet me halfway, Ida," he said, taking slow steps down the hallway. "Just halfway. Please."

Her smile began to fade, and tears filled her dramatic, dark eyes. "She knows 'bout me." She nodded. "You can't be selfish."

Who knew? She was his secret. Who could possibly know that she was here? His wife?

"No," he said, shaking his head. "No, she doesn't know."

Some things were sacred. Ida was sacred. This house was sacred. The man he was when he came here was sacred.

"No, she doesn't know, Ida."

"Buried deep."

He shook his head in confusion. What she was saying wasn't making any sense.

"You can't be selfish."

Ida slowly began backing up into the darkness.

"No, baby!" he yelled, hurrying to her. "Don't go! Don't leave me, Ida."

But by the time he got to the doorway, she was gone, and he was a broken man all over again. He dropped to his knees, lowered his head, and gave in to the emptiness in the hollow of his heart.

Selfish. She'd called him selfish. And she was right. He was the most selfish man that ever was, selfish for wanting her when he was married to another. Selfish for wanting to be here in this small house with her more than anyplace else in the world. He'd always been a fighter, and until now, he'd always won. He'd prided himself on his determination and drive. So many doors had been closed in his face, but he'd always find a new way in or build his own door. He'd never wanted anything the way he'd wanted her, though. Desire had driven him back here, time and time again, but it had come at a cost.

"I'd just like to look around."

He raised his head to see who was speaking. Familiar. A man's voice that sounded familiar, reminiscent of his own. He looked down the hallway into the living room, shrouded with darkness. Heavy footsteps resonated as they came closer, and for a moment, he was scared. And then there was nothing. No more voices. No footsteps, but something else lingered, alighting on him like a mist. He couldn't name it, but somehow he knew that circumstances had changed. The spirit of renewed determination revitalized him, and he stood up.

She wasn't gone from this house or from him. This was their home together, and it always would be if he had anything to say about it. Ida needed to accept that, and she needed to come to him. She needed to cling to him. To be close. Close.

Finally Seen the Light

A GUN FIRED. *And then it fired again. He sank to his knees and then lowered his hands to the floor, gasping for breath. He struggled to raise his head and, for a moment, looked into her eyes.*

"Jordaaaan!" Olivia cried out, reaching for him. "My sonnnnn!" She glanced helplessly at Edgar. "Help him!" she cried. "Do something—Edgar! Please!"

It isn't true that your life flashes before your eyes when you're dying. Disbelief does. Shock. Doubt that this is really going to happen, that your life is over and that you're powerless, completely and utterly powerless to stop death from coming. Claire, his wife. He thought of her and was reminded of the guilt he felt. Random thoughts flashed in his mind. Jordan thought about the password to his computer and about the meeting across town that he was supposed to attend in the morning. Someone needed to tell his housekeeper that there was no need to have the pool cleaned now.

"Jordan? Oh, God! Jordan!"

It's a sinking feeling, literally. His body pressed down into the floor, like it was being swallowed. The sounds of chaos swirled around him, but too far away from him to matter. Heaven? Hell? Did either of those places really exist, and if they did, which one would welcome him? His chest filled with fear and anxious regret. Jordan was suddenly remorseful for every terrible thing he'd done and been. He hated the man that he'd become, and for the life of him, he couldn't figure out how he'd become that man. Did it matter anymore?

He inhaled, or at least, he tried to, but the pain shot through him like a knife. Breath caught in the back of his throat and was trapped there. Jordan's lungs burned; they were on fire, yearning for a taste of cool air. His heart drummed so loudly that he thought for sure it would burst.

"Stay back! Get back, please!"

"Mr. Gatewood? Can you hear me? Nod if you can hear me."

Jordan couldn't nod. He couldn't raise his arms like he wanted to do to loosen his tie. He could see, barely. Blurred images swirling around him. Shit. Shit. Shit. This is what dying felt like. It was never supposed to happen to him. Jordan was invincible. Untouchable. Death was supposed to have been afraid to come near him, and he was appalled now, knowing that it wasn't.

"He's going into cardiac arrest!"

"Jesus!" someone yelled.

No. Jesus wasn't even close. Shit.

Olivia Gatewood was a ghostly beautiful woman. Well into her seventies, she looked like a portrait, hand painted with consideration and patience. She was used to being stared at because people had been doing it her whole life. She'd come to expect it, and she was always unfazed by it. The last several months had been difficult for her. They'd taken their toll, and it showed in the fading of the vibrant blond of her hair. Natural brown and gray hair streaked through what was left of the hair color she'd worn for so long. She'd lost so much weight that it was alarming, even to him. Olivia hadn't said a word to anyone since the night she'd shot Jordan. She just sat, for hours on end, staring out at nothing, imprisoned in some other realm far removed from her physical space. She should've been an actress.

"Good afternoon, Mother," Jordan said, leaning over her and planting a soft kiss on her forehead.

Of course, she didn't respond in any way. Jordan didn't expect for her to even acknowledge that he was in the room. Growing up, he had loved her more than he thought it was possible to love another human being. He'd adored her and promised to take care of her, protect her, and to cherish her. She was a goddess, and he worshiped her.

She was under a doctor's care here. Olivia Gatewood stayed in the best assisted-living community that money could buy, with a private suite, a staff, and nurses available to tend to her every need around the clock. She was surrounded by the kinds of things that she loved, silk curtains and imported bedding, crystal, lace, French and Moroccan antiquities. She was a woman of privilege and had been her whole life.

A large vintage photograph of a young Olivia hung prominently on the wall in the main living area. Framed in heavy mahogany, the black-and-white photograph of the woman was stunning. Back in the day, her beauty had been compared to that of Lena Horne and Dorothy Dandridge. And it was true. All men, black and white, stopped dead in their tracks when she walked by, staring lustfully at her.

She had been the daughter of a rich man, so it only made sense that she was married to one. She'd almost made a mistake, though, when she was younger. The first time she married was for love instead of money. But Olivia quickly remedied the error and set her life back on the right track, leaving the poor man, Jordan's biological father, behind and latching possessively onto the one more deserving of her.

Despondent, they'd called her. And she'd been that way ever since the night she'd shot Jordan. All sorts of theories abounded as to why she'd put two bullets into her son. In one version, her longtime and now deceased friend Edgar Beckman had said, "*She didn't know what she was doing. She thought she was protecting herself, son. You know how she slips in and out of the present. She would never intentionally hurt you, Jordan. It was an accident. That's all it was.*"

Olivia's doctor had pretty much said something similar. "*A woman in her condition could easily slip in and out of reality and not know that she's doing it. Quite simply, she was not cognizant of who she was or where she was, Mr. Gatewood. She should be watched closely, at all times. I'd recommend constant supervision and monitoring.*"

Olivia had aimed her gun at Desi Green the night Jordan was shot. She was upset and beside herself in a rage when Desi confronted her about the fact that Olivia had actually been the one who killed Julian, thirty years ago, and had set up eighteen-year-old Desi to take the fall. Desi had spent twenty-five years of her life in prison for Julian's murder, and her mother, Ida, had died keeping the secret of what really happened that night. It was the only way she could ensure that Desi didn't get the death penalty.

When Olivia took aim at Desi, something unexpected happened. Jordan put himself in front of that bullet meant for Desi Green. The second shot she fired, Jordan knew instinctively, was meant for him. He'd betrayed his mother, and Olivia Gatewood was having none of that.

Jordan casually took a seat across from his mother staring out over the beautiful gardens, seemingly unaware of his presence. But he knew better.

"Mother," he said calmly, studying her for the slightest indication that she'd heard him.

Olivia played her role well, convincingly well. But then again, she always had. She'd been so good at pretending that he suspected she believed her own lies. Jordan had put all his faith into the love he'd held for her, and he'd lost. But still, it was her blood flowing through his veins. He'd grown up watching her every move, hanging on the gospel of the words that fell from her lovely lips, catching every single one of them in his pockets for safekeeping. Jordan had paid attention, perhaps too much, to all the lovely and wistful things that were Olivia Gatewood, dismissing the unsavory traits of the woman that were her true nature.

"We're so close, Mother," he said earnestly. "So close to winning this deal with the feds and taking Gatewood Industries to a whole new level."

He was so proud of his accomplishments in recent years with running his father's corporation. And he'd always shared those accomplishments with her before sharing them with anyone else, because he knew just how much she understood what they meant to him.

Jordan was introspective for a moment, studying her, half expecting for her to snap out of this facade she insisted on playing out for the world to see, just for a moment, even if it was just a smile, showing her appreciation for all his hard work. But he quickly pushed that hope aside. Olivia was so gotdamn impressive.

She was a work of art, a genius, and a master manipulator. She deserved a standing ovation.

She had tried to kill him. And not because of any mental lapse from reality. Jordan had betrayed her. He's chosen the side of her enemy, or in this case, he'd chosen not to stand by and do nothing while she shot a woman who'd found the courage to stand up and call Olivia out on her lies. Jordan was no saint, but there were moments when even he could no longer stomach a lie that was nearly thirty years old.

"You've been declared legally incompetent," he coolly explained to her. "And per your will, all your assets have been assumed by June and me."

June was his younger sister living back in Atlanta with her two children to be closer to her ex-husband. Everything in Olivia's will had been divided between the two of them per her specifications, and their mother was now under Jordan's charge.

He waited for some sort of reaction from the woman, but deep down, he knew she'd never reveal her secret. Jordan stared at her.

"That gives me controlling shares in Gatewood Industries," he said unemotionally.

She had intentionally tried to kill him. It was a fact that had taken him three months to come to terms with.

"History repeated itself damn near verbatim," he said more to himself than to her.

Jordan had thought about the night he'd nearly died every single day since it'd happened, and one truth kept coming back to him over and over. "Do you ever think about that?" he asked, staring quizzically at her. "Two separate times, separate stages, different circumstances, and yet, the scenes seemed to play out almost identically with you as the common denominator."

It was an eerie thought, but one that clung to him, taunting him with the notion that these two events were more than coincidence. He had never considered himself a spiritual man until now. Jordan's thoughts ran deeper than ever before. He was more in tune with instincts and feelings that he'd never paid much attention to. That near death experience had enlightened and scared the shit out of him because he had no idea what that meant or what he was supposed to do with this new insight. This second chance.

"Your aim was true, Mother," he said regretfully. "But unlike Julian, I'm still here."

Olivia blinked, and that was enough to confirm what he'd known since the day she'd shot him and had become immersed in this catatonic state. She was full of shit.

He still loved her. It was likely that he always would. But Jordan was tired and finally ready to put her and the rest of his past behind him and to move on.

Don't Spare Me

FRANK ROSS STARED OUT of the passenger window as his attorney drove through the streets of Dallas to the studio apartment Frank had spent the last year staying in.

"For a guy not in handcuffs on his way to death row, you seem a little down."

Frank huffed and shook his head. "I may not be the brightest bulb in the pack, but even I know that a hung jury ain't nearly as good as an acquittal."

"Yeah, well, it's better than a guilty verdict."

Was it? The district attorney had vowed to the city of Dallas, the state of Texas, the United States, and God that he was going to retry the Lonnie Adebayo murder case against Frank. He felt like Wile E. Coyote with an anvil about to drop down on top of his head. This shit wasn't over, and Frank wasn't free. He was just living on borrowed time.

This apartment wasn't much bigger than a shoe box, but for the last year, he'd called it home. Cotton, Texas, was where he'd lived before turning his life into scrambled eggs. Frank was an ex-cop, and not a very good and upstanding one, an ex-husband, and an ex-cohort in crime to the now deceased Ms. Adebayo. She'd managed to convince him to set up his half brother, millionaire Jordan Gatewood, and reveal Jordan's secret that Jordan wasn't a Gatewood by blood. The point was now defunct, because Gatewood couldn't care less who knew that he and Frank shared a biological father in Joel Tunson. It was a fucked-up puzzle with too many pieces and looked a hot mess no matter how you put it together.

Frank warmed up two-day-old pizza in the microwave and sat down to eat in front of the television. Every local news channel had his face on it.

"This reporter is as stunned as anyone at the announcement that the jury presiding over famed photojournalist Lonnie Adebayo's murder trial was unable to reach a verdict. They said that there just wasn't sufficient evidence to convict former policeman Frank Ross of first-degree murder. A representative from the DA's office promptly responded with the statement that they would retry the case as quickly as the system would allow."

Frank's phone rang. It was his father. "Yeah?" he answered.

"Well." The old man sighed. "How you feel 'bout all this?"

"I feel like I've always felt. It's bullshit."

"At least you're not in prison, son."

"It's about perspective, Pop. One man's prison is another man's studio apartment in Dallas fuckin' Texas. And I'm stuck here over something I didn't do."

Lonnie Adebayo was murdered at the Fairmont Motel in Dallas just off Highway 635. She was shot, along with two others, and a year later, Frank was still suffering the consequences for the fact that he'd used a credit card to pay for a room he'd been staying in. He hadn't killed her, but he had a feeling that he knew who had. The trouble was, he had to keep his mouth shut or risk losing that fancy lawyer and ending up convicted.

"There's no guarantee they'll retry you," Frank's father offered.

The man was doing his best to step up and be that considerate father Frank had been missing out on for most of his life. This last year, the dude had been bending over backward to care. It was almost admirable, but not really. Still, old Joel was better than nothing, which was exactly who Frank had. He had no money, job, friends, woman. He had nothing except this fragile-ass freedom that could vaporize and disappear into the air at any moment.

"They've made it clear that they would," Frank said wearily.

"I hear they're going to have to get some better evidence if they do. Everything was circumstantial, Frank."

Frank was tired of talking and thinking. "I'm, uh . . . I'm gonna lay it down, Pops," he eventually said. "It's been a long day."

"All right, son. I'll be in touch."

"Yeah," Frank said before hanging up.

He'd been a fuckup for most of his life. Becoming a cop was supposed to have changed him into an upstanding citizen with purpose. Frank had taken money he shouldn't have taken, and yes, he'd taken lives he shouldn't have taken. So, what was happening to him now wasn't anything else but karma. He was lucky to be out of prison. But luck was running thin in his corner.

He stood up to head for the shower but stopped by the window first. Reporters were camped out in front of the building, hoping to catch a glimpse of him. He stepped back from the window, and for a moment, the thought came to him to just go. He had half a tank of gas in that old car of his, forty bucks in his pocket, and the desire to get out from underneath the umbrella of a shitty existence. Lonnie had been a big deal. She was some fancy journalist before dying, and because of who she was, folks knew who he was. So, he probably wouldn't get very far without someone recognizing him. But then again, that depended on which way he went. Didn't it?

Frank was on parole for drug trafficking, a little crime he picked up during his police officer days. And it was because of a miracle and friends in high places, so to speak, that he wasn't locked up waiting for that retrial. But he wasn't under arrest. Mexico had always seemed to be calling to him. Actually, anywhere in South America had always seemed like the place to be for a guy like him. He sighed and headed to the shower and stood under the hot running water, hoping it would wash some clarity into that thick head of his.

Lonnie Adebayo had come to him to with a plan to blackmail Gatewood. It turned out that Frank shared a daddy with the man, and Jordan Gatewood had no intention of letting the world know that he wasn't that rich oil man's son by blood. Frank needed money. Lonnie knew it, and together, they figured out a way for her to get back at him for whatever the hell he'd done to her and for Frank to make the money he needed to get the hell out of Texas. It should've been easy. But, Lonnie ended up dead. Frank was arrested for her murder, and Gatewood came out of the whole thing absolutely unscathed. It was their old man, Jordan and Frank's father, Joel Tunson, who'd impacted Gatewood enough to encourage him to pay Frank's legal fees, with the understanding that Frank would keep his mouth shut, nod, and go with the flow.

He could stay here scratching his ass while the DA drudged up some new evidence and dragged him back to trial. Or he could take his chances out on the road somewhere, enjoy some sunshine, beaches, tequila, and pretty women until he was burned to a crisp, drunk off his ass, and his dick fell off. If he was lucky, he'd die in a dramatic shootout with the cops and go out in a blaze of glory.

If he wasn't lucky, he'd go to prison for parole violation, then stand trial again for Lonnie's murder.

Frank chose blaze of glory. He'd give it a few days to let the circus outside his building die down, but the first chance he got, he was rolling up out of this town for damn good. If they did bring him back here, it'd be in a pine box.

What You Need

ROBIN SINCLAIR HAD LEFT work early to get ready for her dinner date tonight. She had lost track of how long she'd been staring at her reflection in the full-length mirror in her bedroom. She looked perfect. Robin always looked perfect. She was turning forty this year, but looked a decade younger. Sultry hazel eyes often caught others by surprise. She had done away with the blond highlights, which aged her, and had since gone back to her natural brunette hue. Robin preferred to straighten her natural curls, except when she vacationed. Tonight, she'd wrapped her long, straight tresses in a messy bun, leaving wisps to frame her slender face, her sepia complexion glowing.

Tonight, she needed his attention. Jordan had been distracted the last several months, more than usual, and she needed for him to truly see her instead of glossing over her the way he'd done lately. Robin was five nine and slender, but her best assets were her long and shapely legs. He loved her legs, and tonight, she'd make sure that he saw them. Blue was his favorite color. The royal hue draped her frame in satin, stopping midthigh. Matching the custom-made red bottoms ended the luxurious journey at her feet. Robin didn't bother with a bra and panties. If things went her way tonight, they would just be an unnecessary hindrance.

He was worth every moment of her effort. Jordan Gatewood was the grand prize, and Robin was so close to the finish line that she could taste it. Together, they were a beautiful couple. How many times had she heard people say that? How many times had she heard them whisper it? Robin and Jordan were even more beautiful together than Jordan and his first wife, Claire. Since her suicide, however, she'd heard that he'd been aloof, cool, and remote to any woman attempting to get close to him. He'd let down his guard with Robin, and he'd let her in. All she had to do now was be patient.

The six-foot-three-inch gorgeous man stood up as she was escorted to the best table in the house, in the back of the restaurant next to the window overlooking the city. His strength, his power resonated throughout this crowded room, and every eye traveled back and forth between the two of them, transfixed and watching in fascination the union between these two flawless people. A slight smile curled the corners of his mouth as he locked onto her. God! He was everything.

"Hello, sweetheart," he said warmly in that rich and deep voice of his, leaning in slightly to kiss her cheek.

Jordan didn't kiss on the lips. He had a thing about it, he'd told her once, but never elaborated. She could live without his kisses, but she couldn't live without him.

"Sorry I'm late." Robin smiled.

"No worries," he said, waiting for her to be seated before he sat down.

He wore a simple black blazer, a crisp white shirt, and slate-gray slacks. His dark, penetrating gaze raked over her, and Jordan subconsciously licked his lips. "You look gorgeous, as usual."

"Thank you," she said humbly. "So do you."

He was an anomaly. Jordan had been through so much in recent years that he'd retreated inside himself and left everyone else cold and wondering and hovering around him, desperate to be let in.

Distant. Preoccupied. Distracted. He'd been all these things for the last few months, and she longed to awaken him.

"How was your day?" she asked engagingly.

The server abruptly appeared at their table. "Good evening. Would you like something to drink?" he asked Robin.

She ordered a glass of wine. Jordan had his signature lager already on the table. The server left to get her drink. *Don't let him slip away*, she thought, looking at Jordan. *Touch him.* She reached across the table and intertwined her fingers in his. "I'm listening," she said gently.

She studied him each and every time she saw him. Jordan's close-cut hair and beard only highlighted his perfect features.

"Interesting," he said simply.

She listened patiently as he spoke, mesmerized by the movement of his lips, wanting like hell to tug on them with hers, to mate her tongue to his. She listened, or rather, she heard him, but he might as well have been speaking Greek. The two of them ate dinner, finished, and later that evening in her apartment, she got her wish.

Jordan stood naked over her, at the foot of her bed, with his hands on her knees.

"Jordan," she whispered weakly, helplessly, as he trailed his hands from her knees to her shins, then wrapped those long fingers of his around her ankles and slowly straightened her legs, pushing them back toward her head until he'd folded her into the position he wanted her in.

Robin was always so pliable for him, so accommodating and weak. Her mouth watered at the sight and anticipation of his thick and rigid cock, tickling her labia. "Don't tease me," she begged.

Robin was one of Gatewood Industries' top corporate attorneys. She negotiated multimillion-dollar contracts on a daily basis and had the reputation of being a beast of a lawyer. She was a powerful woman in her own right, except when it came to him. She was his toy, his slave, his whatever he wanted her to be.

"Make me believe you want it, sweetheart." Jordan's piercing, dark eyes bore down to her soul.

He inched the tip of his dick in between the folds of her pussy.

"I'm convinced," he whispered. "You are so fucking wet, Robin." Jordan moaned.

She hated the thin wall of latex between the two of them. Robin wanted all of him buried deep inside her. She wanted his seed, his babies, his hopes and dreams. She wanted to be his refuge, the place where he could let down his guard and feel safe. He pushed into her so slowly, so completely, that she couldn't help but to cry out and came, the first time, almost immediately.

Hours later, Robin lay quietly in his arms, with her head on his chest, the deep, methodic beating of his heart lulling her into fantasies so lovely that she never wanted them to end. And they all centered around him. He was her man, her husband. He couldn't keep his hands off her, couldn't stop kissing her. "I should've married you first," he would tell her over and over again. In her dreams, it was all he said.

Eventually she dozed off, and he was gone when she woke up.

The text on her phone said what it always said when he left in the middle of the night.

Have an early day tomorrow. I'll see you at the office. Had a lovely time as usual.

She rolled over to his side of the bed, buried her face in the pillow, and inhaled the scent of his cologne.

"Just be patient, Robin," she said out loud.

A man like him couldn't be rushed. He couldn't be tricked or fooled into doing something he wasn't ready to do. He had to want to marry her. Robin needed to be the woman who saved his life and his soul. He had to know, without a doubt, that he loved her more than he loved himself and to wonder how he had possibly lived without her his whole life. But for these things to happen, she needed to stay the course.

Ringing My House

SOOTHING LIGHTING ILLUMINATED THE SPACE inside his penthouse as soon as he stepped off the private elevator. It wasn't yet dawn. He'd drifted off to sleep at Robin's, but it was a restless sleep, one that he couldn't let himself sink too deeply into, because he knew that he didn't want to spend the night.

Jordan was becoming more peculiar with age, or maybe just more particular. He was a man with more money than he could spend in his lifetime. *Gatewood* was more of a status symbol than a last name these days, and there were plenty of women standing in line to have it wrapped around their ring finger on their left hand. Jordan was a commodity. A year ago, he relished the position, but damn near dying had a way of putting things in perspective.

Robin was gorgeous, the sex was amazing, and still, those things weren't enough for him. She had worked hard to satisfy Jordan, making herself available whenever and however he needed her. She was making it crystal clear that she wanted to become a permanent fixture in his life, and all the while Jordan pushed back, reminding her that he wasn't ready to make a commitment to her or anyone else. Still, the accommodating nature of a beautiful, intelligent woman like her would've been more than enough for any man, just not him.

Jordan was forty-nine. A widower. His wife, Claire, had committed suicide more than a year ago because of him. Claire, like Robin, wanted more than anything for Jordan to love her. Not an unreasonable expectation for a wife of her husband. In the nearly six years that they were married, Jordan cheated, lied, dismissed, ignored, and cheated some more on Claire, and still she stayed. Begging. Pleading. Crying for him to be the man that she needed him to be. He excused his behavior by justifying it and by using the excuse that he didn't know how to be any other kind of way. The bigger truth was that he purposefully chose not to be that man.

Claire had been a trophy. Beautiful, compliant, pliable. She made it too damn easy for him to be an asshole. So yes. He used her as an excuse and blamed her every chance he got for his indiscretions. And every now and then, that beautiful face of hers flashed in his mind and tortured him, reminding him of how cruel he was capable of being, so it was a fair trade as far as he was concerned, a lifetime of guilt for him over her death in exchange for six long, painful years of marriage to him for her.

Jordan walked upstairs to his bedroom, undressed, and took a shower. Women were never an issue for men like Jordan. He'd been through more than his fair share, and each and every time, thinking back, he'd been left completely and utterly empty inside. He'd come close to loving one woman, or perhaps it had just been a dangerous obsession that, in the end, got her killed. Not a suicide like Claire. It was an age-old story of love, lust, betrayal, and a gun.

Scalding water washed over him until he could shake loose

that memory. Self, and the preservation of such, were everything to him. Self-centeredness. Self-absorbtion. Self-loathing? No. Not quite. He was a mogul. A big, black, dangerous motha fucka of a mogul who had had plenty of cringeworthy and self-loathing moments, but that's all they were—moments. Besides, ego wouldn't allow him to loathe himself. He had plenty of that from outsiders.

He was an oilman, born and raised in Texas, and his so-called counterparts, his peers, despised him. Arrogant, they called him. A black man wasn't allowed to think too highly of himself, unless he could catch a football or rap, and even then, he was frowned upon unless he came heavy with humility. To his peers, Jordan was void of humility. It was a dirty word and an even dirtier feeling. Humility was a silent and embarrassing plea for acceptance and approval. He didn't want or need their fuckin' approval. That's why they hated him. Arrogant black bastard without a hint of humility, a privileged niggah with no soul. And they were right. If he had a conscience, then he kept it hidden from them, but more importantly, from himself. A conscience was a liability in this business. Fuck every last one of them.

Half an hour later, Jordan was down in his living room, sipping on a cup of coffee, standing at the floor-to-ceiling window, and watching the sun begin to rise over the city. His penthouse was conveniently located in his corporate building. Jordan's office was on the floor beneath him. He'd owned other houses all over the world, but after Claire died, he'd sold just about all of them and called this place home. It was the only place that felt like it. Gatewood Industries Inc. was a multimillion-dollar corporation because of him. He lived and breathed this place.

Jordan's net worth was hundreds of millions of dollars, but being the CEO over GII was never about the money. It was his birthright, thanks to some creative marrying done by his mother.

Jordan's biological father was a man named Joel Tunson, and he was Olivia's first husband. She left him, though, when Jordan was two years old. That's when Julian Gatewood caught sight of her somewhere and started sniffing around. He married her, but it didn't take him long to regret it. Still, he stayed married to her until his death. Jordan was twenty, a junior in college, when suddenly, he was snatched up by his jockstrap and planted behind Julian's desk in that leather chair of his adoptive father. Back then, it was too damn big for him. It took years, a whole lot of mistakes, and some hard lessons before Jordan finally began to fit the mold of CEO, and he eventually tossed his father's seat out and bought his own gotdamn chair.

It had been weeks since Jordan's trek to Ida Green's old house in Blink, Texas, but he couldn't stop thinking about the trip. That house, there was something about it. Jordan left there with the residue of old memories on him. Julian had lived a completely separate life in that place. As a kid, he grew up being told that his father was away on business, but now, he couldn't help but wonder how much of his business had taken him to Blink.

He wanted to go back. But what the hell was he looking for? What did he expect to find in Blink that could possibly have anything to do with the man that Jordan was now? This nagging curiosity was becoming irrational. He was chasing ghosts and whims, and for what? Julian didn't have any answers for him when he was alive; he surely couldn't have any for him now that he was gone. Thirty years. The man had been dead for nearly thirty years, and only recently had Jordan become curious about the meaning of his death, and more importantly, his life. He was losing his mind. That had to have been it. Jordan was going fuckin' crazy, and he needed to hurry up and snap out of it before someone noticed and had him committed.

Abby. Was it just the house? Or was it her? Not a day since he'd first seen her had his curiosity about her not stabbed at him. He held an odd fascination for that woman, an unyielding anticipation of seeing her again, and he had no idea why. He felt like he was on the brink of something, a breakthrough, an answer to some question that he didn't even know to ask. Every time he recalled her face, her pretty, animated, un-made-up face, it felt as if she held the secret to something he'd been searching for all his life, and it bothered him because he had no idea who she was or why she should compel him so. There had been an energy between them. And it had flowed solely and powerfully between the two of them. She'd felt it too, and it made her uneasy. He'd seen it in her eyes. It was an odd revelation, but true. Jordan was changing, evolving. Into what or who, he had no idea.

Fifteen minutes later Jordan finished his coffee and then went upstairs to get dressed. When the call came in, he knew instinctively who it was. Jordan had his phone system wired throughout the house.

"This is Jordan," he said, triggering the answering capability.

"What time did you leave?" Robin asked, sounding as if she were still half-asleep.

"Early or late, depending on your perspective," he said, walking into his closet.

"Why?" she asked, almost pleading.

"Early morning meeting, Robin," he lied.

"Another one." She sounded disappointed but like she knew that it was just an excuse that he'd used to leave.

"Yes." He sighed. "You know how it is."

She paused and then sighed. "Yeah. I know."

The Moon in Her Eye

HAVING A MASTER'S DEGREE in structural engineering with an emphasis on architecture was wasted in a small town like Blink, Texas. Abby was basically a construction worker. But she owned her own contracting business, and she was the boss. At the end of the day, that's all that mattered.

She'd been in this house for almost two months, tackling renovations in between building decks, renovating bathrooms and kitchens, and laying new floors for clients. Abby had gutted the kitchen and had single-handedly built her own custom cabinets and stained them with a warm, off-white hue, and dark brown glazing details. She'd replaced all the old countertops with a light gray soapstone instead of your typical granite. She was still waiting for her appliances to be delivered, though, but in the meantime, she had a microwave that she'd get more use out of than a stove anyway.

"Careful with my walls, Doug," she said, helping PacMan carry out that old, musty, stained carpet and stepping over Doug kneeling on the floor, removing baseboards. "I don't want to re-place 'em if I don't have to."

Doug grunted.

Abby held up one end of the roll of carpet and followed Pac-Man outside to the huge Dumpster that had been sitting in front of her new house for months. Without bothering to be asked, Doug magically appeared at her side, took hold of her end, and helped PacMan get that thing inside the Dumpster.

"Thank you," she said, dusting her hands off on her jeans. "If I were taller, you know I could've handled it."

Doug brushed past her and grunted again. He was a man of few words. Always had been, but he was one of her best work-ers. He and PacMan had offered to help renovate her new place without being paid. Abby did agree to pay for pizza and beers the next time they met up at Charlie's Bar. Abby had practically finished the kitchen in just under two months, doing most of the work herself. New hardwood would be arriving for the floors in three days, and Doug and PacMan had replaced every window in the house in a week. Other than laying hardwood through-out, the only other major project was the bathroom. It was tiny, much too small for the tub, which she'd had the fellas take out as soon as they started demoing the place. Abby was erecting a standalone shower and replacing the sink to allow for more storage.

"No wonder I haven't heard from you," Skye said, standing in the doorway of the small bedroom. "Dang! You took down the wall?"

Abby grinned and planted her hands on her hips. "Looks good, doesn't it? It's gonna be my office."

"So, it's a one-bedroom house now," Skye said skeptically. "You sure you want that? It's gonna be hard to sell a one-bedroom, Abby."

"I'm not sure I'm gonna sell it," she said, shrugging.

"I thought that was the plan."

It had been the plan, especially when she found out that the place was haunted, but these ghosts hadn't given her a lick of trouble since she'd been here. Abby had been sleeping here for the last few days, and not one bump, boo, or creak had disturbed or scared her.

"I mean, if I do decide to sell it, I can always put the wall back up," she said matter-of-factly. "No big deal."

Skye laughed. "To you it's no big deal. Knocking down and putting up walls scares the mess outta people like me."

Skye was a paralegal, so yeah, Abby could see how construction work might bother her. Plus, Skye insisted on wearing unnaturally long nails. How that woman wiped her ass without cutting herself was miraculous to Abby. So yes, construction work for a woman like Skye was out of the question.

"Abby," Doug said, reaching over Skye's head to hand something to Abby. "Found it between the wall and the baseboard."

It was a picture of a woman, smiling, dark skin, with long, thick hair with long spiral curls cascading down her shoulders. She had on a floral dress and was sitting behind a small table with a votive in the center of it, burning a small candle. Several glasses sat on the table in front of her.

Skye leaned in and looked at it, too. "She's pretty. Who's that?"

Abby shook her head. "I don't know."

The picture had been torn in two. The woman in the photograph looked like she was being held by someone.

"It looks old, like maybe from the seventies."

"Maybe she lived here," Abby suggested.

"You should get one of those rain showerheads," Skye said, changing the subject. "You know the kind I'm talking about?"

Yeah. Abby knew.

A few hours later, Abby stepped out of the shower in a room at the Barton; it was the fanciest hotel downtown Blink had to offer. After buying the house, Abby had rented her other house to Lewis and Donna Franklin. While Donna was busy getting ready to give birth to twins, Lewis worked here, at the Barton, and had graciously offered to let Abby use one of the rooms until her new place was livable. She'd been staying at the house as often as she could, but until the bathroom was finished, she had to split her time between the two.

She had no idea why the picture of the woman fascinated her, but it did. Abby got dressed, stuffed it into the pocket of her jeans, and drove to Marlowe's to see if she could provide any psychic insight into the matter. Abby expected that Marlowe would have to touch the picture or something to get a good read on it.

It was getting late in the day, but Marlowe had her boo thang on top of the house fixing her roof.

"Hey, Plato," Abby called out, climbing out of her truck. "How's it coming along?"

"It's coming."

Plato just kind of showed up and saved Marlowe's life, and the two of them had been inseparable ever since. No one knew the details, and no one probably ever would. Like Doug, Plato was a man of few words, and Marlowe just smiled a lot these days. Abby had just placed her foot on the first step leading to Marlowe's front door when all of a sudden, Marlowe's blind and seventysomethingyear-old aunt Shou Shou came bursting through the front door with Marlowe right behind her, catching her by the elbow before she tripped stepping out onto the front porch.

"Don't you bring that into this house," Shou Shou commanded.

Abby stopped dead in her tracks and immediately lowered her foot back down to the ground. "What?"

Shou Shou was so overwrought that she was shaking.

"Auntie," Marlowe said, "calm down."

Shou Shou pointed her white cane in Abby's direction. "Why'd you bring it here? You shoulda left it where it was."

Abby was confused. She had known Shou since she was a little girl, and she'd never seen the woman so angry.

"I-I don't know—"

"Yes, you do, Abigail," Shou retorted. "You do know."

Abby had that picture in her pocket. Was that what Shou Shou was referring to? The old woman was really sweet, but she could be creepy as hell when she wanted to be.

"What do you have, Abby?" Marlowe asked, still holding on to her aunt.

Abby reached into her back pocket and held out the photograph. "It's just a picture," she said sheepishly. "I found it in the house."

"And that's where you shoulda left it," Shou Shou said tersely, jerking away from Marlowe.

"I just wanted to know if maybe she's the ghost, Marlowe," Abby quickly explained. "I was hoping you could touch it or something and tell me."

"I'm not touching that, Abby," Marlowe said gravely.

Shit. Abby had touched the hell out of it.

"You need to take it back to the house, Abigail," Shou explained evenly, more calmly this time. "You need to hurry up and put her back. You hear me? You take her home, and don't take her out again before she's ready."

Shou Shou's words resonated with Abby like bee stings. "Yes, ma'am," Abby murmured.

The older woman turned to Marlowe. "Do me a favor, baby," she said unexpectedly tender.

"Yes, ma'am."

"Go in the house, fill a plastic bag with ice, and wrap it in a dish towel."

Marlowe tilted her head to one side and stared back at her aunt. "Ma'am?"

"Gotdammit! Fuck!" Plato cried out from the roof. He'd been hammering, when the hammering abruptly stopped. "Marlowe?" he called out.

"Hold on, baby!" she yelled back. "I'll get you some ice," she said, disappearing inside.

Shou Shou started to follow her.

"Miss Shou," Abby said, stopping her.

She turned to face Abby.

This whole meeting had left Abby absolutely terrified. "Am I in danger?"

Shou sighed and hesitated before finally responding. "Well, there's danger, and then there's danger, Abigail." She paused again. "Depends on your perspective."

Abby swallowed.

"You take her home, and don't take her out again until she's ready."

It was a strange statement to make. "H-how will I know when she's ready?"

"He'll come for her and she'll go."

Abby stood out in front of that house long enough to see Shou find her way back inside, and Marlowe coming out carrying a bag of ice for her man taking a seat on the steps.

"That old lady scare the shit out of you?" Plato asked while Marlowe took his hand, placed it in her lap, and pressed the ice bag onto it.

Abby nodded. He looked at her as if he understood.

Marlowe smiled. "Get her home, Abby."

Where You Are

JORDAN WAS ON HIS WAY out of his penthouse and headed to his ranch when he got the call. All the key players filed into the conference room: Vince Wilkins, Gatewood Industries' chief of operations; Mike Stevens, chief financial officer. Jordan's right hand and personal assistant, Phyl Mays, sat down next to him. And finally, newly appointed Dave Morris, director of federal acquisitions, followed by his lead attorney, Robin Sinclair, who coolly entered the room and sat down, exchanging a brief glance with Jordan.

"So, what's going on?" Jordan asked without wasting any time.

Dave cleared his throat. "First, I'd like to thank you for taking a chance on Robin and me to head up this new division, Jordan. An opportunity like this doesn't come around often, and when it does, well, it's truly an honor to have been trusted with—"

"Get to the point, Dave," Jordan interrupted.

He didn't need his ass kissed today.

"We received word ten minutes ago that the Department of Defense has narrowed down consideration from the dozens of bid packages they received for the research and development of the new rocket engine to three contenders."

"As you know," Robin added, "we worked day and night putting together a tight and compliant proposal bid package, Jordan. We've collaborated closely with procurement and sales to pull together numbers as fair and as tight as we possibly could."

"Robin's poured damn near all her blood, sweat, and tears into all those terms and conditions and flowdowns and"—Dave laughed and looked at her—"shit. They've thrown everything into this proposal request but the kitchen sink."

"What's the bottom line?" Vince Wilkins interjected.

Dave took a deep breath. "Ours is one of the bids in the running."

Dave looked at Robin, who suddenly smiled so wide it was blinding.

"Damn!" Jordan blurted out amid applause and whoops. He shook his head, leaned back in his chair, and grinned.

Jordan had gambled big-time on a fucking impossibility. He'd established a whole new division in Gatewood Industries, a division focused solely on contracting opportunities with the feds. He'd had a headhunter track down Dave Morris and had practically stolen him from a competitor. Dave had searched high and low for a government contracts attorney with a stellar résumé, and he'd found Robin.

He relished what this could mean for his corporation. The competition for this endeavor had been incredible. All the big dogs had thrown their hats in the ring—Langson, NiVan, Brewster, giants in the industry of aerospace and transportation. Jordan was a guppy in a sea of killer whales, and he was not supposed to even be able to play in this game.

It took a few moments for him to realize that all eyes in that room were suddenly on him.

"We can do this," his CFO, Mike Stevens, said. "We can fucking do this."

"Who are the other two?" Jordan finally asked, looking at Dave and Robin.

"Langson and Brewster," Dave told him.

"Langson worries me the most," Jordan admitted. "They're so in bed with the feds it's not even funny."

"Yeah, but the feds are getting pressure to let go of some of those incestuous relationships they've been having for decades," Robin added. "And besides, we're the little guy."

"A little guy worth hundreds of millions of dollars," Vince reminded her.

"Langson and Brewster are worth billions," Mike said. "Either one of them could swallow us whole like we were nothing more than a snack cracker."

He was right, and everyone in the room knew it.

"They're not taking us seriously," Jordan said introspectively. "Langson and Brewster are looking at each other, convinced that one of them will be awarded this contract."

How many times had Jordan been down and nearly counted out? How many times had he gotten back up to fight another round? He was a fighter. And he was convinced that he had a real shot at this.

"We've formed some serious partnerships with engineering and physics rock stars," he reminded them. "Those motha fuckas at Langson and Brewster have no idea how serious we are, how prepared we are to win this gotdamn bid and to deliver."

Everyone nodded. Jordan had gone into this endeavor knowing that it would catapult Gatewood Industries to a whole new level. Oil and gas were one thing, but it wasn't enough. Not anymore.

"We're turning this corner and taking this corporation to a whole other level. And I don't care if it's this contract or the next," he said emphatically, "but we will not stop until GII casts a shadow over anyone who currently considers themselves my competitor."

Jordan owned at least a dozen vehicles, most of them exotic, but his favorite was a beat-up 1998 Chevy pickup truck that he usually drove when he went to his ranch.

"I'm disappointed," Robin said over the phone as he drove. He'd put her on speaker.

Needless to say, he wasn't surprised she'd called.

"I thought you and I would be celebrating this weekend," she said softly.

Of course that's what she would think. It seemed like the thing to do for two people intimately engaged in business as well as their personal lives.

"And we will when there's something to celebrate," he casually explained, hoping that he wasn't being too harsh. Evasiveness was a tactical skill he liked to think he'd perfected through the years. It wasn't that her company wasn't wanted, but Jordan had a lot on his mind, and getting away from the distractions of Dallas, the office, and Robin was necessary sometimes.

"Maybe I should rephrase," she countered. "I thought that you and I would spend time together this weekend whether we had something to celebrate or not."

So, he'd failed. Apparently he was rusty in the area of tact, because Robin sounded a bit put off.

"I have some things that I need to take care of at the ranch,

Robin," he responded coolly. "I'll see you as soon as I get back in town."

A long pause filled the air.

"Promise?" she finally asked.

"I do," he said before saying good-bye and hanging up.

The harder she pushed, the further back he seemed to move. It wasn't intentional. Jordan couldn't think of one reason why he shouldn't want to spend every waking hour with that beautiful woman. Intelligent, witty, soft, and polished, she was exactly the kind of woman a man in his position should want to spend his life with. She hadn't come out and said it, but he knew that Robin had marriage on her mind. The thing is, marriage was the furthest thing from his.

Once again, he drove past the exit leading to his ranch, but instead of turning around, Jordan kept driving until, an hour and a half later, he came to the exit for Blink, Texas. It didn't make sense for him to come back here. There was nothing for him in this town, not the meaning of life from his dead father or the explanation for why Jordan lived when he should've died a year ago. He'd found no enlightenment inside that old house of Ida Green's, but still he drove, compelled by curiosity, by some unexplainable desire just to see if this strange obsession was a fluke, some odd and temporary fascination that would disappear the moment he saw her again.

The best thing that could happen, he thought as he stopped and parked in front of that house, was that he'd realize that the woman, Abby, was nothing more than a pretty, petite country woman that had caught his whimsy for a brief moment. The worst thing that could happen was, well, the same thing.

And She Was

"YOU KNOW HOW MISS SHOU is," Abby said to Skye over the phone. "She can scare the hell out of you if you let her."

"I don't go near that old crazy witch," Skye said. "My momma told me she was evil and put a spell on my uncle Jake years ago for killing her cat."

Abby stopped pouring soil into a planter, set the bag down on the table, and put her hand on her hip. "Well, if he'd killed my cat, I'd would've cursed him, too, Skye."

"He didn't kill it on purpose. Damn cat ran out into the road at the last minute while he was driving. It was either hit the cat or run into a ditch and tear up his daddy's car. Shou found out he did it, and he's been prone to boils ever since. Never had a boil in his life until she found out he killed that cat. He said she said some gibberish, waved her hands around in the air, and *bam*! All of a sudden, boils came out of nowhere and erupted all over his back. They went away, but every now and then one will just pop out of the blue."

"Well, she scared me so bad I put that picture back in this house and left. Stayed away for nearly a week, but I've been staying here for three days now, and I ain't had no problems with the ghosts."

"How you can even think about staying in a haunted house is crazy to me, Abby. Sane people don't think that's a good idea."

The truth was, Abby loved this house. She hated being away from it, but for some reason, she felt a sense of loneliness and longing that left her melancholy and sometimes even sad. She was about to turn thirty-seven soon, and for the first time in her life, she felt grounded in a place. Everywhere else she'd lived she'd always felt like she was just passing through, but not here. This was home.

After hanging up from talking with Skye, Abby started potting small plants into the large vases she'd bought to put on her deck by her back door. You'd think she'd stolen her daddy's playlist with all that old-school blasting from her small speaker on the table—Aretha Franklin and Sam Cooke among others. On rotation now was Johnnie Taylor's "Who's Making Love," which Abby sang at the top of her lungs. She was so busy singing and planting that she didn't hear him the first few times he'd said her name.

Abby turned abruptly and froze. Dear Jesus Lord! Tall, beautiful cowboys only show up in dreams. Don't they?

"I didn't mean to startle you," he said in a voice that rolled with the rumbling of thunder behind it. "I was here about a month ago," he reminded her. "You and your friend let me take a tour of the house."

For a moment, Abby had forgotten how to speak. This man in a cowboy hat held some kind of magical power over her, and all she could do was stand there with her mouth hanging open, gawking at him.

"Jordan," he said. "Um . . . Abby, isn't it?"

She thought she felt herself nod, but she couldn't be sure. *Say something, Abby. Speak!* "Yes," she finally responded, startling herself a bit. *Keep going.* "I remember you."

He looked past her to the large ceramic pots on the ground around her. "I'm interrupting."

Without thinking, she glanced at them, too. "Yes. I mean, no," she said, turning quickly back to him.

"I knocked, and when I heard the music coming from back here . . . well, I don't mean to be intrusive."

She wished Marlowe were here, or Skye, or somebody who could be the buffer between him and her. It wasn't that she was shy or anything. Abby worked with men, big, strapping men, all day long. Her industry was filled with them, and so she wasn't so easily swayed by muscles and good looks, because she was always too preoccupied with trying to get them to take her little five-foot-two-inch ass seriously. But he was different.

Abby had to make a hard mental shift to her business mind-set and get far away from her lustful thoughts right now.

"What can I do for you, Mr. . . . ?"

"Jordan. You can call me Jordan."

Calling him Mr. Something-or-Other would've made this whole encounter much more comfortable and impersonal.

"What can I do for you, Mr. Jordan?"

Was he this tall the first time she'd seen him? Was he this exceptionally handsome?

And just like that, the tides turned, and he seemed to be the one at a loss for words. All of a sudden, Abby realized just how tightly she was gripping that trowel, when it dawned on her that she was alone in her backyard with a stranger who could easily snatch her up and have his way with her and then kill her.

He seemed to sense that Abby's internal alarm was starting to go off, and he took a hesitant step back.

"My father died in this house," he admitted after a long pause. "Thirty years ago, he was shot and died in the living room."

The man seemed taken aback by his own admission as much as Abby was. The first thoughts that came to her mind, of course, were the ghosts Marlowe had said lived here and Marlowe's strange reaction to him showing up that day. This was all getting to be way too creepy, and Abby would be kicking herself in the ass later for buying this place.

"I came here the first time, out of curiosity," he finally continued. "I'd never been here before, and I just . . . well, I needed to see it."

Abby studied him. "So, you came back to see it again?"

So was this man's daddy haunting her house? And thirty years later, his son shows up out of the blue to finally see the place. Had his daddy somehow called to him from the grave and told him to come here? Dammit, she needed Marlowe here.

"Some very personal and dramatic events have happened in my life recently that have compelled me to . . . my father and I weren't close, but for some reason, I feel a need to . . ."

"Find some closure," she said, summarizing his torment.

Yes, he was tormented. Abby could see it in his eyes. Even though she wasn't psychic like Marlowe, she did have a strong intuition about people that was usually dead-on. Something bad had happened to this man, and he was looking for closure and maybe some peace. Abby decided to try to put aside the ghost aspect of all of this, and focus on a more reasonable, rational explanation for him being here. She was good at being rational. It was more in line with her nature. Gradually she began to relax.

"Perhaps that's it," he said.

She took a deep breath. "So, he lived here?"

Again with another long pause. "He lived in Dallas; however, he was seeing a woman who lived here."

Jordan was really careful how he explained that to her, which raised more flags for Abby.

"He was having an affair," he reluctantly admitted.

Abby nodded slightly. "He was? And this woman killed him?"

The image of that woman's picture immediately came to mind. Maybe she was the mistress.

"No."

She waited for him to elaborate, but he didn't.

"Can I show you something?" she asked, surprising herself with that question.

Abby started toward the back door. "Wait here, please," she said over her shoulder as she went inside, emerging moments later carrying that photograph. "One of my guys found this when we were renovating," she explained, holding it out to him. "It's old. Do you know if this is her?"

The look on his face spoke volumes. It turned stone cold, and Abby could tell just by looking at him that he hated her.

"What was her name?"

He glanced at Abby and held the photo back out to her. "Ida. Ida Green."

Abby took a deep breath. Maybe she'd just met one of her ghosts. "What was your father's name?"

"Julian," he said. "Gatewood."

You Want a Lover

"OF ALL THE GIN JOINTS, in all the towns, in all the world, she walks into mine."

"Really?" Robin said, turning in her seat to look up over her shoulder. "You're still using that old *Casablanca* line, believing it's going to work?"

Alex Richards laughed and bent to kiss her cheek. "I keep hoping you'll find me too handsome and charming to resist and that, yes, it will work."

Without waiting to be invited, he sat down at the table in the chair next to her.

"Still as classically polished as ever, I see," she said, smirking.

Alexander Richards was never seen out in public in anything that wasn't Italian made, expensive, and tailored to fit his tall, lithe frame like he'd been born in it. Piercing blue eyes hid under heavy, dark brows. A perfectly trimmed goatee framed surprisingly full lips, and sharp, chiseled features gave him an animated appearance, almost sinister until he smiled. Then he looked downright adorable.

"What in the world are you doing sitting here all alone?" he asked, taking hold of one of her hands between his.

Robin and Alex had gone to law school together and then became inseparable friends all the way through graduation. After that, their respective careers carried them both off in different directions, Robin to her beginnings as a corporate attorney in California, and Alex to the world of criminal defense, mainly for celebrities, politicians, and CEOs.

"What does it look like I'm doing?" She smiled. "I'm having lunch."

He gave her an inquisitive side eye. "All by your lovely self?"

It was never a secret that Alex had a crush on Robin. But even though she'd considered being more than friends with him, she could never seem to get past that point.

"No," she responded. "I'm waiting for a friend."

"You should never have to wait for anyone, my lovely friend." He raised her hand and kissed it.

"What are you doing in town?" she eventually asked. "I thought you were in New York."

Just then, a waiter appeared. "May I get you something to drink, sir?"

"No," Alex said, leaning back. "I'm on my way out. Thank you." The waiter left, and Alex continued. "A case brought me here."

"Still saving rich bad guys?"

"Actually, this one was a poor bad guy, or alleged bad guy," he explained. "I defended Frank Ross, the defendant in the—"

"Lonnie Adebayo case," she said, finishing his sentence. "I had no idea that was you. He got off?"

Alex shrugged. "Hung jury."

"So, when'd you start doing pro bono work?"

Alex never took a case for any client not worth a few million dollars, and for him, even that was considered charitable work.

"You know better than that." His eyes twinkled.

"From what I remember hearing about the case, the guy was far from rich. Some ex-cop or something. Right?"

"With friends in high places."

"Ah," she said with a dramatic nod. "So, someone is paying that high price tag of yours."

He just smiled.

"Hung jury. Is the DA going to retry?"

Alex sighed. "That's the plan."

"Any idea when?"

He shook his head. "They're going to need a whole lot more than the circumstantial shit they've got now if they stand a chance in hell of getting a conviction."

"Still as cocky as ever, I see."

"That's confidence that you're seeing, Robin my love. There's a difference."

"So, are you going to take up temporary residence in Dallas until the next trial?"

"Not likely," he said with a distasteful expression. "I'm more of an East Coast man. Too many cowpokes in this town for me."

"Don't let the cowpokes hear you say that."

"Indeed."

"Robin?"

Her lunch date had arrived and stood next to her.

Alex took a deep breath. "My cue to leave?" He stood up, adjusted his jacket, and held out his hand to the other gentleman. "Alex Richards. Robin and I are old friends."

"Donovan Adams," her lunch date responded, shaking Alex's hand. "Robin and I are new friends."

The two locked gazes for a moment like bulls before Alex finally leaned down to kiss her hand again. "It's been good seeing you again, Ms. Sinclair. Enjoy your lunch."

"Call me before you leave," she told him.

"Absolutely."

Donovan waited until Alex left before taking a seat at the table. "I apologize," he immediately said. "I must've gotten the time mixed up. I thought we'd agreed to meet here at one?"

"We did," she assured him. "But I was close by, so I arrived a bit early."

Donovan Adams, star wide receiver for the Dallas Cowboys, six two, dark and gorgeous, was seven years her junior and, as young as he was, was starting to consider retirement to pursue a commentator role in the NFL.

Before saying another word, he leaned back and openly admired Robin.

"You're going to make me blush," she said, shifting in her seat.

He looked a bit surprised. "Me make you blush? I'm the one blushing. You finally agreed to break bread with me. I'm feeling pretty good."

She laughed. It was true that he'd been pursuing her for months. The two had met at a fund-raiser where he was the featured speaker. The man was a celebrity and hero in Dallas who literally had his pick of just about any woman he wanted. Robin had finally accepted an invitation from him a week ago.

"Good afternoon, sir," the waiter said, returning. "May I get you something to drink?"

"Just water, please."

"How was practice?" she asked after the waiter left.

"Practice was practice. Tough, as usual."

"Yes. But so are you."

This was her attempt to be interested in someone else besides Jordan. She needed the distraction from him, because he was still sending a message that he wasn't ready to commit. Sometimes, Robin felt that she pushed too hard, came across as too eager and too desperate, which would only push a man like him further away. Besides, begging wasn't her style. Loving Jordan was frustrating, and Robin needed to back off, for her own sake more than his. This was her attempt at doing just that.

"For so many years, my career came first," she found herself explaining as they ate. He was easy to talk to, and Robin relished letting her guard down with him in a way that she'd never been able to do with Jordan. "Time gets away from you," she said reflectively. "The next thing you know, you're forty and wondering where it all went. Marriage, family." She shrugged. "I always believed that those things would come naturally. They haven't."

"It's not too late. You're a beautiful, intelligent woman, Robin. A man would be lucky to be married and have a family with a woman like you."

He was dropping not-so-subtle hints, and she was flattered. For all the wonderful things that he was, however, Robin couldn't ignore the fact that she had spent the whole hour that they'd been together anticipating the vibration of the phone in her purse with a call or even a text from Jordan. Donovan was wonderful, but he was not Gatewood. And that was a realization she just could not shake.

They finished eating, and Donovan paid the bill and walked her outside, where she handed her ticket to the valet and waited for the driver to bring her car around.

"Can we do this again?" he asked, hopeful.

"I'd love to," she lied. "Call me?"

He smiled. "I definitely will."

SEDUCING ABBY RHODES | 71

Tears filled her eyes as soon as she drove away. She should've spent her Saturday afternoon with Jordan. She should've been spending Saturday night with Jordan and waking up next to him on Sunday morning. Half an hour later, Robin pulled into the parking garage of her building and pulled out her phone. She'd gotten nothing from him, so she decided to take the initiative.

Her call went to his voice mail. "Hey," she said, hiding her frustration. "Just wanted to check in to see how your weekend is going. How's that ranch of yours? Anyway." She swallowed and wiped a rogue tear from her cheek. "Call me. Maybe I could come out and, I don't know, help wrangle some horses or something."

She hung up knowing good and damn well that the next time she heard from or saw Jordan would be in the office on Monday.

How High She Flies

PRETTY, DOE-EYED ABBY RHODES. It wasn't this house he'd come to see. Jordan had come to satisfy an unusual curiosity about her. Following the sound of the music coming from her backyard, Jordan had stopped inside the gate and watched her without her realizing it before finally approaching her. She wore cutoff jean shorts, and a black T-shirt with a Batman insignia on the front. Abby's tousled hair was pulled together into a puff on top of her head, and she was barefoot.

Why did he feel like he was in some sort of trance when he was close to her? Her looks weren't dramatic or overtly striking, just comforting, easy to take in, and difficult to ignore. He began to understand that the attraction to him was not solely physical. Jordan felt like he needed something from her, but for the life of him, he didn't understand what or why. He had a feeling of expectation with her. As if she might say or do a certain thing that would become his own personal revelation. As if she were the key to unlocking a door.

He and Abby had gone inside the house, and he waited patiently on the sofa, sitting across from her while she did an Internet search of Julian Gatewood, which, of course, would ultimately lead to Jordan. In a little over a month, she'd turned this place into a dream house compared to what it had been when he'd first seen it. Abby had taken down walls, replaced floors, and remodeled the whole kitchen in that short period of time. It was charming, bright, and comfortable. It was indicative of what he suspected her personality was like.

"Oh, my goodness," she murmured, slowly raising her gaze from the laptop screen in her small office to look at him.

Jordan looked back at her, knowing instinctively what her next words would be.

"You're Jordan Gatewood?"

"I am."

Abby swallowed. Her eyes widened with disbelief. "You didn't tell me that the first time we met."

"No," he said without elaborating.

"It said in one of these articles that you were shot not too long ago. That you almost died."

He didn't respond.

"So, that's what made you want to come back to this house? You weren't close to your father, but I guess the fact that he got shot and you got shot would make you curious about him?"

Not everyone from Texas spoke with the twang, but Abby seemed to relish the accent, and it rolled off her tongue like a melody. He liked the sound of it.

"I suppose you could say that," he agreed.

He could almost see the curiosity churning behind her eyes. "Did you know her? Ida Green?"

"I saw her, at the trial," he explained.

"The article says that her daughter, Desdimona, was on trial for killing him. She went to prison for it."

"Her daughter didn't kill him."

"But she went to prison."

"She didn't kill him."

"Ida killed him?"

Jordan had hated that woman his whole life, believing that she was ultimately responsible for his father's death and his mother's heartache. But now he knew better.

"My mother killed my father," he continued.

It was so important for this woman to know the truth for some reason. And of all the people in his life, she was the only one that he didn't seem to have a problem confessing it to.

Abby's lovely eyes widened in astonishment. "Whoa," she whispered. "But it doesn't say that in any of these articles."

"And it never will," he simply said, deciding to leave it at that, even if she did pursue the subject.

He saw no need to weigh down this conversation with all the details of what had transpired here three decades ago. Abby seemed to understand that and closed her laptop.

"What is it that you hope to find here, Jordan?" she asked earnestly, as if she really expected for him to have a clear and concise answer.

He actually hadn't truly pinpointed the answer inside himself, and Jordan had to think about it. "I think I've misunderstood my father," he finally admitted.

Shit. He'd never been to therapy a day in his life, but all of a sudden, that's exactly what this felt like.

"I believed that I knew him, but circumstances, recent circumstances, may prove to the contrary." Jordan searched for answers internally. "I don't know what I expected when I came here. For some random reason on that random day, something drew me here."

Jordan reached for Ida Green's photo on the small table in front of him and stared at it.

"He spent a great deal of time here with her, Abby. If you knew my father, then you'd know that it doesn't make sense that he would." He looked up at her again. "Julian Gatewood was a grand man, larger than life." Jordan could hardly remember a time when Julian wasn't wearing a custom-made suit and tie. He spoke with such authority, commanding attention when he walked into a room.

"He would not fit in a place like this, in her life. And I'm not talking about physically. But it seems that he was happier here than he was in that Dallas mansion I grew up in. My mother is a beautiful woman—always was. On the surface they were perfect. It made sense for him to be with her."

"But not Ida?" she asked softly, looking almost as if she had personally been insulted by his explanation.

Jordan looked at Ida's picture again. Ida was not the beast of a woman he'd remembered during that trial. Jordan had been a kid; he was in college, twenty, maybe twenty-one years old. Back then, he thought she was hideous, too dark, fat, an ugly woman. But looking at this picture now as a grown man and not some confused, angry kid, she was none of those things.

"He loved Ida," he concluded. "He loved her so much that he'd rather have been here with her than at home. A man who had absolutely everything would rather spend his weekends in this small house with this small and insignificant woman than in the kingdom he'd built in Dallas."

"Then Ida wasn't insignificant," Abby responded protectively.

"You can't see it because you're not him. He saw something in her that no one else in the world did, and he needed it. Whatever it was, it was important enough to keep him coming back."

She was a romantic. Jordan never had been.

"If you knew my father, then you'd know that the idea of love being the reason that he was obsessed with this woman was ludicrous. Julian loved Julian," he said shrugging. "He loved his business. I guess, I'd be stunned to know that he risked everything to be with Ida over something as basic as love."

"But what else could it be?"

"I'd like to know."

"Why do you have to know? It was private between the two of them. Maybe it's not meant for you to know."

Too much of his life had mirrored that of a man that he'd come to realize he hardly knew. Jordan had inherited the man's business, his legacy, even the care of his wife. He'd almost inherited his father's demise, but by some stroke of fortune, he was still here. And he'd inherited a void. Julian had had one, too, Jordan was positive. But he'd filled his with time in this house and with another woman. Why this woman? Why this town, this house?

"I need to understand," he said, trying to sound reasonable, even though he was starting to unravel inside. "He died trying to protect her. He sacrificed everything for her and I've never been able to grasp that."

"People do things like that when they're in love. You've never felt that way about anybody?"

No, he hadn't. Jordan decided not to say that out loud. From the look on his face he concluded that his expression had answered it for him.

"I wish I could help." She shrugged. "It makes sense to me that whatever he felt for her died with him. It's not like finding a photograph or a trinket, Jordan. Sounds like it was just love. And maybe it really was that simple."

Was it his imagination or was the air slightly warmer around Abby? Was the world a bit quieter when she spoke? Jordan felt easy in her presence, that constant hum of defensive energy flowing through him felt stalled and even unnecessary for the few hours he'd been here with her. Abby distracted him and not in a bad way.

A few minutes later, Abby walked him to the door.

"I hope that you can find whatever it is you're looking for, Jordan. I mean that."

He towered over her by at least a foot. Jordan wasn't ready to leave, but he wasn't quite sure how to let her know that he wanted to stay. It was an odd revelation. He reached for his wallet, pulled out a business card, and held it out to her. A gut feeling was telling him that this wasn't over, whatever *this* was.

"I appreciate your time, Abby," he said as she reluctantly took it.

"Oh, it was no problem. I wish I knew how to help you find what you're looking for. I'm sure it's frustrating."

"Maybe there's nothing for me to find. Maybe what went on between those two is none of my business."

She smiled. "Well, have a safe drive back to Dallas. And it was good meeting you. I mean, the real you."

He nearly smiled, turned, and left. But Dallas was the last place he wanted to be. Jordan would make his way back to his ranch and try not to think about when he might see this woman again.

Just Look

". . . THE SAME THING. He's like him."
"I can't know that. How can I know? What?"
"Buried. Buried deep."
"But where?"

Abby's dreams these days were fragmented and cryptic. In the dream she had last night, she vividly remembered talking to someone about something that seemed so urgent and profound, but for the life of her, she couldn't remember who or even what the conversation was about. Morning came, and everything that had been so crucial while she slept had become a blur.

After meeting Jordan, she spent the next few days just surfing the Internet about him. The notion that a man like him had been sitting in her living room was absolutely unbelievable. Jordan was worth hundreds of millions of dollars according to *Forbes*. *The Forbes*. He was forty-nine, though; she'd have never guessed he was that old by looking at him. He was the same age as her brother

Wesley, except that Wesley looked every single one of his forty-nine years. Actually, he looked like he'd had a couple of extra ones thrown in for good measure.

Jordan had been married for over five years before his wife died. She'd committed suicide. Abby had even found pictures of his mother, Olivia, and she was a beautiful woman. The difference between her and Ida was definitely night and day. Julian Gatewood did a whole one-eighty when he chose Ida, who apparently died a very sad and lonely woman. Abby's heart broke for her.

During Julian's murder trial, Ida was painted as the harlot, the sleazy other woman who did everything she could to steal him from his wife, Olivia. Looking at her in those old photographs from the newspapers on the Internet, Ida looked like a broken woman and so sad. The man she loved was dead, and her only daughter, a very young woman named Desdimona, was charged and convicted of his murder. So, not only did she lose him, she lost her, too. Years later, before her daughter was released from prison, Ida died alone in this house. No wonder it was haunted.

Jordan was a Taurus. She wasn't surprised. He seemed like a Taurus. Determined and solid, he had a strong air about him. But in the little bit of time that the two of them had actually talked to each other, it was obvious that he desperately needed to find this connection to his father. He didn't even fully understand why, and maybe he wouldn't until or unless he found it. But it was important to him. Things like this just proved that money wasn't everything. To Abby, it was simple. Julian Gatewood came to this house and spent all that time with Ida because he loved her. She added value to his life that wasn't there before, despite everything else he had. Love was like that. At least, that was Abby's best guess. She still hadn't ever really found it, only managing to skirt around it a few times, but she'd never experienced the full-blown, head-over-heels love.

Jordan Gatewood, on the other hand, only needed to open up those muscley arms of his, and love would fall right in them. She'd seen so many pictures of him with so many beautiful women, it was a wonder that he had time to be looking for any damn thing. Between running a whole, entire corporation and going out on dates, the fact that he had time in the day to come down to Blink chasing history was absurd to Abby. There had to have been at least ten women standing in line waiting to be the next Mrs. Gatewood. If she ever spoke to him again, she might suggest that he slow down a bit and pay attention to what he had available at his finger-tips. Maybe then he'd understand what his father had seen in Ida.

"Hey, Auntie Rue." Abby smiled and wrapped both arms around that woman as soon as she walked into her father's and stepmother's house.

"Hey, baby." Rue laughed and patted Abby warmly on the back. "Oh, it's good to see you."

"It's good to see you, too." Abby sat down next to her. "How was your flight?"

Rue was her father's oldest sister, and she lived in Virginia with her daughter and her daugher's husband. She was in town for the next few weeks visiting family.

"Too damn long. Next time, y'all need to come see me. I'm getting too old to be flying down here every year."

Abby shook her head. "Ain't nothing old about you."

"Tell that to my knees and hips." She laughed.

"You bring that drill, Abby?" her father said, coming into the living room.

"Yes, sir. It's in my truck. Want me to go get it?"

"No. I'll get it."

"I heard you bought another house," Rue said, impressed.

"Yes, ma'am." Abby smiled.

"How many you got now?"

"This is my fourth. I just finished renovating it—well, most of it. There are still a few things to do on the outside, but I've got most of the inside done."

Rue shook her head and smiled. "Chile, you are just like yo' momma. Between you and me, she was the smart one in that marriage to my brother."

Abby laughed. "She said the same thing."

All day long, cousins and aunts and uncles filtered in and out of the house to see Rue. Food appeared out of nowhere like magic. They laughed, joked, and teased one another. It was one of those unexpected treats in life that would linger with Abby for weeks afterward. She loved her family and being close to them. Of course, the question of her social life always managed to come up in these situations.

"You seeing anybody?"

"Why not?"

"Having your own business is nice and all, but . . ."

"You a cute girl. It shouldn't be that hard to find anybody."

"Ever think you might be too picky?"

"I'd like to see a grandbaby or two before I die, Abigail."

Abby was a master at deflection. So, whenever the conversation turned to her and her love life and her empty womb, she changed the subject. After everyone had eaten, Abby found Rue sitting outside on the porch with some of her old neighbors.

"Auntie Rue, do you know who she is?"

Abby had taken Shou Shou's warning to heart. She didn't dare ever take that picture of Ida Green out of that house again, but she did take a snapshot of it with her cell phone. Back when Rue used to live here, she knew a lot of people. Abby hadn't intended on asking her about Ida. She'd meant to ask her father, but she decided to start with Rue.

Rue stared down at the phone through her reading glasses. "That Ida?"

Abby's heart thumped hard in her chest. "You do know her?"

Rue adjusted her glasses. "That's an old picture."

"I found it in my house."

Rue looked at Abby. "That house you bought?"

Abby nodded. "Yes, ma'am. You knew her?"

She passed the phone to one of her friends. "That's her, all right," the other woman said. "Where's the rest of the picture?" she asked, looking at Abby.

Abby shrugged. "That's all I found."

That old woman handed it back to Rue, who studied it some more. "This look like it was taken at Smitty's."

"Smitty's?" Abby asked.

Rue laughed out loud. "Boy, did we have a good time at Smitty's." She looked at her friend, who lowered her head and pressed her lips together, like she was trying to keep the secrets from running past them.

"What's Smitty's?" Abby asked.

"An old disco off Smith Road, all the way down to the end near the lake."

"There's a building back there?"

"Probably not much of one anymore, but yes. There used to be a building back there."

"And we partied our asses off," the other woman finally said, laughing, too.

Okay, so Abby had to sit here and accept the fact that these old broads hadn't always been old, and to surmise that from the twinkles in their eyes, they'd done some things she was probably better off not knowing about.

"It looks like the picture has been torn in two," Abby explained.

Rue sighed. "Julian was probably in the other half," she said dismally.

Abby played dumb. "Julian?"

"Some old rich man she was fooling 'round with."

"You couldn't tell her nothing," the other woman said. "She clung to him like lint on a black sweater."

"Naw. She did try to break it off with him, but he wouldn't leave her alone," Rue explained.

"I still think she's the one that shot him," the other woman said. "That girl of hers just took the blame to save her momma. That's what I think."

"That could be," Rue said introspectively. "But I do think she loved him too much. He knew it. And he took advantage of her because of it."

The Calm I Feel

"HEY, BABY," ROBIN PURRED OVER the phone.

Jordan had been driving lazily through Blink for the better part of forty-five minutes when she called. "Hey, you," he responded warmly. "I was going to call," he lied.

"Oh, really? When were you going to call me?"

"Soon," was all he'd say.

"Well, since I beat you to the punch, how about you come and pick me up and take me out for a drink, talk about our busy weeks, and then come back to my place?"

He sighed. "I'd love to, but I'm not in town."

She paused. Knowing Robin, she was probably setting up a task on her phone to call his assistant in the morning to find out where he was. "I thought you were just going to your ranch."

"Yes."

Her hesitation was a sign that she expected him to elaborate.

"I could come there."

"I'll see you in the office tomorrow, Robin. Bright and early."

Of course, her mind was reeling. A part of him felt as if he should've been willing to just tell her the truth, but Jordan didn't want the questions; he didn't need the attention or for Robin to try to psychoanalyze him and his daddy issues. And she was the type to do just that.

"Is everything all right, Jordan? Are you all right?"

"Why would you ask me that?"

"You just sound a bit distant, preoccupied. That's all."

"No, I'm fine, Robin. Like I said, I'll see you in the morning, and after work, I'd love to take you out for that drink."

"Promise?" she asked seductively.

"Of course."

This town forced him to drive too slowly. The very air here was saturated with an unhurried pace. He almost felt high off it, but he wasn't complaining. After leaving Abby's, Jordan had stopped at a corner store and picked up some essentials, a toothbrush and toothpaste, deodorant, soap, and a newspaper. When was the last time he'd actually bought a newspaper?

The clerk at the counter was an older woman with perfectly coiffed curls, pink lipstick, and faded blue eyes. "The weather's real nice today," she said engagingly as she took her time ringing up his items.

"It certainly is," he felt compelled to say, surprised that he actually meant it.

"Will that be all?" she asked, taking the time to stop, look up at him, and smile.

"Yes, ma'am," he said politely.

Anonymity was a treat that most people took for granted. Jordan's life had played out in the public for as long as he could remember. He'd been in Blink since yesterday, and he was no one special. Had it been that way for Julian? Did he relish this small pocket of the world where he was just a man and no one in particular? Small towns had a way of wrapping themselves around the residents like blankets, keeping them warm and safe. A brief stay here could be comfortable, but too long would be stifling.

Jordan had stayed the night because he wasn't in any hurry to get home. He'd spent most of that first night and today using his cell phone to check some e-mails from work. But his thoughts kept drifting back to Abby Rhodes. He wasn't crazy. There was something about her—Jordan had just decided to get back on the road and head home. He'd told Robin that he wouldn't be home until Monday, but Jordan needed time alone and alone in the comfort of his own home instead of some cramped hotel room.

Just then, his phone rang. "This is Jordan."

"Hi."

Hi was not the kind of greeting he was used to when he answered his phone. "Hi?"

"This is Abby."

"Abby. Hello." Needless to say, he was certainly surprised. Pleasantly.

"So, I spoke to my aunt Rue," she began.

Immediately, he wondered what her aunt Rue had to do with him. Jordan pulled over to the side of the road and put his truck in park.

"She knew Ida Green, and she knew Julian."

Jordan was caught off guard. "You spoke to someone else about this?"

"Yes, but I didn't mention you. I didn't think that would be a good idea. I just . . . well, I had Ida's picture, and so I . . . I don't know. I just thought I'd take a chance and ask her if she knew her. They'd be about the same age, and Aunt Rue knows everybody in Blink. Just about literally."

Jordan felt a sense of resentment that she'd take the liberty to talk to anyone about this. Then again, he found himself appreciating the fact that Abby hadn't let go of this quest—of him completely. Perhaps she was just curious about the relationship between Julian and Ida. A part of him hoped that it was more than that, though.

"I could take you somewhere," she reluctantly offered.

Her statement caught him off guard. "Where?"

"It's kinda silly, really, but, well, it might help you to get a feel for your father and how he may have been when he was here. I don't know. He didn't just sit up in the house with Ida when he came to Blink. They weren't a secret, Jordan. Not here."

Jordan thought about it before responding. "I don't know if that's going to be much help, Abby."

"You're probably right," she said much too anxiously. "I just thought I'd at least mention it. But yeah. I agree. It's silly, like I said."

Was it silly? He'd been driving through town wondering how it must've felt to Julian driving through these streets. Maybe that's what he'd been doing all along, trying to retrace that man's steps.

"What did you have in mind?" he asked.

"Well, when you get back into town, there's this place where he and Ida used to frequent. It's a night club. Probably barely standing anymore, but I know where it is, and if you want, I can take you there or give you directions."

Julian Gatewood, multimillionaire, partying with his mistress in an old club in the backwoods of Blink, Texas. Sounded like some kind of bad comedic skit, and he was suddenly very curious.

"I'd appreciate it if you could take me."

"Well, just let me know when you're in town again and—"

"I'm in town now." Jordan pulled away from the curb. "On my way to your place."

Smitty's was literally just a shack, deep in the woods on the edge of a lake. It couldn't have been more than two thousand square feet of space inside, at the most.

"Wow," Abby said in awe, following Jordan inside. She laughed. "Can you believe this place?"

The few windows in the place were broken out. Wood floors creaked with each step, the parts that weren't rotted out.

"Be careful," he warned her.

"Oh, I'm being careful."

There was a dilapidated bar against the far south wall, topped with peeling linoleum, and behind that were empty shelves where liquor bottles had probably sat. Old and broken wooden chairs and tables were scattered throughout. It was almost as if she could still smell stale smoke and beer over the mildew.

"This must've been the dance floor," Abby said, standing in a small open space covered with the same material that covered the bar top. She looked at him and smiled. "I'll bet you can't even imagine your daddy in a place like this, doing the bump and the robot, or whatever dance they did back in those days."

She was right. He absolutely could not. Julian was tuxedos and polished shoes, elegant dinner parties and the theater.

"They probably had live music," she continued, slowly walking over to one corner of the room with a small platform. "Do you think they'd have a DJ?" she asked, turning to him. "Playing records?"

He found her question amusing. "We're talking eighties here, Abby."

"Eighties?" she asked, stunned. "They had records in the eighties. Right?"

"They did," he said nonchalantly. "When were you born?"

"Seventy-nine."

He stared at her. She was twelve years his junior. Young enough for him to almost feel like a dirty old man.

"Aunt Rue said that this was the place to be back in the day. There were nicer discos, but folks preferred this one because the music was old-school. You know. Like music from the sixties and seventies."

Jordan found himself mesmerized by the sound of her voice and her description of the place, almost as if she had been there.

"She said that they'd get here early, around six for happy hour, on Fridays, mostly, and start off by playing cards and dominoes."

Abby walked slowly through the room, grazing her fingers over the backs of chairs and across dusty tables. She wore a delicate blue dress, cotton, the hem stopping at the middle of her thighs, the top fitting the contours of her breasts, with a thin, black belt cinched at her waist. Her curls fell loose around her face, touching the tops of her shoulders. Jordan hung on to the sound of her voice, fixated on the delicate trace of her fingers, and allowed himself to be caught up in her reimagining of this place.

"They'd drink and smoke and laugh," she said, staring out at the expanse of the room, beyond him. "And then at some point, the music would start playing, and one couple would get on the floor and just start dancing, then another and another until it was packed and they could barely move."

Jordan could almost hear the music and see the bodies moving from side to side as one collective.

"Catfish and french fries," she said, closing her eyes and inhaling like she could actually smell it. "Doused with plenty of hot sauce, of course. And some of the best coleslaw in Texas." She laughed and looked at him. "They ate like kings and queens and drank until the world moved in slow motion." She laughed again. "And the best dances were the slow ones." Abby looked enviable and lost in her thoughts. "The night always ended with a slow dance."

It took every ounce of restraint in him not to reach out for this magical woman who'd transported him back to a time and place where life was simple, pure, and easy. An image flashed in his mind of Julian, sweaty and high on cheap liquor, catfish and cole-slaw, wrapped around Ida like second skin, staring deep into her eyes, whispering promises, and grinning like he'd won a prize.

He met her gaze and held it. He could tell that she wanted to look away, but hoped she wouldn't.

"I imagine that for a man like him, a night like that would be a reprieve from all those big responsibilities that he had back in Dallas. And I'd imagine that spending it here with the woman he loved made it even more special." She shrugged. "Not that I con-done the fact that he was cheating on his wife," she added.

"No, there's no excuse for that," he said. Infidelity was one of those things he and Julian had always had in common. Jordan had been a shitty husband, too.

"This place wasn't much, but tucked back here in the woods like this?" She smiled. "There's something mysterious about it. Don't you think? Forbidden and secret."

Abby looked uncomfortable all of a sudden as she slowly winded her way out of fantasy.

"We should go," she finally said to him, hurrying and leading the way out. "I'm sure you need to get back home to Dallas."

And that was too bad.

Witchy Woman

TWO DAYS AGO OLIVIA GATEWOOD had stunned the hospital staff when she asked her caregiver to warm her tea. The woman nearly fainted before rushing to get nurses and doctors who crowded around Olivia like she'd just woken up from a thousand-year sleep.

"I need to see him," she said to the woman bathing her. "I need to see my son."

You'd have thought from the expression on the woman's face that Olivia had asked to see Jesus.

"My son," she repeated, more determined. "I want to see him."

Olivia had rested long enough. That silly son of hers had been away for too long. Her doctor had assured her that he'd phoned Jordan alerting him to recent events surrounding her. Her daughter, June, had called several times and was making plans to come and see her mother as soon as possible. Jordan obviously wasn't in a rush to see her.

"I've been waiting for two days."

Olivia saw no need to begin this visit with cordial and wasteful pleasantries. Jordan casually walked into her living room, unbuttoned his suit jacket, and sat down in the chair across from her as if he hadn't kept his mother waiting all this time.

"Tell me that you've only recently received my message," she challenged.

Jordan's unconcerned expression started to anger her.

"Glad to see you've finally snapped out of it," he said with a casual sarcasm.

Olivia raised her chin defiantly. "Attitude, Jordan," she said with warning. "Remember who you're talking to."

"How could I possibly forget?" he responded indifferently. "But it is good to see that you're feeling better, recovering nicely, they tell me."

Olivia released a soft and heavy sigh. "I've been resting, Jordan. My condition sometimes takes its toll. But that's no excuse for you to stay away for so long or to act like an ass when you do decide to finally show up."

He turned his handsome face slightly to one side and peered intensely at her. "No, I truly am happy to see you're faring well and I'm not acting."

Again with the cloaked sarcasm. A mother knows her child better than she knows herself, and Jordan was purposefully callous.

"So, you're angry with me," she eventually concluded.

The amused expression faded from his dark, hooded eyes. "Angry? How could I possibly ever be angry with you, Mother?"

If he had bothered to hide the malicious tone of his question, he hadn't done a very good job. And yes. She was hurt by his behavior, by his lack of attention to his mother. Jordan had always been so devoted to Olivia, even more than June. He had been the one that Olivia could always count on. He had been her prince; even when he was a little boy, he had doted on her. She could only conclude from his attitude that he was somehow disappointed with her.

"My memory can be so deceptive at times, son," she tenderly tried to explain. "There are gaps, moments missing that I can't account for. So much has been lost in those moments—people, time, and events. If I've somehow caused you any grief, Jordan, believe me, it was never intentional."

"Is that right?" he eventually asked.

Yes. Olivia had done or said something hurtful to him during one of her blackouts. Studying him, she could almost see the pain in his eyes.

"You have always been my one true love, Jordan." She smiled warmly. "The love of my life."

"I'm honored," he said curtly.

Now he was starting to piss her off, but Olivia decided that pursuing an argument wasn't worth the effort since she hadn't seen him in ages and there was so much for them to catch up on.

"I've been told that you're working on finalizing some kind of contract with the federal government to develop a new fuel alternative. Is that true?"

It was next to impossible not to be impressed by her son. In so many ways, he was even more brilliant than his father.

"Who told you that?" he asked casually.

It was easy enough for her to still put her finger on the pulse of Gatewood Industries, even in the two days since she'd recovered from her "episode."

"Does it matter?" she replied coyly. "It's my understanding that this could be the collaboration of a lifetime if it plays in our favor."

"Yes. It could be," he confirmed. "The alternative fuel project would be in conjunction with design and development of a new rocket engine."

She smiled and clasped her hands together. "Since when does Gatewood Industries build rocket engines?

"Since the government expressed a need for one," he said nonchalantly.

"How impressive!" Olivia exclaimed.

She had nothing but faith in this resourceful young man. Of course he could build engines for rockets. Olivia was as convinced as she always was that there was nothing he couldn't do when he set his mind to it.

"How close are you to finalizing the agreement?" she asked excitedly.

"Two other businesses are in the running, Mother. All we can do is wait and see."

"And if you win, Jordan, how much is it worth to Gatewood Industries?"

Jordan paused. "Billions."

He was her golden child. Always had been and always would be. She'd known it from the moment she handed over the helm of the corporation to him after her husband's death, nearly three decades ago. Jordan had grown up with Gatewood Industries. He'd turned it into something Julian could never have fathomed.

"And what about your social life?" she asked, changing the subject.

Of course she was concerned about how he was managing all aspects of his life. He was too wonderful to just bury his head in business.

"Claire's been gone for some time now, Jordan. Maybe we've

spoken about this and I don't remember, but have you been seeing anyone?"

He raised a heavy brow in response.

"Not that I'm prying, son, but it's just that I want you to be happy. You know I do."

Just then, his cell phone vibrated. Jordan pulled it from the inside pocket of his jacket, glanced at it, and looked at her. "Excuse me. I've got to take this."

She nodded. "Of course."

"Yes?" he answered and paused, listening to the caller. "Please do. I look forward to receiving it. Thank you."

A mother knows her child, and Olivia couldn't hold back the sheepish grin spreading her lips as she listened to his exchange with the other person. Of course it was a woman.

"I'll read it as soon as I get back to the office. Good-bye."

"So, there is someone?" his mother brazenly asked.

"Someone I've met recently," he admitted. "Yes."

"Good," she said without probing for details. It was too soon for that. "I'm glad that you haven't closed yourself off to the possibilities, son. You have so much to offer some lovely woman and you deserve every happiness."

Jordan seemed to ponder her comment before abruptly excusing himself.

"I really do have to get back to the office, Mother. I've got several meetings this afternoon that I must attend."

"Of course, Jordan," she said enthusiastically. "But I would like for you to come back soon. We should have dinner together. I'll have my chef prepare your favorite."

He stood up, walked over to her, and leaned down to kiss the top of her head. "That would be interesting."

It was an odd choice of words, but he left her little time to challenge them.

"I'll call you," he said over his shoulder as he left.

Olivia watched admiringly as her handsome son walked out of the room, disappearing into the foyer. He had always been her heart and soul. There had been times in his life when he sometimes seemed to forget that, and she had had no choice but to blame herself. Olivia oftentimes allowed distractions to get the best of her, to the detriment of their relationship. But Jordan was the most steadfast and dependable person in her life. He always had been, even in the worst of times. He forgave her for her sins and devoted himself to her more than she could ever truly comprehend.

Suddenly, an unexpected image flashed in her mind of herself screaming. A gun firing. She inadvertently jumped at the sound that wasn't real now. Regret immediately washed over her as she took a deep breath to cleanse away the residue of unpleasant thoughts. Some memories were best left to the dark corners of the mind, forgotten and put away. She'd always been selective about such things. He was angry with her still. But Jordan loved her beyond what was reasonable, and in time, he'd forgive her. He always did. She rested in that knowledge.

Echoed Voices

JORDAN HAD WATCHED ABBY'S video several times, to the point of damn near having it memorized.

"Hey, boss," his personal assistant, Phyl Mays, said, knocking lightly on his office door before entering. "Jennifer's gone for the day?"

He glanced at the time on his computer screen. It was after six in the evening. "Yes."

Phyl took a seat. "Just a few things before I head home," she said, powering up her tablet. "Ms. Sinclair wanted me to remind you about Senator Wilson's fund-raiser a week from Saturday. Got a tux all dusted off and hanging in the closet for you." Phyl winked.

"Thank you."

"Did Jenn put the interview and photo shoot on your calendar for the first for the *Houston Maverick* magazine?"

He glanced at his calendar. "She did."

"Because she's good like that," Phyl joked. "Mark Allen will be conducting the interview, and I forwarded you a list of questions earlier today."

"I'm surprised that he gave you a list of questions," he said.

"I told him you wouldn't agree to do the interview without them."

"Thank you."

"And I did some research on Abby Rhodes like you asked," she finally said. "So, she's a general contractor in Blink, Texas. Owns several properties—three single-family homes, which she rents out to tenants. She runs a small business called A&R Contracting, where she mostly does things like household renovations. You know, kitchen and bathroom remodels, decks, that sort of thing. Has a net worth of around three hundred thousand, which for Blink is actually pretty impressive. Single. Never been married. No kids. Not even a dog. Thirty-seven—this weekend." Phyl smiled proudly. "And she's cute. If I weren't in sort of a committed, lusty relationship with a big-bosomed brunette, I might make a play for her."

"Is that it?"

She sighed. "That's it, boss. Can I go home now?"

"Have a good night, Phyl."

Phyl was efficient, overly sarcastic, quick-witted, and she never asked more questions than she needed to. He didn't always act like it, but he liked her and, more importantly, he trusted her.

Was he losing his damn mind or what? Jordan was too busy to be traipsing up and down the highway to Blink fucking Texas, but it was like he was on automatic pilot, and the very next afternoon, Jordan had checked into his hotel and, two hours later, was sitting down at a restaurant called Belle's for a steak dinner, watching the video that Abby had e-mailed to him again.

Jordan played Abby's video on his cell phone. She'd recorded it from her home. Abby's hair was pulled back like before and her face free of any makeup. Actually, he couldn't remember if he'd ever seen her wearing makeup.

"So, I was going to e-mail you but then thought that'd be like sending you a book. And I don't think you want to read that much, just like I don't want to have to type that much."

Jordan didn't realize he was smiling, but the sound of her voice did that to him.

"I'm just going to be forthright with you," she said taking a deep breath. "My house is haunted. No, I'm not crazy. Just hear me out. I believe that it's haunted by Ida Green and maybe even your daddy, which is why I have become somewhat obsessed with learning who these people are, just like you have."

She licked her full lips, and Jordan fixed his gaze on them.

"It seems to me that maybe if you knew more about her, it would tell you more about him. Right? Does that make sense?"

It did.

"I spoke some more to my aunt Rue. But don't worry, Jordan. I have not mentioned your name at all. If anyone in town knew that I knew somebody like you, they'd be camped out in my front yard just to get a good look at you and they'd be all over you like fire ants," she concluded. "But I did speak to her about Ida. And the two of them went to school together. They graduated a year apart and were friends, as much as anybody could be friends with Rue." She shook her head and sighed. "But Ida was shy. A lot of the kids made fun of her because she was so dark and her family was so poor. Anyway, after high school, she got a job working at a hotel in downtown Blink. Before that she'd worked as a seamstress in her mother's shop. She met Julian at the hotel, though."

Abby looked off to the side and flipped through a notepad sitting next to her computer.

"Um, I guess he must've been passing through town on business, decided to get a room one night while she was working. Rue couldn't be sure, but she thinks she remembers that he came back to town a couple of times. This was in 1970, by the way."

Julian formally adopted Jordan in 1970, maybe '71. He'd married Olivia in '68. Damn. Jordan had never stopped to do the math, but it made sense. Julian was barely married to Olivia when he started seeing Ida.

"Now here's the delicate part," Abby said apprehensively. "Ida sorta got pregnant right away, Jordan," she said broaching the subject cautiously. "And she had a daughter, Desi, who is the one who went to prison for killing Julian. Lord, I hope you know that."

Abby's eyes widened.

"I so hope you do."

He knew.

"So, I don't know if any of this helps you. I know it's helping me to understand that this wasn't just a fling. I mean, he was with her until the day he died, eighteen years later. But I can imagine that he was pretty overwhelming to her. A shy young woman meets a big-city businessman."

Once again, he sensed that Abby was very protective of Ida's memory.

"I'm sure he was real slick, said all the right things, and impressed the hell out of her. It couldn't have been hard. But he didn't just, well, to put it mildly, hit it and quit it. He stayed with her, had a baby with her. I'd say that whatever he felt for her was genuine. I'd say he definitely loved her." Abby shrugged. "And I find comfort in that for some reason. Anyway, I hope this helps."

———

"Hey, Mr. Rhodes. Mrs. Rhodes."

Jordan looked up from his phone and saw an older man and woman coming in to the restaurant and stopping at the bar to talk to the woman who owned the place. "Belle," the old man said. "How you been?"

"Good. Good. Y'all need menus?"

"Naw. We waiting on Abby," the woman said.

The man wasn't quite six feet tall, slender, and was dark like Abby. The woman looked to be Latin.

"The two of you look real nice," Belle said. "What's the occasion?"

"Abby's birthday," the man said. "We're taking her out."

"She thinks we're having dinner here," the woman chimed in. "But we're surprising her and taking her to Clark City to that new seafood restaurant they just opened up."

"Sounds good. I'm not even going to say that I'm offended that you're not eating here; if it were me, I'd rather try out that new seafood place myself." She laughed.

Abby walked in at that moment, wearing a form-fitting, floor-length dress, patterned, showing off a lovely back, beautiful teardrop behind, and cleavage of those bountiful breasts. "Hey, Daddy," she said, hugging and kissing the old man on the cheek. "Hey, Birdy." She hugged the woman. "Sorry I'm late. Hey, Belle."

"Don't you look sexy," Belle teased. "You sure you're just going out to dinner with your daddy and stepmomma?"

Abby smiled. "I am not spending my birthday in steel-toed boots and a utility belt. That's for damn sure. I don't care if we were going to Wally's Burger Kingdom, I was gonna dress up no matter what."

"You look beautiful, honey," her father said, kissing her cheek.

She certainly did.

"Belle, I think there are going to be about six of us," she said, questioning and scanning the room, he assumed, looking for a table, when she spotted him.

Once again, Abby's expression froze in astonishment as if she were seeing him for the first time all over again.

Abby gave a pensive wave in Jordan's direction.

Her father turned and looked, too, then turned back at her. "Who's that?"

Jordan saw her mouth move, but he couldn't hear what she told him. The next thing he knew, the three of them were making their way over to his table. Jordan stood up and shook her father's hand and then her stepmother's as the three of them were introduced.

"Hey," her father said. "I'm Walter Rhodes, Mr. Tunson. This is my wife, Birdy."

Birdy, a very short, round Latina woman with big brown eyes and a warm smile, nodded.

"How do you do," she smiled.

"Um, I see you managed to find the best steak house in Texas," Abby said.

"Yes, it's pretty good."

"Abby says you're thinking about buying that old farmhouse on Paris Road, Mr. Tunson."

Jordan looked at Abby, staring back at him with a slight squint.

"Thinking about it."

Jordan guessed her father to be in his seventies. Jordan's father would've been in his eighties by now, so the two men probably didn't know each other. But then again, they could've.

"How long you in town for?" he asked Jordan. He had no idea what kind of story she'd told her father, but Jordan decided to play along.

"Just until tomorrow."

"From Dallas, right?" he probed.

"Yes, sir."

Sir? Strange how that subtle show of respect rolled off his lips so effortlessly here in this town.

"Hey, everybody. Sorry we late."

Another man holding the hand of the woman with him showed up all of a sudden, too. "We still going?"

"Going?" Abby asked, looking confused. "We're here already, Wes. Duh."

"She don't know?" Wes asked, looking at his father.

"I told you she didn't," the old man fussed.

"Know what?" Abby asked.

Watching this conversation take place was like watching something akin to the Abbott and Costello. *Who's on first?*

"We're taking you to that new seafood restaurant that just opened up in Clark City, sweetheart," her mother told her.

"Really?" Abby's eyes widened. "Seriously?" she asked excitedly.

"Too bad you're almost finished eating or we'd invite you to come along," her father offered to Jordan.

Abby looked mortified and relieved. She'd be mistaken if she thought he didn't notice.

"Thank you. I appreciate the consideration."

"What time are you leaving tomorrow?" he asked.

"Daddy," she muttered with a warning.

Jordan's curiosity was suddenly sparked. "I'm not sure."

"Well, we're having a family cookout at the house for Abby's birthday tomorrow at noon, if you'd like to come."

Jordan glanced at Abby just in time to see a tidal wave of fear well up in that woman's eyes. "Daddy, I'm sure he's not interested."

"Don't speak for the man, Abby," he gently scolded her, then turned his attention back to Jordan. "Like I said, you're more than welcome to come if you're interested. Got a brisket on the smoker now, and I'll be up early smoking ribs and sausages. We'll have plenty of food. But it's up to you. Abby can get you the address."

"I'm sure you're probably going to be heading out by then," she said, nodding at Jordan.

He was so fucking amused by her pretty face and the dread in her eyes that he couldn't resist.

"No," he said, sending shock waves through her lovely body. "No, I think I can make it."

Abby opened her mouth to protest, but her father chimed in before she could.

"Sounds good." Her father nodded. "We'd better go, honey. Got reservations for eight," he said, reaching out to shake Jordan's hand one more time. "It was good meeting ya, and I'll look for you tomorrow."

"Looking forward to it." He was polite for the benefit of her father, but he gloated for Abby's benefit.

He watched them leave and saw her turn one last time to him with a strange look on her face before being ushered out the door.

Trust in Your Dream

EVERY YEAR, FOR AS long as Abby could remember, her family held a cookout in September for her birthday. Every year, every cousin, aunt, uncle, niece, nephew, and in-law showed up to partake of her father's famous smoked brisket and ribs, barbecued chicken, hot links, burgers, and hot dogs. His oldest sister, Auntie Rue, and their younger sister Amelia came bearing tubs of their to-die-for macaroni and cheese, potato salad, turnip greens, and homemade biscuits. Everybody else brought food, and in the end, it was a feast fit for the gods with enough to feed battalions for weeks.

"Come on, T!" Abby shouted, out of breath and frustrated, walking back to her team from the end zone. "I was wide open!"

She was thirty-seven years old today, and for the last thirty years, since the first time they let her play in the Rhodes family traditional touch-football game, which they had started in honor of her birth, she'd been chasing the one birthday present that had always eluded her—a touchdown. Abby had never once, in all her years of playing this game, scored one single point, and her legacy was turning out to be downright embarrassing.

She made it back to her team, which consisted of her twenty-six-year-old cousin, Tauris, who played quarterback, and five other cousins, male and female, ranging in age from ten to thirty.

"I know you saw me," she said, frustrated, planting her hands on her hips and rolling her eyes.

Abby had been standing in the end zone, by herself, jumping up and down like a fool, yelling, "I'm open! I'm wide open!" until she was exhausted. But T's dumb ass had decided to hand the ball off to Marshall, a kid no more than thirteen, who managed to gain maybe two yards before his flag was snatched.

Tauris was about to call the next play when Abby interrupted. "I'm wide open, T," she reminded him. "Nobody's covering me."

"That's 'cause they know you ain't gonna catch the ball," one of those little assholes blurted out. Abby glared at him.

He smirked and looked away.

"All right," T said, motioning for everyone to huddle close. "I'm keeping this one. Try to at least get the first down."

Abby was livid. "You keep just about all of them."

"Which is why this drive has lasted as long as it has," he shot back.

She shook her head. So, she wasn't the fastest one on the field. She certainly wasn't the best blocker, and her pass coverage was so-so, but still.

"All I'm saying is for us to take advantage of the situation," she reasoned. "They're not covering me because they don't think I'll catch it." She glared at that kid who'd said it. "Which is exactly why it'd be a smart move to throw it to me."

Everybody looked at each other and then finally back at her.

"Y'all hurry up!" someone shouted from the other team.

"No, man," another baby cousin groaned. "Just run the play you just called."

"Would you be quiet?" she retorted to the kid.

"I'm keeping it," T reiterated.

They broke huddle and took their positions across from the other team. T faked a handoff, kept the ball, turned to run, and just like that, his flag was snatched.

"Nice call," she said sarcastically.

So, she was a sore loser. A really good one.

"Who's that?"

"Anybody know who that is?"

Abby knew who he was, and she had been up praying all night that he wouldn't show up here today. She must've done something terribly wrong to offend God. Here it was, her birthday, her blue team was losing in the most embarrassing way to the red team, and multimillionaire CEO of a huge corporation Jordan Gatewood, pretending to be Jordan Tunson, shows up on her football field. After talking to Tauris, he took the football from him and suddenly became the quarterback for Abby's team.

It took everything in her not to cry.

"They changing players?" Abby's brother Rau asked one of their cousins.

The cousin shrugged. "They could bring in Jesus, man. It doesn't matter."

And he was right.

Jordan motioned for his team to huddle and knelt down on one knee. "You all know that you're not winning this game. Right?"

Everyone nodded except for Abby. Dealing with Jordan off the field was one thing. But having him here, at the house where she'd grown up, on her birthday, was something else. Her father shouldn't have invited him, and he should've had the decency to decline when he did. But she knew that from the look in his eyes last night when he'd accepted that invitation that the only reason he'd done it was to get under her skin.

Jordan turned his attention to Abby. "Nobody's covering you."

"Because she can't catch," that portly little cousin of hers said again.

Abby glared at the little boy. "How would you know if nobody ever throws me the ball?" she shot back.

"If they think that you can't catch, then we need to use that to our advantage," Jordan said calmly.

"It's not that they don't think she can't catch," the boy continued. "She really can't catch."

Jordan looked at Abby, who immediately looked away. No one had thrown her the ball in, like, years. Back when they had thrown it to her, she'd tried to catch it, but because of one reason or another, she hadn't. So, since then, nobody would throw to her.

"I want you to get to the end zone, Abby," Jordan continued. He was still watching her. She could feel it. "And I want you to wait."

"What do you want us to do?" one of the kids asked.

"You get to the end zone, too. The rest of you, keep the other team off me," he said simply.

Abby's gaze slowly drifted to Jordan.

"I'm putting it in the air, sending it right to you. All you have to do is wrap your arms around it when it comes," he said to her.

He was going to throw her the ball. A lump formed in her throat. Abby's stomach filled with butterflies.

"Tell me you can do that?" he asked her.

Abby took a deep breath and nodded. This was it. This was her chance, her shot, finally, to prove all these people wrong that she wasn't the worst player on the field. That's what they all thought.

That's why she was the last one to be picked and why no one trusted her to run with or catch the football. The general attitude where she was concerned was "Just stay out of the way, Abby," which was horrible, because she was the most passionate player on the field.

"We know you can build a skyscraper, Peanut, but you suck at sports."

Everyone took their positions on the field. As soon as that ball was snapped and Abby took off running, she didn't look back. It was just her out there by herself, running toward that end zone at the end of the yard, because no one thought of her as enough of a threat to cover. And then she stopped, turned back to her quarterback, and waited.

Jordan ran left, pumped the ball once, but didn't let it go. Her brother Rau nearly had him, but Jordan twisted out of the way. Just before Rau could grab one of the flags off Jordan's hip, Jordan ran right and let it go. Abby watched the ball sail through the air like a bird, coming right at her. The sounds of voices faded. She locked onto the ball, held out her arms, and then, just as it began to descend into her arms, she closed her eyes.

"No!" someone yelled.

Time stopped. What had happened? Silence. And then— slowly, she opened her eyes and realized that she had that ball squeezed tight against her chest. Abby had scored, and no one was more shocked than she was.

"What the—"

"Whoa," the mouthy cousin said, standing and staring mes-merized at her.

"Whoa," she murmured.

"Finally! That's my baby!" she heard her dad call out, clapping. He whistled. "You did it, baby girl! You did it, Peanut!"

And she had. "Yes!" she yelled, spiking the ball and then

jumping out of the way before it hit her in the face as it rico-cheted back up. "Woooo!" She pumped her fists in the air.

Abby ran to Rau. "What, fool?" she said, taunting him.

"Really?" he shot back sarcastically. "You know your team still lost."

She shook her head, patted her hand against her chest, kissed two fingers, and raised them to the sky. If she was a sore loser, she was obviously even a worse winner. Abby skipped, did cartwheels, jumped, and ran to each person on both teams, taunting them and thrusting her personal victory into each and every one of their faces. They'd had no faith in her. They'd written her off years ago, and now she'd just proven them all wrong.

Laughing, jumping, and skipping, she made her way over to the tall and beautiful Jordan whatever-his-last-name-was, who had vision and faith in her the way no one else ever had, and without thinking or hesitating, without realizing what she was doing, Abby hurled herself into his arms, wrapped both legs around him, and kissed him flush on the mouth.

And just like that, she snapped out of it, their eyes met, her mouth gaped open, and Abby slowly lowered herself back to the ground and stared up at him, in disbelief, shock, and awe.

"I am so sorry."

Could she just faint? Or better yet, could she just curl up and die right here in this yard at his feet at this very moment? Please? Abby abruptly broke eye contact, turned, and walked back toward the house and went inside. She was never coming out again.

Too Headstrong

PEANUT. HE GOT IT. Peanut was happy that she'd scored her first touchdown at the annual family flag football game. Peanut gloated like she'd just won the Super Bowl. Peanut forgot that she and Jordan barely knew each other, hurled her lovely little self into his arms, wrapped her legs around him, and planted a wet and sloppy kiss on his lips. Peanut suddenly snapped out of it and practically ignored him for the next hour until Jordan finally said his good-byes and left.

It took all of five minutes to get his things from the hotel room and check out. Jordan had been on the highway for a little over half an hour, headed back to Dallas, thinking that it was no big deal that she'd kissed him. It was cute. Funny. But it didn't mean anything. He'd hoped that the two of them could talk more about the video she'd sent him. Peanut—Abby had actually claimed that her house was haunted. Jordan had never given much thought to the existence of ghosts. Apparently, however, she did believe that it was true, and he was curious as to how she'd reached that conclusion. At least, he told himself that he was. In reality, if talking about ghosts gave him another opportunity to see her again, then he was willing to listen to a few tall tales about all the otherworldly things she wanted to discuss.

That kiss. He was amused by the memory of it. It was like they were two kids on the playground—a bit awkward, unexpected, and sweet. Is that what Julian had seen in Ida? Country-girl sweetness?

Julian Gatewood was a slick sonofabitch. He probably saw that pretty little country Ida Green and swooped down on her like a hawk. Shy. Abby had said that Ida had been shy. He remembered a very reserved version of the woman sitting in the courtroom while her daughter stood trial for Julian's murder. Ida seemed to never make eye contact with anyone. Jordan remembered staring so hard at her at times that it was a wonder he didn't burn a hole in the woman with that laser-sharp gaze of his.

He blamed her. She was the reason behind all those nights that his parents argued and for his father's death. Ida had tried to steal his father from them, to take him from Jordan, his mother, and his sister and Jordan hated her. He hated everything about her.

Of course, back then he had only seen her through the eyes of a very distraught young man. The situation was easier to understand now, though. Jordan was a grown man, and he knew the minds of grown men. Ida was young and sweet and innocent and shy when Julian got his hands on her and made a baby with her. He was shiny and gleamed like a brand-new silver dollar to that young woman. Of course she fell in love with him. It wouldn't have been hard. But what about Julian? Was it love for him, too? True love? Or was he just enamored by the hero worship of a very young woman? Abby wanted to believe that the two shared the love of a lifetime. Jordan wondered if it really mattered.

Twenty years later, Julian was still there, still spending time with Ida and their daughter, the same daughter accused of murdering him, although no one knew at the time that she was his biological daughter. Jordan learned the truth many years later.

Jordan absently licked his lips as the haunting sensation of Abby's kiss lingered, along with other things like the weight of her and the warmth of her wrapped around him. He needed to let that go. Jordan was dwelling on things that meant absolutely nothing or that should've meant nothing. She was a nice woman trying to help him find his damn self. At nearly fifty, he shouldn't even still be looking. Thinking about it now, Jordan felt a twinge of embarrassment creeping up on him.

It was futile to search for answers to questions that were starting to become more vague by the moment. It all started because he believed that he needed to know his father better, but why? Jordan had gone his whole life with assumptions that had served him fine, as much as he had needed them to. He and Julian shared a name, and Olivia and June. They'd shared close to twenty years of Jordan's life and shared Gatewood Industries. Jordan had gotten by just fine with what he knew already. This whole soul-searching endeavor had been a waste of time, and he needed to put it behind him, get his head out of his ass, and snap out of it.

His phone rang, and he saw that it was Robin calling.

"I was just thinking about calling you," he said.

"I just got back in town," she said. "Dinner tonight?"

Had she told him that she was going out of town?

"I'm on the road right now, sweetheart. Probably won't be home for another couple of hours."

"We can eat late."

He sighed.

"Later in the week?" she asked, sounding disappointed.

He felt bad for putting her off so many times lately. Part of the reason was that he didn't want to set expectations that he wasn't ready to meet. He didn't want her to get the impression that there was more to this relationship than there actually was. The other part was that he had been pretty self-absorbed lately, and Jordan was stretched thin enough already. But still, he did enjoy their relationship, and he owed her more than just brushing her off all the time.

"How about I give you a call when I get in tonight?" he said, sounding enthusiastic. "Maybe we can at least go out for a drink."

"I'd like that," she said.

"I'll be in touch," he assured her before hanging up.

Moments after getting off the phone with Robin, his phone rang again, and Abby started in before he even had a chance to say hello.

"I am so sorry that I did that. I didn't mean to, and I wish I could take it back, but I just got so excited, and I was so grateful that someone had that kind of faith in me when no one in my whole entire family has even looked at me twice on that football field since I was ten. I know that I'm not any good, but my heart for the sport is humongous, and I just needed for someone to believe in me and give me the confidence to know that I really could catch that ball and score them points."

Jordan resisted the urge to laugh. "You actually closed your eyes when the ball landed in your arms, Abby."

She hesitated. "Did I? I don't remember, Jordan. That whole thing really was an out-of-body experience for me. It was like I was there but I wasn't. So, I probably did close my eyes, but that doesn't negate the fact that you landed the football right in my arms like it belonged there, like it was destined to be there, and I just got overwhelmed with emotion. If I embarrassed you, trust me, it was nothing compared to the embarrassment that I felt when I realized what I'd done to you."

He decided to go in for the kill. "And then you ignored me the whole time I was there."

"I'm sorry," she said dismally. "I didn't know what else to do. I couldn't face you. I'll never be able to face you again. That's why I'm calling. It's easier to apologize over the phone because I don't have to look at you."

"Come on, Abby. Let's go," he heard a woman say in the background.

"Where are you going?" he asked before he realized it.

"Oh, to Roscoe's. Some friends of mine are taking me there for my birthday. But listen," she continued, "please accept my apology, Jordan. I hope you will. I truly meant no disrespect. I just got overwhelmed with joy and all. It was a huge moment for me. One of the biggest moments in my life."

"Abby!"

"Look, I have to go. Um, you take care of yourself."

"I will."

"Bye, Jordan."

Don't It Always Seem?

IT TOOK FINISHING TWO, almost three vodka-and-cranberry-juice cocktails for Abby to finally shake that anxious feeling in her stomach over her last encounter with Jordan. To say that all she'd wanted to do was to crawl under a rock and die after she'd made a fool of herself all over him was an understatement. Jordan Gatewood was a demigod whom Abby had no business putting her hands on, let alone her mouth. After she'd kissed him it was a wonder that Zeus himself hadn't struck her dead with a bolt of lightning. But before restraint had had a chance to kick in, she'd lost her mind over a stupid touchdown pass and practically sexually assaulted the man in front of her whole family. Getting drunk off her ass was definitely in order for the remainder of the evening. And besides, it was her birthday.

Belly dancing was a celebration of the belly. Abby reveled in it every time she got a chance to do it, especially in public. She had calluses on her hands, and spent most of her days stomping around in steel-toed work boots and dragging a utility belt around her waist. Dancing reminded her of her curves, and of how delicate and fluid she could be when she set her mind to it. And it reminded people who knew her that she was a three-dimensional human being, and not just someone who knew how to hang drywall, run wires and cables, and pour concrete.

Belly dancing was sexy, seductive, and powerful, capable of tugging at the primal nature of man and reminding him of why women were worth starting wars over.

Abby and her other two girlfriends, Skye and Brianna, were stellar, in sync, poised, and fucking hot. The three of them danced in perfect unison to Janet's "That's the Way Love Goes," swirling hips, rolling shoulders and wrists, and jutting breasts sending that whole room into a frenzy. They'd been practicing this all summer in order to have this little number polished and ready to go in time for her September birthday because, yes, for just one night, she wanted to be center stage, beautiful, free, expressive, and drunk enough to where she didn't give a damn what anyone else thought about her, but not so drunk that she'd forget the choreography and fall and make a fool of herself.

She wasn't as lit as she was planning on getting, yet. But by the time the night was over, Skye and her man, David, would have to pour her into a plastic cup, drive her home, and empty her into bed. That was the plan. And it was a beautiful plan. Could've been better, though. Would've been better if it wasn't Skye and David tucking her into bed on her birthday. She was good at looking preoccupied and busy all the time, too busy for a relationship. Too busy to fall in love. She looked the part, but inside, Abby was climbing the walls and had been for a long time. Lonesome.

She regretted kissing Jordan but only because it was in her father's backyard in front of her cousins, brothers, and everybody else, over a stupid touchdown. And of course, because he was Jordan. Because a man like him had women clawing at the hem of his pants to try get to him. High-maintenance women. The kind who spent Tuesday afternoons in spas and sipped high tea with their pinkies up. And the kind that got boob implants, Botox, and brazilian hair extensions. The kind with personal trainers named Josh.

He was strong. Abby recalled the muscle definition on his shoulders that she felt when she wrapped her arms around him. He worked out. Caught her like she was light as a feather and didn't teeter once. Powerful arms wrapped around her waist, pillow-soft lips mated with hers. He smelled so good, and he tasted so . . . like . . . oh . . .

"Abby." Skye elbowed her. "What're you doing? C'mon, girl. Get back in step."

Abby didn't realize that her eyes were closed until she opened them again. The three of them finished up their routine, and the whole room broke out into a maddening applause with whoops and whistles and some *gotdamns* thrown in for good measure. The three of them embraced, slapped each other high fives, and celebrated their own small victory that left them all feeling like rock stars for the night. David came in and grabbed hold of Skye before one of her exes decided to try to win her back because these days he couldn't live without her. Not after shaking her ass in the middle of the dance floor like that.

Brianna was literally picked up off the floor and carried away by some dude Abby had never seen before, but the woman was laughing and hugging on him, so Abby figured she must not have had a problem with it.

"Hey," tall and lanky Ron Pewter said, pushing up behind her. "I keep on falling in love with you, and you keep on pretending like I don't exist." He grinned. Ice-blue eyes sparkled like crystals.

He'd been declaring his love for Abby since the third grade, and two ex-wives and four kids later, he was still doing it.

"Hey, Ron," she said as enthusiastically as she could muster, starting to walk away.

He promptly took hold of her elbow.

"C'mon now. Don't be like that. Let me buy you a drink for your birthday."

Drinking with Ron meant having a conversation with Ron, and the conversation inevitably always centered around how fine she was and how much he wished that the two of them could get together, maybe even get married.

"Oh, it's all right. Skye and David have a tab going, so . . ." She shrugged.

"Marry me," he blurted out.

All of a sudden, Ron looked over her head at something behind Abby, and warm, moist lips pressed in that slope of her neck as it met her shoulder. Abby jerked around.

"I'm so sorry I'm late, sweetheart." He smiled at her.

"Jordan," she mouthed, her heart pounding like a foot kicking against a door to try to get it open.

Jordan then looked directly at Ron as if to say, *You can go now.*

Ron vanished like a magician.

An empty bar stool became available behind him, and Jordan backed over and sat down on it, as he gently took hold of her hand, and pulled her into the space between his thighs. Abby had no idea how long she'd gone without oxygen until natural bodily functions took command forcing her to take a breath.

"You dance beautifully, Abby," he said, looking her square in the eyes.

"You saw that?" she asked, feeling absolutely mortified.

Was he joking? Teasing her maybe? It was one thing for the

locals to watch her and her friends putting on one of their dance numbers. They did it all the time, and folks had come to expect it. But it was never meant for outsiders to see. Especially not outsiders like him.

A wry smile spread across his lips. "The whole thing."

Her first instinct was to cover both her ears with her hands and run away screaming, but after swallowing that big old lump in her throat, Abby helplessly explained, "We've been practicing."

Out of all the dumb things she could've said, that right there sounded like it was probably the dumbest. As if he cared that they'd been practicing.

Jordan surprised her and laughed. "And it showed."

"Thank you," she whispered. "What in the world are you doing here? I thought you went back to Dallas."

He'd never looked at her like this before. Not like he was really actually seeing her. "I'd like to buy you a drink for your birthday, sugah."

She stared back at him, waiting for the punch line.

Jordan cocked a thick brow. "Is that all right?"

A hesitant smile spread her lips. "You came back here just to buy me a drink?"

"I did."

This had something to do with that kiss. Her first instinct was to get all defensive and pretend that it didn't affect her the way it actually had affected her. He didn't need to know that she was still thinking about it, and she was not going to remind him of it. She didn't, though. Of course she was flattered. What woman in her right mind wouldn't have been flattered that a man like Jordan had offered to buy her a drink on her birthday? It was the craziest thing, by far, that had ever happened to her, next to buying and living in a haunted house. And next to finding out that a CEO of a huge corporation had died in that house and his son had shown up thirty years later to try to find a connection to the said dead CEO. But yeah. This was the next-craziest thing.

"Okay."

Abby felt like she was being manipulated remotely, like she wasn't in control of her own mind and body. It was like he'd hexed her just by being here. Then again, Abby was pretty close to being really drunk.

Jordan waited and then probed. "What're you having?"

She desperately needed another cocktail, but warning sirens went off inside her. All it'd take for her to get too drunk to think straight would be one more vodka and cranberry juice, and Jordan could bend her over a table and . . . yeah.

"Water."

He looked confused. "Water?"

She felt herself nod. "Please."

Control. Abby needed it like she needed her heart to beat. Self-control was everything because he looked too good and she was vulnerable and surprisingly weak for him right now. So, why'd he have to put his hand on her waist and pull her closer? Did he know? Could he tell that her resolve was pretty much sloughing off her right now?

"You look beautiful," he murmured, his face, his lips dangerously close to hers.

The light touch of his fingers low on her back sent shockwaves down her spine turning her legs into boiled spaghetti noodles.

"Um, thank you. It's new. I just bought it," she said, referring to her outfit.

Was that it? Did he just appreciate her new duds? Abby bought it as set, a fitted knit crop top and matching pencil skirt, both in orange. She'd even found sandals to match. It was more risqué than outfits she'd normally wear, but it was for her birthday, and she decided to step outside of her comfort zone and show a little more skin. She'd thought about explaining all this to him, then realized that she was rambling inside her own head.

He smiled. "It's very pretty."

Jordan pulled her so close that their bodies touched. Abby inhaled the aroma of all of him without meaning to. Jordan leaned in closer and grazed his lips against her neck, then planted a soft kiss there again. Oh, it felt so good, but no. She pulled back and looked at him.

"Please don't do that," she pleaded.

He didn't look hurt, but he looked sincere. "I cannot stop thinking about you," he admitted. "Ever since I met you, that first day, Abby, I—"

She could not believe that he was saying this. Hearing it was amazing, but it was also overwhelming and certainly not expected. Abby tried to take a step back, but Jordan held her in place without even trying.

"It's, uh," Abby began, trying to find a reasonable thought, one that would clear this whole confusing situation up for the both of them. She looked at him, and she had absolutely nothing.

So, he kissed her. But not like the kiss she'd slapped on his face earlier in the day. No. No, this one intentional and even softer than the first time. It was just lips at first. Lips. People don't give lips the homage they deserve. Lips massaging and tugging on lips, slow and easy, delicious and—

He pulled her closer, which seemed like it shouldn't have even been possible, because she'd already thought that she was as close as she could get to him, but she was so close now that she could feel his heart beating. Jordan gently parted her lips and slipped his tongue past them folding it into hers.

Was that her moaning? Or him? Oh, man! He tasted so warm and savory and strong and safe. Those big arms of his cocooned her against him until she felt every muscle underneath his shirt. Abby raised her hand to his face and pressed it against the smooth, low-cut beard. She hadn't been kissed in so long, but she had never been kissed like this ever in her life. *Please don't stop*, she wanted to say, but in order to say it, she'd have to stop kissing him, so she was kind of between a rock and a hard place. All she could do was say a silent prayer or hope God would answer or that Jordan could read her mind.

Jordan pulled away just barely. "I need to take you home, Abby," he murmured, grazing his lips against hers.

Take her home. He needed to take her home, which was code for taking her to bed, which would be so damn nice, but Abby was a reasonable person. She wasn't one to just hop into bed with a man because he was good looking or kissed her like his lips were made of magic clouds. She was responsible and cautious and careful. Abby was—

"Please," he whispered.

Abby was horny. It was her birthday. He was gorgeous. After processing for a few, brief moments, she responded the only way she could.

"Okay."

He stood up, took hold of her hand, and led the way to the front door. Abby looked over her shoulder just in time to see Skye glance up at her. Abby smiled, waved, and mouthed the word *bye*.

She Held Me Spellbound

THE WOMAN HAD HIM PINING like a teenage boy, without even trying. The natural beauty of Abby was breathtaking. The simplicity of her was irresistible. Everything from her tousled and loose curls to the form-fitting outfit she wore worked together effortlessly, allowing everything that was lovely about her to show through, and tasting her had been his downfall. Jordan wasn't big on kissing and hadn't been since before Claire had died; even with her, though, Jordan just went through the motions. Jordan was consumed with the idea of sampling her, all of her, from head to toe. Kissing was just the beginning for him with her.

Jordan led her out of the club and across the parking lot to his truck. He knew her well enough to almost hear the wheels turning in her head, processing and building up to reluctance and an inevitable change of heart and mind about what they were planning on doing. Abby wanted to be with him as much as he wanted to be with her, but her nature was a cautious one, overly so. And Jordan had to rely heavily on his instinct if this was going to work.

He helped her into the passenger side of the truck, climbed in behind the wheel, started the engine, and headed to her house. He estimated that it would take about fifteen minutes to get there, so he had to think fast, before she talked herself out of spending time with him.

"I'd like to hear more about these ghosts," he said, reaching over and taking her hand in his and resting them on the center console.

Abby looked at him, surprised, as if she'd forgotten she'd told him about them.

He looked back at her. "In your e-mail? You mentioned ghosts in your video."

"I did," she said, staring wide-eyed at him.

"So, you think the house is really haunted?"

Not that he cared one way or another about haunted houses, but he had to get talking, to distract her from the host of second thoughts that he knew were probably already starting to creep upon her.

"Sounds crazy, huh?"

He shrugged. "A bit. What makes you think that it is?"

"Well, it's been rumored to be haunted for years," she began. "But that in and of itself would not be enough for me to believe it. I mean, I'm an engineer, Jordan. By nature, I'm a logic- and reason-driven creature. Know what I mean?"

He was about to respond, but she interrupted him.

"So, after I closed on the house, I went in and made my assessment of what needed to be done—flooring, new roof, updating the electrical and plumbing systems, and the back room, which is the main bedroom, was ice cold. Freezing," she explained dramatically. "Which made no sense, because it was the middle of July and there was no air conditioning. I thought it was odd, but I didn't dwell on it."

He listened patiently as she continued.

"What really got my attention was hearing the floor creak in the living room, when I'd be in another part of the house. And it wasn't just creaking. It was like someone taking steps. Someone walking. Then one day before I'd moved in, I was repairing the drywall in the hallway, and I thought I saw someone out of the corner of my eye standing near the front door. Scared the mess out of me. But when I turned to look directly at it, there was nothing there."

Abby explained how she'd invited a friend of hers, the woman he'd met the day he'd met Abby, who was supposedly a psychic but who denied being a psychic, to confirm that the house was indeed haunted.

"And she said it was. But after you told me what happened there, I started to put it all together."

By the time she'd reached the conclusion to that story, Jordan was parking in front of her house, and Abby froze. Jordan turned off the engine and sat quietly for a few moments before getting out of the truck and walking around to her side to open the door.

"This probably isn't a good idea," she quickly said.

And there it was. That logical and reasonable-thinking engineer. She'd simultaneously told him ghost stories and talked herself out of spending the night with him. Jordan could honestly not think of one time in his life where he had actually not gotten the girl. This would be a first, and if things worked out the way she wanted, at the moment, he'd have a long drive back to Dallas and a vicious hard-on to contend with.

He shoved his hands into the pockets of his jeans and slowly nodded. The look in her eyes said it all. He was definitely not getting the girl.

He sighed. "Well, I'd be lying if I said I wasn't disappointed," he said, trying not to feel as rejected as he amazingly was.

This was one of those things that never happened to a man like him. But apparently, she was going to pat him on the head and send his ass home.

Abby wouldn't look at him. "It's just that we barely know each other, Jordan."

"Well, that's not entirely true, Abby," he said patiently with a hint of optimism still struggling to survive in his gut. "You know more about me than most people."

She finally looked at him. "I just don't feel comfortable with this," she said softly, batting those pretty brown eyes at him.

Jordan realized that he would have to actually concede. "Can I at least walk you to your door?"

"Oh, you don't have to do that," she said apologetically.

On this, he was not taking no for an answer. "I insist."

Jordan held out his hand. She reluctantly took hold of it and climbed out of the truck. Abby stepped onto the first step of her porch and turned to Jordan.

"Thank you so much," she said warmly. "I'm sorry I—I didn't mean to send mixed signals."

Jordan was being dismissed. It was a phenomenon to end all phenomena. He wasn't used to not getting his way and a silent explosion went off someplace deep inside him. Jordan didn't know whether to cuss or laugh. If he'd told this story to anyone of he knew back in Dallas, that he'd been shot down by a cute, little woman in Blink, Texas, they'd have thought he was making the whole thing up.

"You should probably get on the road and head home," she said sweetly. "It's getting late and you've got a long drive."

She was too pretty to not at least try to kiss one last time. He leaned in slowly, cautiously, prepared to back off if she made it clear that she wasn't interested. It was as uncharacteristic a thought as he could ever remember having. Abby accepted him wrapping one arm around her small waist. If this was going to be it, he was going to make sure that it was damn good and that he didn't rush through it. His approach was hesitant, grazing his lips against the softness of hers, pressing hers between his and lulling her into that space where she began to relax and feel comfortable. Abby gradually began to push her soft and warm body closer to his, pushing into him, placing the palms of her hands against his chest. Slow, even breaths escaped from both of them. Jordan held her tighter, more securely in his arms. Her lashes grazed his cheek, and he slipped his tongue between her lips without warning. Abby moaned and mated hers to his. Jordan's erection grew more and more demanding the longer the two of them stood here doing this until he couldn't take it anymore. He was either going to have to leave or . . . damn!

Jordan stopped kissing her and asked breathlessly, pressing his forehead to hers, "Are you sure you want to send me home?"

Abby mercifully shook her head. "No," she confessed, turned around, took hold of his hand, and led the way to her front door.

She was noticeably nervous and perhaps a little awkward. Jordan sat down on the side of her bed while Abby stood barefoot in front of him.

"Do you have a condom?" she asked, looking and sounding more like a young college virgin than a logical and business-owning engineer.

No. He did not have a condom, and Jordan hated the notion that this encounter could end here and now because of it.

Abby read the expression on his face, then leaned over to her nightstand, opened the drawer, pulled out a condom, and handed it to him.

"I-I keep them just in case. I mean, it's not like I'm always . . .

well, but, I replace them every six months. But not because . . . I haven't had sex in four years, Jordan," she finally blurted out, then thought about it. "Or five."

Jordan was stunned but thought better of pursuing that statement with any sort of question. He set the condom back down on top of the nightstand, slipped his thumbs at the waistband of her skirt between the fabric and her skin, and slowly slipped it down past her hips, letting it fall to the floor. His gaze locked onto the lacy pink triangle of her thong and he lightly grazed the tips of his fingers up the curve of her waist until his hands disappeared underneath her top. He looked up into her eyes and gradually pushed the material up, exposing a matching sheer bra, and caught and held his breath. Abby raised her arms and slipped the top off over her head.

Five fucking years? No man had touched this body in five years? Except him. He relished the thought. Jordan pulled her into his chest, then leaned back on the bed with Abby in his arms. This was special, and it needed to last for as long as humanly possible. She was vulnerable and timid and absolutely gorgeous. He rolled her over onto her back, then stood over her, taking in the view of every perfect curve and committing them to memory.

Jordan bent down, balancing himself on his hands on either side of her, and kissed her slowly, passionately, savoring the flavors of the two of them mixed together. Abby pulled on him at the shoulders, coaxing him closer to her.

He pulled away, stood up, and began unbuttoning his shirt, peeled out of that, loosened his belt, and shucked out of his jeans. His dick was ready to explode.

Slow the hell down, man, he told himself.

He lowered himself down on top of her. Abby welcomed him between wide-open thighs, that beautiful mouth of hers, and soft arms wrapped over his shoulders. Jordan pushed himself down until his mouth was in line with her dark nipples straining against the thin fabric of that bra, and he wrapped his lips around one. Abby grabbed him by the back of his neck, arched her back, and gasped. Jordan flicked his tongue against it, grazed his teeth over it, and sucked, and it seemed like it would burst, and then he turned his attention to the other one.

It was tantalizing through the material, but it wasn't long before he craved the warmth and the flavor of it. He reached up to her shoulders and pulled down the straps until Abby's beautiful breasts were fully exposed and Jordan lost his damn mind in a feeding frenzy on both.

She said his name over and over again.

He had always exercised constraint. Jordan's lovemaking was metered and planned, but not this time. This time it wasn't about her. It was about him, consuming her, losing himself in her, and for the first time in a very long time, Jordan was out of control and greedy for this woman.

At some point, he must've reached for the condom and slipped it on. The act of making love blurred into images flashing like snapshots one after another of Abby facedown on the bed with Jordan easing long, deep thrusts in and out of her from behind. And of Abby straddled on top of him, biting and tugging on his lips, raising and lowering her hips against him. It wasn't until he had her pinned underneath him, holding her legs up at the knees against his biceps, pressing down on top of her, slowly and methodically driving into her until, finally, he released so hard, so powerfully that he nearly passed out.

Sounds coming from her disappeared in a vacuum. The room started spinning, and Jordan released the most painful and delicious orgasm he'd ever had in his life. When it was over, he moved his arms, allowing her to lower her legs on either side of him. Jordan almost made the mistake of collapsing all 230 pounds on top of her petite little ass, but had presence of mind enough to roll over onto the bed. And thankfully, Abby rolled over to him and placed her head on his chest. He got the girl. He got *this* girl.

Yes, I Have Known

HIS FACE WAS FAMILIAR.

The sound of his voice was familiar.

But what was he doing here?

He shouldn't be here. Not here.

The memories in this house played out like films. And he watched. And he recalled the details with such clarity, as if he had played a part in their unfolding. But how could that be? His frustrations were growing. Anxious and impatient feelings had begun to consume him and distract him from a focused sense of purpose that he'd had for as long as he could remember.

He stood in the living room.

Home.

Two women, arguing. Angry shadows. Bitter and cold. He stood there watching, squinting to try to get a clearer perspective on the scene in front of him. And who was he? A man in the midst.

Yelling. He could never make out fully what they were saying. Only that their tones were angry, biting.

The curse words came through, though.

Bitch!

Fuck you!

Mother fucker!

Everything else was muddled and vague.

Music. A dance tune, light and laughter.

Boogaloo! Ha! Yes. He remembered boogaloo. That little girl loved to dance. Like her momma.

And there she was. That little dark-skinned beauty with pigtails and a frilly dress. Bouncing. Taking hold of his hand and spinning until she was dizzy. Until she spun like a top and fell to the floor.

Pop! Pop!

He jumped, startled by the sound, and an angry and warm feeling washed over him as he jerked to the source.

This house was too small for all these things to be happening at once.

Pain! Ah!

He raised his hand to his chest. It was . . . hard . . . to breathe.

Oh, and that pissed him off.

No! No. He pulled his hand away from his chest, and blood seeped through his shirt and covered his palm.

No. She could not take this from him. He wouldn't let her.

Fuck you, Oli—

———

They were making love. Panic arose inside him. No! Not in this house. In his house!

He could hear it. Moans and groans. The heat of fucking filled the air. That good kind of fucking.

Sweet.

He knew it well. It was addictive because it was liberating. It set him free. She set him free.

He followed the sounds down that narrow hallway, fearful of what he might see.

Ida with someone else? No. With him. Only him.

The passionate sounds tugged at him and ignited delicious memories of his own, though he could not recall the details.

Only her face. Her beautiful eyes and long, soft hair.

Burying himself in between her thighs was such a treat.

Because he loved her. Because she loved him.

Truly.

This man was in his bed.

The woman he knew, though she wasn't his. Reminded him of her, though. He sighed. Relieved.

Who was this man?

He was familiar. Distant and familiar.

He reminded him of someone. Himself? In a way. Yes. He had a way about him. Even sleeping. There was something about him.

But he shouldn't be here. Not in this room. Not in this bed.

He needed to see the man's face. A closer look. So, he bent down to see who he was.

These eyes of his had grown tired. He squinted, struggling to see the lines and features of this other man's face.

In his frustration, he raised a hand to touch this man's face.

"Julian."

He turned at the sound of her calling his name. Ida stood in the doorway of the room.

"Home," she whispered. "See it?"

See . . . what? This was not his home. This was not another man's home. It was Julian's home.

He turned to the man again. Who was he? And why would she believe that this was another man's home?

Julian turned back to Ida. She was gone.

And when he looked down at the man again, he saw that the man was looking at him.

Jordan's heart caught in his throat. What the fuck? Was he dreaming?

Abby slept soundly with her head still on his chest. He woke up out of a sound sleep and thought he saw something—someone hovering over him. It looked like . . .

Julian? His father's face? He blinked and it was gone. But the air in the room had cooled dramatically. Jordan had been dreaming. That had to have been it. Jordan took a few deep breaths to calm himself. All of Abby's talk of ghosts must've gotten to him. Still, it took several minutes for calm to come over him again. It seemed real, real enough that Jordan thought that if he'd raised his hand, he could've touched—

She stirred in her sleep, and instinctively, he held her tighter and kissed her forehead. She was definitely having one hell of an effect on him. Jordan couldn't remember the last time he'd actually spent the night with a woman or the last time he'd wanted to. But tonight, he didn't want to leave, and he hoped that morning took its sweet-ass time getting here.

He'd called Robin back earlier after finding out that Abby was going to be at Roscoe's and told her that something had suddenly come up. Her disappointment was evident and warranted. He had no idea where this was leading, if it would lead to anything beyond this, but Jordan needed to break things off with Robin. She deserved someone who could give her the time and attention she wanted from him. And Jordan had outgrown the need or the desire to entertain more than one relationship at a time.

The startling effects of that dream he'd had, or whatever it was, were starting to wear off, and the need to go back to sleep was starting to creep up in its place. Jordan had never given much thought to the possibility of ghosts one way or another. But this house held something that alighted on him every time he set foot inside it. Maybe it was some kind of remnant left behind from his father's death. He wondered how much any of that mattered anymore. The man had died thirty years ago, taking anything Jordan might've needed from him with him. The only thing he cared about now was this moment right here. It was basic. No frills. But it meant so much to him in ways he didn't quite understand.

Eventually, his eyes fell shut, and he drifted back off to sleep, making sure that she stayed close.

Is It My Turn?

IT TAKES A REAL TIGHTROPE walker to balance on that hair-thin line of being respectful to the boss's girlfriend and straight-arming the woman at the same time. Phyl Mays had mentally begun preparing herself for the task two days ago, when she'd accepted Robin's invitation for a drink.

"Thank you for coming," Robin said graciously, greeting Phyl with a smile as Phyl sat down at the table where Robin was waiting.

Robin's acknowledgment of Phyl had always been cordial, cool, and pretty dismissive before today. The woman was one of the most gorgeous women Phyl had ever seen, and she was almost Phyl's type, except for the fact that she wasn't nearly butch enough.

"Well, of course," Phyl replied, trying not to sound as fake as she felt. "Needless to say, I was surprised by the invitation," Phyl admitted, "but I never turn down the offer for a cocktail if I can help it."

The small talk flowed smoothly enough for the first few minutes of the conversation. Robin complimented Phyl on her shoes, and of course, Phyl raved over Robin's designer clutch. Phyl wasn't stupid. Robin Sinclair was not the type to hobnob with the hired help. This was the longest conversation Phyl had ever had with the woman in the six months since Robin and Jordan had started seeing each other. Now the woman was acting like she and Phyl were sorority sisters. She beat around the bush for as long as she could, but when the moment of truth came, Robin was as smooth as silk when she finally broached the real reason for this meeting, as if Phyl hadn't already figured it out.

Robin started talking about the designer dress she'd had fitted for a fund-raiser that she and Jordan were scheduled to attend Saturday night in San Francisco, finally bringing him into the mix.

"I'm just worried that my knight in shining armor might stand me up," she said, laughing as if she were joking. "He's been impossible to get ahold of lately."

Phyl did that seesaw kind of nod thing with her head. "Yeah. He's been pretty busy lately," she said indifferently.

Above all else, Jordan's privacy was sacred. His business was his business and was to be shared with absolutely no one unless he gave explicit instructions to the contrary. He'd made her raise her right hand, put her left hand on the Bible, and swear on her mother's grave to keep that oath. Then he'd pulled out a huge serrated bladed knife, sliced her hand across the palm until it gushed blood, did the same to his, and made her his blood brother. Not really, but he'd made it a point to be certain that she understood just how important it was for him to know that he could trust her. And he could.

"Usually, he tells me when he's traveling," Robin said, studying Phyl for some sign to confirm or deny her suggestion that he was on the road.

Phyl held her gaze. "You know how he can be." She smiled. "Jordan gets so wrapped up in things that he gets tunnel vision." She took a sip of her vodka tonic, a long, slow sip.

Robin was as steady as a rock. "I just worry because he seems to be a bit removed," she continued. "Busy or not, he usually gets back to me pretty quickly when I call. I've left several messages, but . . ."

The truth was, even Phyl didn't know what Jordan had been up to lately. She had no idea if he was traveling or not. His comings and goings were as much a mystery to her as they were to Robin. Periodically, he called her to "just check in," but other than that, Jordan disappeared for days at a time and then would suddenly appear like a rabbit popping out of a magician's hat with no indication whatsoever of what he'd been doing or where. Despite what Robin wanted to believe, Phyl worked for Jordan, he didn't work for her.

"I have the same problem," Phyl admitted. "He's got a sixth sense about things, though, Robin. Jordan always shows up in the nick of time to save the day." She raised her drink to her lips again. "Just like Batman."

Robin's blank stare gave a clear indication of the fact that either she had no idea who Batman was or she just didn't care. That easygoing, friendly demeanor of hers gradually faded, and Robin's steely gaze gradually put Phyl back in her place.

"I need confirmation from him that he's still planning on taking this trip with me to San Francisco this weekend," she said curtly.

Phyl had a feeling that she was going to be paying for her own drink.

"I'll reach out to him," she assured her.

"My feelings will be hurt if he's more responsive to you than he's been to me," she said coolly.

Phyl let loose a nervous chuckle. "Well, you know? I'll be sure that he knows how important this is."

Of course he'd respond to Phyl. She held his life in her planner, mostly. At least that part of his life that he wanted her to keep track of. But she got it. Ms. Sinclair wanted the whole Jordan, lock, stock, and barrel. And Jordan was being, well, Jordan. He was doing his thing, whatever that was. He didn't feel compelled to answer to Robin or anybody else because after all, he was a mogul. And moguls had minds of their own.

Robin's glare made Phyl severely thirsty, and she tossed back what was left of her cocktail.

"Please let him know that I'd like to speak to him as soon as possible."

"Oh, of course."

Without uttering another word, Robin picked up that expensive clutch of hers, stood up, and left. As soon as she did, the server appeared out of nowhere and placed the bill down on the table. That bitch had left Phyl to pay for both drinks. She gave the server her card and immediately called Jordan. Yeah, she was definitely expensing this one.

"Hey, boss," she said, leaving a message on his voice mail. "Now it's my turn to check in. Wanted to let you know that Robin contacted me wanting confirmation from you that you're still flying to San Francisco this weekend. She hasn't heard from you, and, well, she's concerned."

More like pissed.

"She wants you to call her as soon as you can. Your tux was delivered yesterday, and the captain has the jet fueled up and ready to go, so, I guess I'll just wait to hear back from you."

She hung up and wondered where it was written in her job

description that she would have to referee lovers' spats. Knowing Jordan, it was probably in there somewhere.

It had been several days since the last time Robin had seen Jordan, and even then, he was short with her, almost dismissive. Every time she called his office, all his executive assistant, Jennifer, would say was that he was in meetings and asked if Robin wanted to leave a message. Yes, it was only days, but Robin couldn't shake the feeling that he was slipping away from her, and that just would not do.

She was in love even if he wasn't. Robin padded barefoot through her penthouse apartment and sat down on the sofa facing the expansive window overlooking the city. The wine was too warm, and she hadn't eaten all evening. Once again, she'd left a message for him to call her, sounding overtly casual, like it was no big deal if he return her call. But it was a big deal.

"So much has happened in the last year of my life," he'd told her over drinks the first time they went out, *"I'm just focused on the business and seeing where else I can take it."*

Seeing Jordan Gatewood in pictures or from a distance paled in comparison to being up close and personal with him. But it wasn't just about looks with him. It was an air, imposing and electrifying. He effortlessly commanded the attention of everyone when he walked into a room. It was about everything he represented, an extraordinary black man who'd beaten the hell out of the odds and earned the respect of an industry. He was a king, a god, striking and regal.

Robin knew from the moment he'd asked her out that she wanted him, but she was intelligent enough to read between the lines of their conversation that night.

"*I get it.*" She smiled. "*Believe me. Considering everything that you've gone through, Jordan, no one can blame you for wanting to focus on other things besides personal relationships. You need to heal and sort things out. When you're ready for anything more serious, it'll come.*"

"*In the meantime,*" he'd said, gazing into her eyes with those dark, penetrating orbs of his, "*thank you for agreeing to spend some of your evening with me, and welcome to Gatewood Industries.*"

Of course she made love to him that night. She made love to him like her life depended on it, because it did. Robin had been desperately hanging on to him, to their relationship, these last six months, waiting for it to turn a corner and become something more than just casual dating. He teased her with himself, dangling all that he was in front of her, just out of reach, but keeping close enough to make her want him even more.

Robin needed to stop pretending with Jordan. Even if it meant pushing him away, it was tearing her up inside, keeping her true feelings hidden. She'd been so close on several occasions to telling him that she loved him, only to second-guess herself and swallow those words like bitter bile, holding them in just a while longer until the next time, she told herself. Well, next time was here.

The Feeling That I Feel

JORDAN HAD HER COCOONED against his chest with those big arms of his wrapped around her and one heavy leg on top of hers so that if she moved, he'd know it and wake up. Abby was starting to get really close to having to pee. She didn't want him to wake, though. Not yet. Not until she had fully processed what he'd done to her last night. It was savage, frightening, and most incredible. She must've had at least three orgasms, and Abby was a one-orgasm-per-sex-act girl on her best day. He'd had her dizzy in ecstasy, her head reeling, eyes rolling back in her head, grabbing at sheets and pillows and him like a crazed animal. She'd never experienced anything like it, and she hoped that she'd never have to endure that again, because it was absolutely too much, more than her little mind and body could handle. At one point, she may have even cried.

He moved and moaned. She held her breath. Abby was not prepared to face him right now. It was too soon. If she could figure out a way to get out of his grasp without waking him, she'd sneak into some clothes, pee, tiptoe down the hall to the living room, get her keys, and leave. And she'd stay gone for a couple of hours, until she could be sure that he had left.

"Morning."

She pressed her lips together and squeezed her eyes shut. That heavy and deep morning voice resonated to the depths of her soul. Please, God. Let him think she's still asleep.

"You ignoring me on purpose?"

She couldn't help it. Abby nodded.

He laughed, held her tight, and rolled her over on top of him. Abby pressed her face into his chest, refusing to look at him.

"Aw, baby," he chuckled. That voice that rivaled Barry White's. "Last night was lovely, Abby." Jordan put his hand under her chin and raised her face, forcing her to look into his. "You are lovely," he said, smiling.

Abby dared to open her eyes and stared back helplessly at him. "Why are you torturing me so?"

She was weak for this man, absolutely pitiful, and it was downright embarrassing. He seemed to know it and revel in it. Jordan stared so deep into her eyes that it felt like he could see every single secret, fear, hope, and dream. She felt so helpless.

"I think it's the other way around, sugah," he said, soulful. "I think I'm the one being tortured."

"Now you're teasing me."

His expression turned serious, and he pulled her up until her mouth touched his. "Never," he said, his lips grazing hers before sweeping his tongue against hers. All of a sudden, Abby started to get warm all over, and Jordan's sizable appendage started to harden again, and it became immediately clear to her that they were about to pick up where they had left off the night before.

"Condom," Abby said, abruptly and reluctantly breaking away from that kiss.

Even his morning breath was perfect.

He reached over to the nightstand, opened the drawer, and pulled out something that wasn't a condom and that he wasn't supposed to see.

"What's this?" he asked, holding her vibrator in that big old hand of his.

Abby was mortified. "Put that back!" she demanded, attempting to snatch it out of his hand.

Jordan held it out of her reach. "What is it?"

"None of your business, Jordan. Put it back!" Abby was beyond humiliated, attempting to crawl across him to try to get to his outstretched arm, but he had a tight hold of her around her waist, and she felt and probably looked like a fish flapping around on dry land.

"What's it do?" he asked, fumbling with it.

"Will you give me that?" she shot back angrily. How come she had the feeling that he knew exactly what it was and what it did? "C'mon, Jordan. Just give it to me," she demanded.

Jordan found the on switch and pressed it.

Abby grimaced and buried her face in defeat against his chest. "This is so humiliating," she muttered mortified.

"Whoa!" he said, feigning surprise.

"I'm starting not to like you so much," she declared in dramatic fashion.

Somehow she found the courage to raise her eyes to his to let him see just how badly he was embarrassing her.

Jordan turned it off and placed it back inside the drawer. "I sincerely hope that's not true," he said, warmly brushing her hair back away from her face and kissing her forehead.

And just like that, she wasn't mad at him anymore.

Abby was the keeper of the biggest secret in Blink and maybe even all of Texas history. She had a tycoon in her house, a larger-than-life head of a major corporation, worth boo-coo millions of dollars, a major celebrity whose picture had been in *Forbes*, *Time*, *Money*, and who knows what other magazines, sitting in her breakfast nook, eating bacon with her.

Of course, Jordan had to ask about the belly dancing. She blushed a little when he asked her how she'd come to be interested in it.

"Well, I was in grad school," she began with an exaggerated sigh. "Geeky girl, surrounded by a ton of geeky boys, and none of us knew how to talk to the opposite sex unless the topic of conversation was about calculus or metal alloys." She rolled her eyes. "Know what I mean? So, one day, I was passing by the bulletin board outside the lab and saw an ad from this Turkish girl who was teaching belly dancing classes to earn extra money. I figured, why not?" She shrugged. "I mean, what better way to fuel-inject my estrogen than learning to do one of the most feminine dances in the world? Right? Most of my life, it had been all clogged up."

"Your estrogen," he confirmed.

"Yes. Which is understandable when you consider all the circumstances. I mean, there was a pattern." Abby raised one finger. "Only girl raised in a houseful of men. That was the first problem. Two," she said, holding up the next finger, "one of only two females in my whole graduating classes majoring in structural engineering." She held up a third finger. "And three, summers and school breaks spent working construction, for crying out loud." Abby grimaced. "Belly dancing reminded me that I had been born and still was, despite circumstances to the contrary, a woman," she finished with a smile.

Finally, he laughed. "You most certainly are," he said, pulling her to him and kissing her.

He sure liked kissing her. She liked kissing him, too.

"I tell Skye everything," she said to him.

He was patient and listened to her ramble on without interrupting. It was nice.

"But I still haven't told her about you, that I know you."

Right now he looked just a regular person, sitting there with his shirt off, his jeans slung low on his hips, leaning on the table, sipping on a cup of coffee. If she didn't know who he was, he'd be a guy. An average, everyday, severely handsome, overtly sexy guy.

"That's good," he said.

"Oh, it is. I trust her implicitly, but I don't think she's strong enough to keep you a secret. And then the next thing you know, everybody in town would be bugging me about you. I wouldn't even be surprised if news reporters showed up at my door."

"We wouldn't want that."

"How do you get used to something like that?" she asked, studying him. "How do you ever get used to people probing into your private life, wanting to know every single thing about you, and publishing it whether you want them to or not?"

He thought about it before finally responding. "That's how it's been my whole life, Abby," he said introspectively. "Julian Gatewood was a man before his time. He was a big deal, and it was impossible to ignore him."

"So, even when you were a kid, the media followed you around?"

He sighed. "Him more than us. And my mother, because she was his wife and because she was beautiful. My sister and I watched it, and to us, it was normal. It didn't really affect me directly until he died and I was made CEO."

"You were so young," she said sympathetically. "Too young."

"I was the man of the house," he clarified. "It was my job to pick up where he left off. So, I did."

"Do you have any privacy?"

He looked at her and smiled. "You're private."

"And I'd like to keep it that way," she said emphatically. "I've never been one for the limelight. I'm small-town," she said proudly, "through and through. And there's something to be said for that."

"I agree."

"I wonder if they had this conversation," she said, suddenly thinking of Ida and Julian. "I wonder if Ida was more comfortable living her small-town life here in Blink than being closer to Julian?"

Jordan seemed to think about it. "This place is a haven, Abby. This town is nowhere. Maybe it was his way of escaping his world. I'm starting to wonder if he didn't prefer it here as much as she did."

"Is it a haven for you?"

He surprised her and nodded. "It is." Jordan took hold of her hand, raised it to his lips, and kissed it.

It was hard not to consider the similarities, the parallels between her and Jordan and Ida and Julian. Of course, Abby was not going to be anybody's side chick, and after today, she and Jordan might not ever see each other again. They had no reason to, really. He had his big life in Dallas, and she had her manageable life here in Blink. They were literally two different worlds.

Besides, she'd seen those pictures of him on the Internet with all those women that looked like Victoria's Secret models. He had his pick, and for now, he'd picked Abby. And she'd picked him. That was about it. No expectations. She'd had the night of her life, though. After five years of unintentional celibacy, she deserved him—it.

"You want some more coffee?" she asked, starting to get up.

"Please," he said politely.

Burned by the Fire

THE EVENT WAS HELD AT the St. Regis Hotel in San Francisco, and Jordan and Robin had flown in on his private jet. Tonight was a fund-raiser for someone's foundation to support some cause that Jordan couldn't recall. He'd gotten the invitation months ago and had actually forgotten about this thing until his assistant, Phyl, had reminded him of it a few days ago.

People gave their customary greetings and nods. Jordan returned them in kind. He knew most of these people. Jordan had attended many of those types of events with these same people but would not count any of them as his friends. He was the dark horse. The stepnephew that none of them would purposefully choose to associate with. They tolerated him because of who he was. The name *Gatewood* drew more cringes than praise. But his money was green, he had lots of it, and green money at fund-raisers for causes he couldn't remember always secured him a spot on the invite list.

Robin Sinclair was gorgeous as usual. Jordan waited and watched in awe as the tall, lithe, elegant woman glided across a crowded room, her eyes fixed on his while she made her way over to him. She'd been poured into that red dress. A deep and dangerous V neckline barely held her breasts in place. The slit exposing one of those long legs of hers ended midway on her thigh. And when she leaned in to kiss his cheek, Jordan pressed his hand against bare skin low on her hip.

She was extraordinary in every way. He glanced over her shoulder, staring back at men in the room staring at her. Robin was the ultimate trophy. For a man like him, she was the perfect match. All of them envied him, as they should, because he would be the one leaving with her tonight.

"You look breathtaking, as usual," he whispered, ogling her.

She fingered his lapel. "So do you, baby. As always. I love you in Armani."

Of the two of them, it was Robin who was really the star, charming and engaging. She knew the script well, laughing at the right jokes, remembering everyone's names. Always with an anecdote to offer, entertaining and personable to whoever it was she was speaking to. Jordan stood over her like a brooding gargoyle, doing his damnedest to pay attention, to at least try to appear that he was interested in what was being said, and when he failed, which was often, she came to his rescue with some excuse usually related to all the late hours and weekends he put in at the office or some silly shit like that.

When it came time to sit down for dinner, once again, Robin commanded the attention of everyone at the table. All eyes and ears were on her, the consummate social butterfly. She reveled in this circus. Robin had come from money. Her parents had been wealthy, like Jordan's, and this world really was all she knew. *Privilege.* But of course, that's all that ever showed up at these events.

Three days ago, he'd had the most restful and satisfying sleep of his life, in a tiny bed in Blink, Texas, holding the soft, warm body of a petite and shapely woman in his arms. And Jordan longed to be there again.

"Are you all right, Jordan?" Robin asked, whispering in his ear at the dinner table. "You seem preoccupied."

A woman like her deserved so much more than he was willing to give her right now.

He smiled. "Just tired," he told her.

Robin leaned in and planted a soft kiss on his lips, which caught him by surprise. She looked at him until he satisfied her with some kind of a response, a curt smile.

"We don't have to stay the whole evening," she told him, staring seductively into his eyes. "In fact, I'd rather not."

She wasn't the one he wanted. And Jordan had no right to shortchange her like this. She had been sweet and patient with him, and he'd tried to be direct from the beginning that he was not interested in pursuing anything more serious than a casual relationship. He'd thought he'd made it clear, but more and more, Robin seemed to be pushing another type of agenda onto this relationship. He wasn't being fair to her, and he was standing in the way of someone else who could be.

This was and it wasn't about Abby. Jordan had no idea where or even if that relationship had a future. The two of them came from very different worlds and lived very different lifestyles, and he had no indication that either of those worlds and lives would ever mix. More than being about another woman, this was about Jordan trying to do the right thing where a woman was concerned, for once in his life. He'd ruined Claire. Now he had to be more careful than ever not to ruin someone else.

———

Two hours later, Robin had Jordan by the hand, leading him into her hotel suite. After he'd closed the door behind him, she tossed her handbag on a chair, turned to him, and wrapped her arms around his waist. "Okay, cowboy. Now that that's finally over, why don't you peel me out of this dress and have your way with me?"

He smiled affectionately at her. "Be still my heart."

"No, it doesn't have to be still." Robin pressed her sensuous body against his.

She was so very tempting and willing.

He kissed her forehead. "It's time for me to go, sweetheart."

Her disappointment wasn't immediate. It was as if she paused momentarily for the punch line before realizing that he meant it.

"Why on earth would you leave, Jordan?" she asked, staring up at him, hoping that he was teasing.

More affection, time. More attention. Robin wanted more of him, and Jordan honestly didn't have it to give, at least, not to her.

Maybe he'd get lucky, and by the time he'd finished saying what needed to be said, Robin would casually wave him off like he never mattered. Or perhaps she'd get angry, curse him, and throw something at him on his way out.

"I think we need to stop seeing each other," he said as quickly, clearly, and compassionately as he knew how.

She looked as if he'd blindsided her, but that couldn't have been true. Jordan had been gradually putting more distance between them on purpose these last few weeks. A part of her had to know what was coming.

"I haven't been able to dedicate much time to you and this relationship, Robin."

"But I understand that," she immediately responded, taking a step back from him. "There's a lot going on right now, Jordan. I get it."

"And it's not fair to you."

He resisted the urge to tell her that he'd met someone else. Telling her that would be a slap in the face. But it would also be putting the cart before the horse. He had no idea what the future might hold for him and Abby, if anything at all. But she held the place in his thoughts, in his heart, that Robin wanted to hold. He couldn't say that, though.

"I'm a big girl, Jordan," she said boldly. "I admit, at first I was fine with the idea of a casual relationship with you. It was easy, and there was no pressure. I'm a grown woman. I knew that I could handle it," she explained.

"Then how come I get the feeling that casual is no longer acceptable?" he challenged.

Robin blinked.

"How come I get the feeling that you want more?"

Had he been wrong? Had Jordan thought so highly of himself that he'd misread this woman and believed that she felt more for him than he'd come to believe?

"Because it's true," she finally admitted.

He'd hurt her more than he'd ever feared he would.

"I love you, Jordan. I didn't mean to fall in love. I didn't try, but it happened. We're perfect together. You have to know it, too," she said earnestly. Robin motioned to the door. "Those people at that banquet know it. They saw it tonight, how we interact, and how we are together, like two pieces of a puzzle—we create such a beautiful picture together."

She was right. Robin was the kind of queen that everyone expected Jordan to be with. Hell, a year ago, he'd have expected it. He'd have embraced it. She was a perfect follow-up to his perfect dead wife, Claire. Robin was the sequel.

"I know that you don't love me," she continued as tears began to flow. She paused, waiting and hoping for him to assure her that she was wrong. "But you could," she continued when he didn't. "I know this. You're still wounded by Claire's death and by what happened to you with your mother. Trusting love again is hard for you, and I understand that. But I'm willing to wait and give you the time you need to work through those things."

"And what if I never do?" he asked.

Robin believed that she'd psychoanalyzed his ass, and she didn't sound too far off the mark, if he were being honest with himself; however, he already knew that she wasn't his remedy. The last thing he wanted to do was to be cruel and say that to her, but it was the truth. Robin was status quo in Jordan's world. She was a cutout of his wife who believed that Jordan would someday miraculously love her, too. And he tried. And he failed. And she died because of it.

"You can trust me," Robin argued. "All I want is to be here for you."

"Stop it, Robin," he argued, hoping to help her to salvage some of her dignity. "A woman like you should never have to beg a man for his time and attention. You're too beautiful and intelligent for that."

"But I'm not beautiful enough or intelligent enough for you?" she snapped.

Now she was getting angry. Good. She needed to get angry at him. She needed to hate him, for his sake and for hers.

"I'll understand if you choose to leave the company," he eventually said. "The last thing I want is for you to be uncomfortable."

"Uncomfortable, Jordan?" she asked bitterly. Robin shook her head in dismay. "That's the understatement of the year. I am more than uncomfortable. How about humiliated? Destroyed? Distraught?"

What else could he say? It was over between them, and Jordan was almost ashamed at how relieved he felt. He'd never meant to hurt her and he was ashamed of that, too. Jordan turned and started walking toward the door before stopping and turning to her one last time. "I'm sorry, sweetheart. I truly am."

"Why don't you shove *sweetheart* up your ass?"

Atta girl, he thought, proud of her for standing up and being the queen that she was as he left.

If I Have to Take a Part

THE ROBIN SINCLAIRS OF THE world didn't cry over selfish bastards like Jordan Gatewood. They didn't ask themselves questions like, *What did I do wrong?*, *What could I have done differently?*, *Was I not attentive enough or beautiful enough?*, *How did I fail him?*, *Was I too needy or clingy?*, or, *Was I too passive?* But that's exactly what she did after he left. Being dumped was foreign territory for a woman like her.

She'd stripped out of her dress and sat on the sofa filling her stomach with glass after glass of chilled Belvedere she'd ordered from room service. If she was drunk, she didn't notice. Robin was too hurt to be drunk, too bitter, full of regret and disbelief. It didn't seem real that he had said those things. For her whole life, it had always come down to a matter of choice in the man that she would marry and spend the rest of her life with. She had had her pick of the litter—other successful businessmen, scholars, and artists, all bent on wooing her and on winning the prize that was Robin Sinclair.

Jordan wasn't even the richest man who'd courted her. He

wasn't the most successful or powerful. Royalty had begged for the gift of her time. And of all those opportunities, she'd laid eyes on him, and she had chosen.

"This shit doesn't even make sense," she muttered, taking another sip from her glass.

The vodka was starting to sour in her mouth, and she cringed at the taste of it and at how much of herself she'd wasted on Jordan. Not just her mind and her body but her talents, her negotiation skills she'd poured into those gotdamn contracts. Funny how now that the hard part was done, he had no use for her anymore. Robin chuckled and immediately picked up her cell phone and dialed his number.

"Did you really pimp yourself out for a damn contract?" she asked before giving him a chance to say hello.

"It's late, and you sound drunk," he said indifferently.

Indifference. Yes. Jordan had been indifferent with her from the beginning, only she'd been too stupid to notice it.

"I'm good and drunk," she shot back. "But not so drunk that I don't know when I've been used."

"We'll talk when you sober up."

"No, Jordan. We will not." Rage erupted in her like a volcano. "How dare you casually toss me aside like some trick you met in a club." Hot tears stung her eyes. The vodka boiled in her belly. "How dare you think of me as disposable and expendable after all I've done for you and your fucking company!"

She expected him to hang up on her, but he didn't. He owed her this, the right to speak her piece. "I made no demands on you. I sat by and waited for you to grace me with your sorry-ass time, to see me, to fuck me. I would've given you all of me, you selfish sonofabitch! Do you understand what that means?"

"I do," he said quietly, infuriating her even more.

158 | J. D. MASON

"You were a waste of my time, Jordan. And I have no doubt that had this relationship gone on any further, you'd have driven me to suicide, too, you selfish bastard."

Jordan remained silent, but she'd spoken her mind. And Robin was done.

"You'll have my resignation Monday morning," she said angrily before ending the call.

Jordan was on his way back to the airport when she called. Her words resonated with him long after she'd hung up.

"... *you'd have driven me to suicide, too* ..."

Women had loved him. Good women. Too many women, and Jordan had always taken it for granted. For most of his life, he'd never quite embraced the depths of what that meant for him or for them. Losing Claire the way he did had been clarifying and resounding, settling into his soul like a railroad spike. She had literally loved him to death, and all the way to the end of her life, Jordan had never reciprocated. Was he even capable of such a thing?

"Mr. Gatewood." His pilot, Stan Moore, greeted him with a handshake at the jet.

"Stan."

"We'll be taking off in half an hour, sir."

Jordan started up the steps. "Thank you."

He settled into his seat, realizing that he was alone. But then that was usually the case. Even when Jordan was surrounded by people, he'd always felt isolated, unable to connect emotionally to anyone. For most of his life, Olivia had been the exception. Of course, she'd tried to kill him. Shit like that had a way of severing ties. Jordan's relationship with his sister, June, had never been close, and even after learning who his biological father was and that he had brothers, Jordan still felt detached.

Robin had been in the same room with him, in bed with him, and he hadn't fully been present with her. God! How could she not know that? How could she not sense that he was just a shell of a man trying to care, to relate and connect to another human being? None of this should've been a surprise to her. All that he could hope for was that one day, after her anger and pain subsided, she'd finally come to terms with the fact that she really and truly never was the problem and that he was.

He dozed off for about an hour on the flight home. Jordan took the private elevator up to his penthouse, set his bag down in front of the elevator inside, and stood there, looking out over this empty home. This place represented exactly who he was. Expansive in size, filled with expensive things, and void of any warmth. He lived on top of a tower, far removed from the rest of the world, only interacting with it and the people in it when he had no choice. Jordan had been lonely his whole life. And he'd been alone. But Jordan had no right to feel sorry for himself because people had tried to love him, good people, and he'd always found a way to damage them.

It was after two in the morning, and he couldn't sleep. Jordan sat up on the edge of the bed, missing the warmth of Abby and that small-ass house of hers. He was much too big to ever believe that he could be happy in such a place. The place wasn't much bigger than his master suite. But she was in it, and just like this place represented him, hers was a reflection of who she was, and right now, he desperately needed to share it with her. Robin had been right about one thing: he had been selfish. The trick with Abby was not to ruin her the way he'd ruined so many others. He had to be extraordinarily careful with her. Could he be?

Jordan dressed quickly, hurried downstairs, and got the key to that old pickup truck of his. It'd take him two hours to get there. Maybe less.

Can't You See My Desire?

OF COURSE THE HOUSE WAS dark when he pulled his truck into the driveway. It was almost four in the morning. Jordan was exhausted, and all he wanted to do was to crawl in that tiny-ass bed next to her, pull her close to him, and sleep. He'd been rude enough to try to call to let her know that he was on the road, but the call went straight to voice mail, so he decided to take a chance that'd she'd let him in when he arrived. And what if another man was inside with her? No. There was no one else. Was he staking a claim on this woman already? It was a ridiculous thought, but one he harbored anyway. There was something between the two of them, thick and rich. Whatever it was lingered with him long after the two separated. There was something about her, about this particular woman that resonated with him in a way no other woman ever had. He liked the taste of it, the smell and the feel of it. And Jordan wanted more of it.

Abby was absolutely unexpected for someone like him. She went against the grain of the world he lived in. She'd awakened a part of him that had been dormant perhaps his whole life. A renewed curiosity for the unexpected. Everything about her was peculiar to him, odd and even quirky. She didn't follow any rules that applied to how he lived. She wasn't polished or pristine. She lacked "bearing" as his mother would say, an attitude born of privilege and wealth. Yet, she was her own kind of queen, undefined by things or people around her, by upbringing. He doubted that she even realized how noble she was.

He climbed out of his truck and made his way up the steps to her front door. Just as he was about to ring the doorbell, he heard the dead bolt click. He almost laughed out loud. They shared a frequency, him and her, he confidently concluded. Abby somehow knew he was coming. Maybe she'd heard his truck pull up. Whatever. He waited for her to swing open the door and to either curse at him for not calling first or to jump into his arms and smother him with kisses, or both. The door opened slightly, but if Abby was behind it, she kept herself hidden.

"Abby?" he asked softly. "I take it this is my invitation to come in, sugah?"

He concluded that she was being coy. Women did shit like that. Abby had unlocked the door and had run back into her bedroom. She was probably hiding underneath the covers, hopefully naked.

He pulled open the screen door and walked in, then quietly closed the main door behind him and locked it again. A sudden and unexpected wave of apprehension washed over him, causing him to stop and stand right where he was. Something was wrong, and Jordan felt disoriented, as if he were moving, but he wasn't. The space moved around him.

Home . . .

Come to m . . .

Voices, but not coming from any one place, filling his head, dizzying and chaotic whispers.

Ghosts? Abby's ghosts? She'd talked so much about them, though, that more and more of her stories were starting to have an effect on him. That conclusion made sense. Nothing else did.

Not over!

A man's voice. Angry.

Crying. A woman was crying.

Show him!

Jordan wasn't afraid as much as he was confused and anxious. This wasn't supposed to happen. What? What wasn't supposed to happen? A wave of panic washed over him. Regret and anger.

Show him . . . what?

Show . . . home?

He took a step farther into the living room. Screams echoed through the small space, but they weren't real. They couldn't have been. Jordan looked all around and up. Fuck! Was he dreaming? Exhausted?

He wasn't ready. *He* wasn't ready. Emotions flooded him as if they were his own but they couldn't have been.

He meaning Jordan? No. No, that didn't make sense. Where was Abby? Alarm swelled in him for her safety. Was she all right? He composed himself and began making his way down the hall to her bedroom at the end of it. The door was closed. His heart raced as he began to worry about what he'd find behind it. Jordan managed to quietly push the door open and saw her sleeping.

How could she have slept through all that? He turned and looked back down the dark hallway, and there was nothing. All that turmoil, all that commotion was gone. Jordan looked back at Abby, quietly stirring in her sleep. What the fuck just happened?

he wondered, staring back down the hallway and then looking back at her.

It took a few minutes, but he eventually pulled himself together. Jordan sat in a chair across from the bed, watching her sleep, and it made him realize just how exhausted he was. He'd been up since five the previous morning and hadn't slept in nearly twenty-four hours. It was after 4:00 A.M. He must've sat there for ten minutes trying to find a rational answer to what he'd just experienced. The thought occurred to him that she could be right. It wasn't fear that had consumed him in her living room just now. Jordan felt the strain of loss, losing. Desperation had taken hold of him and anger at not being able to keep what he'd wanted more than anything else. His gaze rested on her.

Jordan undressed without waking her and then stood over her, realizing that he was about to scare the shit out of her. There was just no way around it. And of course, she should be afraid. He showed up in the middle of the night, naked and in her bedroom, without calling, magically getting in through the front door without a key. Yeah, she was bound to be terrified.

As Jordan carefully lowered all six feet three inches of himself onto the bed, Abby naturally was startled awake, looked at him with wide, frightened eyes, and her mouth gaped open to scream.

"It's all right, sugah," he said immediately, staring back at her quickly trying to reassure her. "It's all right, Abby. You're safe, baby. It's just me."

"Jordan?" she asked, stunned and trembling, gradually relaxing and letting him pull her against his chest. "Jordan?" she repeated again, breathless.

"It's me, baby," he said again. "You're fine, Abby."

The two of them eventually relaxed, took a couple of deep breaths, and settled into position.

"H-how'd you get in here?" Abby finally managed to ask. "How'd you get into my house?"

He thought about it, and the only answer he could come up with sounded absolutely foolish, but as much as he knew, it was true. "Your ghost let me in, Abby," he finally admitted, staring at the dark passageway beyond the bedroom door.

And that's when he saw it—him. He stood at the end of the hall closest to the living room, wearing a white button-down and dark slacks. Jordan couldn't make out his face, but he recognized his shape, his coloring. And he froze. *Julian.*

The longer he stared, the more the image began to fade, until it was completely gone. All of a sudden, he became aware of Abby and how quiet she had gotten and how still.

"Did you see that?" he reluctantly asked.

After a pause Abby nodded, wrapped her arm tightly around his waist, and buried her face in his chest.

Need.

He'd felt it before. And it was powerful. Addictive. He was weak to it. All men were. It was love, but not certain at first. Like this one. Like him. Like her. Like Ida and Julian.

Show him. She kept saying that, over and over again. Show him. Show who? Show him what? He didn't know. And it frustrated him and pissed him off. But he understood the overwhelming need. Because it was the same as his.

Show him!

Oh, Ida! Stop with these games. I got no time and no patience for your silly games, woman. Tell me what you want from me. Tell me what I need to do to have you with me again.

His soul ached, damn near crippling him. Weary and lost, he

was starting to lose hope. It was all he had—hope. Hope that one day he could touch her and hold her again, and love her. Taste her. But she seemed to be moving away from him. What had he done wrong? How could he fix this?

Fix it, Julian! He scolded himself. *Hurry the fuck up and fix it before it's too late!* But how?

They shared something. He knew this man. But he couldn't recall him by name. They shared a need.

He looked down the hallway at Ida standing in the doorway of the bedroom, watching. Watching. How many times had he run down that corridor to her, only to lose her before he could touch her? Too many.

Selfish.

Her voice carried through the house.

Tell him. Show . . . him.

Julian walked with him down the hall to her room. Step for step. Loneliness. They shared that, too. It felt good connecting again to someone, even to this other man in his house. As they drew closer to Ida, closer than he had been in so very long, she began to disappear, and Julian's sorrow returned. But he'd gotten so much farther than he had before. Somehow, he'd managed to get within reach of her. Julian had been fingertips away from a touch. He stopped just outside the bedroom as the other man entered, and he waited. Enviably. He looked on with envy as the man climbed into the bed and pulled her into his arms.

Yes. Julian knew how good she must've felt.

I need you, Ida. Please. Please baby, tell me what to do.

Watch Us Play

IT WAS AS SCARED AS she'd ever been in that house. Abby had never actually seen the ghosts before last night, and if Jordan hadn't been there, she'd have run out of the house screaming. He held her until he eventually drifted off to sleep. How he could sleep after something like that was absolutely amazing. Abby didn't dare doze off until she saw the sun starting to rise outside the bedroom window.

Late the next morning, the two of them sat outside in the backyard on Abby's swinging sofa, sipping on coffee. Jordan had been unusually quiet all morning, giving her the feeling that if she didn't bring it up, then he wouldn't either.

"I'm positive that I locked the front door, Jordan," she said, studying his handsome profile.

He sighed and nodded slightly.

All sorts of questions ran through her head. The main one being why that ghost would unlock the door in the first place. She knew that the ghost had to have been Julian. It looked like a man.

"Was it your father?"

He didn't say anything, but his silence on this subject was not allowed. Jordan's father was haunting her house, and if he had an opinion on the matter, then he certainly needed to express it.

"What do you think he wants?"

He sighed and shook his head.

"I may never be able to sleep inside my house again after last night," she said dismally. "What do you think he wants?"

Finally, he looked at her. "How am I supposed to know, Abby?"

"He was your father."

"Who died thirty years ago," he reminded her. "And I don't believe in ghosts. I didn't believe in ghosts." Jordan paused and thought for a moment before continuing. "I honestly don't know what to say about what I saw last night."

So, how was she supposed to live here now? It was broad daylight, and Abby absolutely did not want to go back inside that house. And when it came time for Jordan to leave, she definitely didn't want to go back inside. He must've seen the trepidation in her eyes.

"Let's go to my ranch," he suddenly optimistically offered. "Put some space between us and this house."

She stared back at him, surprised.

"No ghosts there." He smirked. "I promise."

By nature, Abby had never been an impulsive person, but Jordan had been challenging her in all sorts of ways lately, forcing her to step outside her comfort zone. An impromptu trip, even if it was only to Fort Worth, was a major break from the norm for her, but a welcome one, considering that her other option was spending the weekend in the house with Jordan's dead father.

Personally, she'd never seen an actual mansion, but that's exactly what this was. Jordan pulled his truck into the circular driveway in front of the house, and all of a sudden, Abby was starting to get a much clearer understanding of what it meant to be wealthy. It was one thing to read about Jordan on the Internet, but it was another to see him represented on a twenty-thousand-acre ranch with a humungous Mediterranean-style house planted in the middle of it.

"You live here?" she asked, staring in awe of the grand entrance with its dramatic mahogany floors and trim, ornate iron stair rails, and massive windows.

"Sometimes," he said, closing the door behind her.

A cute, round Latina immediately greeted them at the door.

"Señor Gatewood," she said in a thick, Mexican accent.

He handed her Abby's bag. "Please take this upstairs to the bedroom, Lydia."

"Sí." She nodded and smiled as she passed Abby.

"Gracias," Abby said politely.

The woman nodded appreciatively. "De nada."

His home. It was beyond grand. Beyond massive. Elegant and sophisticated. Rich. She was no art collector, but Jordan had pieces worth thousands, maybe even millions. How in the world was she ever supposed to put someone like this in perspective? All of Blink, Texas, could've fit in here. It was an exaggeration, of course, but not much of one.

Suddenly, Abby started to wonder if she wasn't just dreaming. In reality, Abby was probably lying in her own bed, sleeping peacefully, and she had dreamed buying that house, and meeting him that day when Marlowe confirmed that it was haunted. She'd dreamed Smitty's and her birthday touchdown and that kiss. She'd only dreamed they'd made love, because how could she

possibly ever meet anyone like him in real life? And she'd probably dreamed Julian Gatewood's ghost too. Abby decided that, yes,
she was in fact dreaming and that it was a good-enough fantasy
to continue running uninterrupted. She made up her mind that
she wasn't ready to wake up yet.

After giving Abby a tour of the 15,000-square-foot house, Jordan took her to the stables that housed half a dozen thoroughbred horses. Jordan actually raced three of them, but one in
particular, a huge black stallion, was his personal favorite.

"He's beautiful," Abby said as soon as Jordan brought out the
regal horse to introduce him.

"This is Ares," he said proudly.

"Like the Greek god Ares?" she asked, smiling.

He smiled. "Exactly."

Abby stared admiringly at the horse. "Suits him."

The horse was already saddled. "Let's ride?"

Abby was taken aback. "Oh, I don't know how to ride, Jordan."

He smiled. "I do, Abby."

"Scoot back on the saddle, baby."

Abby inched back away from him.

"You're crushing my nuts."

"Maybe this ain't such a good idea, Jordan," Abby said, panicked, wrapping both arms tight around his waist.

Ares was huge, and Abby was terrified.

"Calm down before you spook him. He's sensitive."

Good Lord! She was sitting on top of a giant monster of a sensitive horse who could buck her off at any moment, and he wanted
her to be calm? Abby squeezed her eyes shut and held her breath
as soon as they started to move.

"Relax, honey," he said soothingly.

"Me? Or the horse?"

He laughed.

After about ten minutes, she did relax, even enough to enjoy a short canter to where a massive herd of cows, including some longhorn, grazed as if they hadn't a care in the world. There had to have been hundreds of them.

"Whoa," Abby said in awe as Jordan helped her down off the horse. "What do you do with all those?"

"Dinner," he said indifferently.

Abby jerked to face him. "How could you possibly joke about something like that?"

He chuckled. "You're lovely."

"You're teasing me," she said, rolling her eyes and turning back to look out over the herd.

Abby waited for him to object. He didn't.

Jordan sidled up behind her, leaned down, and kissed the side of her neck. That man in that cowboy hat was mesmerizing.

"Are you feeling better?" he asked.

She nodded. "If you mean, am I recovering from my ghost sighting? Then yes. Are you?"

He straightened up and took a deep breath. "Still trying to figure out what it could mean," he finally confessed.

Abby turned to him. "So, you're not trying to ignore the fact that you saw him?"

He shrugged. "I saw . . . something."

"It was him, Jordan. Why can't you accept that?"

"And what if it was? What difference does it make if I accept it or not? He's dead, Abby. If he chooses to hang around thirty years after that happened, then that's not my problem."

"He let you in my house, Jordan."

"The door unlatched. Faulty lock. You might want to check on that."

"My lock is fine," she argued. "What happened when you walked in? Did you see anything? Hear anything?"

"Not really," he said uneasily.

"What does that mean?"

Jordan was hiding something, but he seemed dead set on keeping it to himself, which was probably for the best. The less she knew, the better as it pertained to last night. Abby was already freaked out enough. She didn't need to add fuel to that fire.

"Me and you aren't that different, Jordan. I don't want to believe in ghosts either, but I know that they're real. I've known since I was a little girl."

He just stared out at that livestock.

"My momma died in a car accident when I was five," she began explaining. "She was taking me to school. It was my first day of kindergarten, and I was riding in the backseat."

"Mexicano negro," she said, rolling a perfect "r."

"Black Mexican," Jordan clarified.

"Sí." She smiled. "She always made it a point to introduce herself to strangers that way, like she was so proud of the fact that she was both."

Abby paused for a moment in reverence to the memory of her mother.

"I don't remember much about that day," she continued. "We were singing my favorite song while she drove. It's still my favorite song to this day." She laughed. *Es el ojo del tigre . . . Elevándose hasta el desafío de nuestro rival,* she sang.

Jordan thought for a moment, latching onto the melody. "I know that song."

Of course he knew it. Everybody knew it.

" 'Eye of the Tiger' by Survivor," she reminded him. "From *Rocky*?"

He laughed.

"We sang it in Spanish, which, by the way, was no easy feat."

Abby paused again to collect her memories, recalling a violent jolt that shook her whole body. "I remember feeling like I was falling, and I was scared because it happened all of a sudden. It felt like I was flying through the air." She stared off at nothing in particular across the landscape. "And then"—she looked at Jordan—"there she was, smiling, holding her arms open, waiting to catch me." She smiled. "And she hugged me real tight, and then moments later, she sat me down on the sidewalk, kissed me, and told me, 'You be good, Abby. And I'll see you later.'

"I woke up and saw Daddy asleep in a chair across the room, and I called to him and asked him where Mommy was." Her voice trailed off, and tears filled her eyes. Abby blinked and wiped them away before they had a chance to fall. "It was a hospital room," she clarified. "She'd died on impact." She looked at Jordan. "And I should've. No one could understand why I didn't, but later, as I got older, I began to understand."

"You sure you didn't dream that?" he asked tenderly.

She shook her head. "She saved my life, after hers was already gone."

He looked skeptical. Everyone she'd ever told that story to looked skeptical, except for Marlowe and Miss Shou.

"Wanna know what I think?" she asked.

"If I say no, are you going to tell me anyway?"

"Of course."

He waited.

"I think he's trying to communicate with you."

"I doubt that. He's not haunting my house."

"But he's the one who let you in. I'm sure of it. It wouldn't make sense that she'd unlock that door for you."

"What's he trying to communicate, Abby?" he asked impatiently.

"I don't know. But I think he's reaching out to you. Maybe there's something he wanted you to know before he died that he never got a chance to tell you. Things like that happen."

"Again, he's haunting your house, not mine. If I'd never shown up that day when we first met—"

"But you did. Don't you think even that's a miracle?"

"I think it's a coincidence."

So he was in denial or trying really hard to get there. Abby could see in his eyes that he was going to be stubborn about this, and she concluded that probably nothing she said was going to change his mind.

"You said yourself that you came to the house that day to try and learn something about the man. Did you plan on coming or did some invisible pull compel you to come to my house that day?"

Abby studied him, intensely. From his expression, she could tell that she might have actually hit the nail on the head.

"What is it that you need from him, Jordan? What'd you come looking for?"

Jordan gazed out over that herd, quietly pondering her question. Did he know? Maybe Julian knew. Maybe he'd cared more about Jordan than he'd ever let on before he died and now he was trying to reach out to him.

"Maybe he's trying to save your life."

All of this was way over her head, but it was no coincidence that Jordan had come to her house that day and that the ghost of his father was kicking up dust whenever his son came around. Julian had shown up because of Jordan. She was sure of it.

"Don't you believe in miracles, Jordan? That's sort of what this is starting to feel like."

"I'm surprised that you do, Ms. Logical, Reasonable, and Analytical Engineer."

"What do you think science and engineering is if not the discovery and explanation of miracles?"

"Never thought of it that way."

"Not many people do. Science is magic, dissected. That's all."

He stared warmly into her eyes. "I believe that you are magic."

Abby blushed. "You want to dissect me?"

He brought out the naughty girl in her without trying.

"Dissecting you is absolutely one of my favorite things to do."

Abby chuckled. "Well then, let's climb back on that big old horse of yours and head back to the palace."

Your Remedy

THANKFULLY, LYDIA PREPARED A MEAL with chicken instead of beef, for Abby's sake. This house felt different with her in it. Abby had dared to take a step into his world, and all it took was the appearance of a ghost.

When was the last time he'd danced? "I'll Be Good to You" by the Brothers Johnson wafted through the entire house while he and Abby danced outside on the lanai around the fire pit. Jordan held a beer in one hand and had the other wrapped around Abby's waist as they swayed back and forth to the rhythm of a beat that was not much older than she was.

"You're only twelve years older, Jordan," she'd told him earlier when he'd made mention of the huge age difference between them. *"That's actually kind of perfect since girls usually mature faster than boys."*

Jordan wasn't sure, but it felt like she'd mildly insulted him.

He couldn't keep his hands off her. He couldn't stop staring at her. Abby was a different kind of beautiful. Natural and understated, effortless. The kind that settled into his soul nicely. She listened intently as he told her about the contract he was hoping to win from the government. It was an impressive deal in the making, a fact that wasn't lost on her.

"I know you're probably going to have Ph.D.s at your beck and call when you land this deal. But if you *ever* would like the council of a lowly structural engineer with a master's in mechanical engineering, I'm your girl."

"I will keep that in mind," he responded, smiling. "But I'd rather you be my woman. Not my engineer."

She blushed, and masterfully glossed over that part about wanting her to be his. "I'm dead serious, Jordan. That kind of stuff makes my heart race and my palms sweat."

"Is that the only thing that makes your heart race and your palms sweat?" he asked without missing a beat.

Abby sat perched on his lap, straddling and facing him.

"Of course not," she said after a brief pause, her expression subtly becoming more serious.

He lightly grazed his thumb over the skin of her thigh exposed by the short, white sundress she wore.

"Being with you absolutely makes my heart race and my palms sweat," she admitted. "But I figured you already knew that."

He was flattered. "I'd hoped."

She smiled. "If we had gone to college together, you know that you would never have given me the time of day. Right?"

"Oh, I don't know about that," he disagreed.

"Boys like you never did. You, the jock, had girls lined up waiting to get to you. Don't try to deny it. I know it's true."

Jordan sort of shrugged.

"I tutored the jocks. Sometimes, I even wrote their papers for them. For a price, of course."

"Then chances are our paths would've crossed. I needed a ton of tutoring."

She laughed. "Oh, I don't believe that. You can't be dumb and run a corporation."

"I wasn't running a corporation in college. I was chasing footballs and girls." He grinned. "Life was much simpler then."

"I'm sure it was," she said, her demeanor softening even more. "What if he hadn't died, Jordan? What'd you want to be when you grew up?"

No one had ever asked him that before in his entire life.

"What were you majoring in?" she asked when he didn't answer.

"Business," he eventually said.

"Why business?"

Jordan thought about it. "I have no idea."

Abby tilted her head slightly to study him. "I think you're the kind of man who would've been great at whatever he chose." She knitted her brows. "Be it, a doctor, lawyer, fast food restaurant manager."

He laughed.

"Don't knock it. Fast food work is harder than it looks. I know. I worked a whole summer at Whataburger once as a fry and milkshake specialist, and it damn near killed me."

"Oh, I'm not knocking it."

"Resilient and stubborn. Confident." She stared admiringly into his eyes. "Whatever you decided to be, you'd have been the boss."

She was right. On all accounts. The last person Jordan had taken orders from was his football coach in college.

"What do you see in me?" she asked in a more serious tone.

He was confused by the question.

"I'm cute," she continued. "Pretty. Funny. Smart. But I'm sure that you come across women all the time with those attributes. You could be with any woman you wanted, Jordan. And a man like you is far too busy and important to be driving up and down the highway to Blink. So, I don't get it. I like it. But I don't get it."

"I feel good with you," he admitted without hesitation.

"Define good," she said, leaning in close to him and pressing against his chest.

Jordan took his time gathering his thoughts. Abby was forcing him to take a long, hard look at himself and at her.

"Good is not having to walk in an image that's been defined for you, by you, by someone else. It's just . . . being."

Jordan Gatewood had a persona, and he had somehow fallen into the trap of living up to it, intentionally or not.

"You didn't know me, except for what you might've read about me," he said to her. "You know me now as the man I am, not as the man you think I'm supposed to be."

"Because you didn't introduce yourself to me as Jordan Gatewood's predefined image?"

He smiled. "Exactly."

"I'm confused." She laughed.

He wasn't surprised. What he was saying, or trying to say, was confusing.

"I've spent my life believing my own hype," he confessed. "I stepped into Julian Gatewood's shoes and decided that I needed to be him or rather, my perspective of him."

Jordan compiled a list in his head of those things he believed his father to have been. "Unwavering. Unyielding. Cold and detached. Brilliant. I admired those things about him, and I adopted them. I adopted his demeanor, his stance, his attitude and made them mine."

"Those aren't necessarily bad things."

He sighed. "No, but it's exhausting having to be those things every single day, all day, to the point that it's second nature."

All of a sudden, Jordan understood what it was that had kept his father going back and forth to Blink. The revelation was so clear, and it made perfect sense.

"Comfortable," Jordan simply said.

There was no pretense with Abby, no requirement for him to be anyone else but who he was. And it wasn't until he'd met her that he realized how strained he'd always felt in his surroundings, driven by expectations, his own and everyone else's, to live up to a name as tall as his corporate offices in downtown Dallas.

"I am unburdened around you, Abby. I think that I must've felt it the moment we met but I didn't understand at first. I think Julian must've felt it with Ida, a peeling away of the burden of living up to preconceived ideas of who you really are. It's like a peacock fanning out feathers to make the enemy believe he's bigger than what he is. You're not my enemy and because of that, you're addictive."

The look in her eyes wasn't one of pity, but she seemed to understand precisely how much something like being able to be himself must've meant to him.

She planted a soft kiss on his lips. "So, you find peace in me?" she asked earnestly.

Jordan felt himself nod. "I do."

She smiled. "Rest?"

"Yes," he said, locked onto those beautiful eyes.

"Then I will be your refuge, Jordan." Abby closed her eyes and pressed those lovely lips to his, pushed her hips against him, and wrapped her arms around him.

Is this what he'd been looking for? His refuge. His peace. A place for him to rest and just be Jordan.

Abby eventually pulled away from their kiss and whispered, "I'm not wearing panties. Did you know?"

Jordan laughed. "No. But I had hoped."

In the Devil's Bed

"MEN DON'T BREAK UP with women unless they have found another woman, Robin. Relationships 101."

Robin sat across from her longtime friend Liza Atkinson at Station's, an upscale bar in the heart of downtown Dallas. The two of them had worked for the same firm fresh out of law school back when they were baby attorneys, still wet behind the ears.

Contrary to her threat, she still hadn't submitted her resignation, but Robin hadn't been in the office in more than a week.

Liza's words washed over Robin like ice water.

"Don't tell me you haven't considered it," Liza continued.

"Of course I have," she said coolly. Robin wasn't naive. There had to have been someone else. "All of those times when he was out of town, or too busy—were likely times when he was with another woman. But does it matter?" Robin shrugged, angry tears filling her eyes. "We're no longer together."

Hurt feelings really weren't her thing. Robin had broken plenty of hearts in her day, but she'd never had hers broken. Being on this side of the situation was brand-new, and she had no idea of how to feel, except angry.

"But aren't you curious, Robin?" Liza asked, leaning forward, her dark eyes probing. "Don't you want to know what woman could possibly take your place in his life?"

Liza was a notorious shit starter, a gossip, married to a rich man who left her alone with too much time on her hands to fly to Dallas from Los Angeles just to spur Robin into action and drag her ass kicking and screaming out of that pool of self-pity she'd been drowning in all week.

Liza leaned back and smiled. "I would love to know."

Curiosity or ego? Both. It was a futile reaction to a deed that was already done. But Liza had planted a seed that quickly took root and blossomed into an immediate obsession that would likely only lead to more disappointment and deeper heartache for Robin. It was bad enough knowing that there was probably someone else in his life, but knowing who she was, or why he'd chosen someone over her was asking for her pride to take even more of a beating than it already had.

"Dean Rivers," Liza had said over drinks that day as she'd pulled up his contact information on her cell phone. "A good friend of mine and excellent investigator." She had looked up at Robin and smiled. "Consider this an early birthday present."

In a matter of days, Liza's investigator friend had forwarded Robin a file, a photograph, to her phone. And there he was. There *they* were. Robin felt as if she'd been kicked in the stomach, physically ill at seeing Jordan Gatewood sitting at what looked like a bar with a woman standing in between his thighs, holding and kissing her. Even seeing something like this with her own eyes was beyond comprehension at first. Robin couldn't wrap her mind around the idea that he would accept the kiss of another woman when Robin practically had to steal them from him. How was that even plausible?

The woman had dark skin and curly black hair. It was hard to see her face because of the angle that the picture was taken. The photographer must've been far enough away so that they didn't notice him. Additional information accompanied the e-mail from Liza. Moments later, other pictures came through. Four altogether, all taken in that bar of the two of them huddled together, smiling, even dancing.

Jordan was enjoying himself. In just these few pictures she could see and almost feel something different about him, something that wasn't there when he was with her. The reserved Jordan, reticent and aloof, wasn't anywhere to be found in those pictures. This version of him was relaxed, open, welcoming. He looked content, happy.

A paralyzing numbness slowly consumed her, and Robin must have spent the better part of the day staring at that picture, memorizing every small detail, from how the woman stood on the tips of her toes to the familiar black-leather-and-silver bracelet Jordan always wore on his right wrist, to the way he tilted his head, accommodating himself to receive her kiss.

Negative thoughts cycled through her the way blood circulated through veins. Robin wasn't good enough for him. She wasn't beautiful enough. He didn't like her sex or the way she laughed or talked. It had to have been those kinds of things that had turned him off, made her unattractive to him. He didn't like the way she dressed—or what? What else? But this one, this Abigail that he held in his arms, that he kissed—that he loved?

What made this other woman better to him? What was it

about her that compelled him to show her that side of himself that Robin had hoped he'd show to her? Robin had been waiting for the moment between them when Jordan would put down his armor and bare his heart and soul to her, but it never came. Somehow, someway, she was better to him than Robin. He'd chosen her over Robin because she was who he wanted to be with?

"Why?" she muttered softly to herself, truly perplexed by the multitude of questions circling her thoughts.

It made no sense. And Robin was the kind of woman who desperately needed to have things make sense. She showed up the next morning in his office and immediately closed the door behind her. Jordan looked surprised to see her.

"Who the hell is she, Jordan?" she blurted out, standing in front of his desk.

Jordan furrowed his thick brow. "Now's not a good time, Robin."

"Who is she?" Robin asked, still numb, still broken, tossing printouts of the pictures onto his desk.

Jordan glanced at them and then looked up at her like she'd lost her damn mind. And she had. "She's no concern of yours, Robin."

"The hell she isn't," she said with a smirk. "How dare you say that to me. Of course she's my concern, Jordan. She's the reason you dumped me in a San Francisco hotel. She's the reason you've been too busy to return my calls. The reason behind you standing me up or canceling our dates at the last minute. She's the reason for me sitting around feeling sorry for my damn self ever since you fucking left me humiliated. So don't you dare tell me she's of no concern to me."

Cool and calm as ever, Jordan's demeanor didn't even ripple.

"That wasn't my intention. You know it. What I said to you in San Francisco was the truth. I never intended to hurt you."

"But you did," she snapped. "And for what? Some random little bitch in a bar? A nobody, Jordan? Seriously?"

"What I do and who I see are none of your business," he shot back coolly.

It was as if she were a stranger to him. He spoke to her like she was some random person off the street. There had been moments between them, intimate and raw moments that left even the great and mighty Jordan Gatewood begging for more of Robin. She'd held him in the palm of her hands on more than one occasion, teasing him, torturing him with the kind of passion that that little country cow of his couldn't possibly match. Or had he forgotten?

"Because you'd rather be with her than me."

"Because I would," he admitted. "Yes."

That was it. Gloves off. "What is it, Jordan? Trying to relive the glory days of your father? Didn't he have a dark little morsel of a side piece, too? Where was she from? Some small, insignificant town in the middle of nowhere, if I recall correctly. Is that where you've been disappearing to lately? Smothering your balls in greasy country pussy to drown your filthy-rich sorrows like he did? And her little black ass probably worships the ground you walk on. Is that what you need?"

Jordan's expression turned dangerously ominous, and Robin relished it, because she'd obviously hit a nerve. Finally.

"Get the fuck out of my office," he demanded.

Robin bowed slightly and graciously at the waist. "Oh, I will get the fuck out of your office, Jordan. The last thing I want is dick that's been slathered in hog slop."

Satisfaction slithered up her spine when she realized she'd insulted his girlfriend and it struck a nerve. "If slumming is what gets you Gatewood men off, then so be it. Because you are absolutely right. I do deserve better than your ass. And one day, you're going to think back on all of this bullshit, and what you've done to me, and regret that you ever turned your back on me. You will miss me when I'm gone. I swear to God you will."

Robin stormed out of his office to the elevator. She took it a few floors down to her office and began packing her things to leave.

She saw it all so clearly now. Jordan and his wistful and whimsical need to fully follow in his dead daddy's footsteps. He was reliving a past that wasn't his, but he romanticized it and wallowed in it until it crippled him. He was no good for her or any other reasonable woman. And in hindsight, he was doing her a favor.

The flood of hot and bitter tears that had erupted when she closed the door behind her in her office eventually stopped. She was not going to feel sorry for herself over Jordan, because he wasn't worth it. No man was worth her sacrificing her self-respect over.

Robin was just about finished packing when her cell phone rang. It was Alex Richards, her old law school friend.

"Hey, Alex," she said, trying not to sound as upset as she was.

"I heard a nasty little rumor," he said after a cordial hello.

"What rumor is that?"

"That you work for Jordan Gatewood at Gatewood Industries."

Robin swallowed. "Yeah," she said, trying to sound upbeat. "It's true."

"Look at the two of us sharing a boss," he said sarcastically.

Robin stopped packing. "What do you mean?"

"That case I've been working on in Dallas," he began, "the Lonnie Adebayo murder case?"

"Right. What's the client's name again? You got the guy off."

"No, I got the mistrial. Frank Ross is his name, but Jordan Gatewood pays my bill. Talk about a coincidence. I had no idea the last time I saw you that you were employed by him, too. What do you do?"

Robin sat down slowly. "Corporate. Government contracts."

"Nice and safe, I suppose. Had enough of the criminal defense bullshit, huh?"

"I did," she said, her mind whirring around why Jordan would be footing the bill for an attorney of Alex's caliber to defend a nobody.

"Oh," Alex said abruptly. "I'm getting on an elevator and will probably lose you. But I'll be in touch," he said before hanging up.

Ten minutes passed before Robin finally logged on to her computer and did an Internet search on Frank Ross and then followed it with another search on Lonnie Adebayo.

With a Silver Spoon

MARLOWE HADN'T BEEN to the house since before Abby had renovated it. Abby had spent three days and nights with Jordan at his ranch because she'd been too scared to come back to this place. But this was her home, and she needed to figure out how to make this situation work, ghosts or no ghosts, at least until she could figure out if she wanted to sell the place or not. It didn't seem fair to sell a haunted house to unsuspecting people. But then again, someone had sold it to her.

"Hey, girl," Abby said, greeting Marlowe at the front door.

Abby had just arrived a few hours earlier, and so far, the place didn't seem any different from usual.

"You want a Pepsi?" Abby asked, heading into the kitchen.

"Abby, stop."

Abby did stop, turned, and saw Marlowe looking at her funny. "What?"

Marlowe slowly approached her and peered hard at Abby's face and then into her eyes. "You got a bae?"

Abby reared back slightly. "What?"

"You seeing somebody?"

She blinked several times in disbelief. "Your psychic abilities telling you that I am?"

Marlowe arched a brow. "Girl, you're glowing. Ain't nothing psychic about that."

Abby laughed. "Sort of," she said, excited as a sixteen-year-old girl. "I mean, yes." She sounded more confident this time because it was true. "I am seeing someone, Marlowe."

Marlowe's mouth gaped open. Her eyes stretched as wide as saucers. "Who, Abby?"

Abby felt so giddy that she covered her mouth with her hands and squealed. "You're not gonna believe it."

"Tell me anyway."

Abby took several deep breaths to compose herself. She hadn't told a single soul in this world about Jordan. Not even her own family knew. Not even Skye knew, and Skye knew every damn thing, except this, about Abby.

"Remember that day that I asked you to come here to tell me how haunted this house was?" Abby paused and stared expectantly at her friend.

"No!" Marlowe exclaimed.

Abby nodded. "Yes!"

"No, Abby! Oh, my . . . what? What?" Marlowe spun away from Abby and pressed her hand to her forehead. A moment later, she turned back to her. "Are you serious? Him?"

Again, Abby nodded, grinning from ear to ear.

"How the . . . what . . . tell me what happened."

"I'll tell you, but you're gonna have to sit down."

It was one thing to tell Marlowe that the man Marlowe and Abby had met that day was related to one of the ghosts in the house. Abby relayed the story she'd read on the Internet of Julian and his mistress and then she told her the part that she'd learned from Jordan about Julian's wife finding out about the two of them and showing up at this house with a gun. It was another thing to watch the expression on Marlowe's face when Abby pulled up Jordan's images on the Internet and zoomed in on the one showing him on the cover of *Forbes*.

"You can't tell a soul," Abby said, concluding her presentation.

Marlowe was speechless.

"Not even Ms. Shou, although it wouldn't surprise me if she guessed it as soon as she walked into this place."

Marlowe stared at Abby as if she were seeing her for the first time. Having Marlowe staring at you, especially after you've told her something that's absolutely impossible to believe, was never a comfortable feeling. Abby always felt as if Marlowe could see things like auras and actual souls.

"Stop it, Marlowe," Abby warned. "You know I don't like you looking at me like that."

Marlowe blinked. "Sorry, Abby. I just—"

Abby held up a hand to stop her. "Don't."

"I'm happy for you," she blurted out. "That's all I was going to say."

Abby smiled and wrinkled her nose. "Really?"

Marlowe grinned. "I am, girl. Truly, I am."

Just then, Abby looked up and saw Belle, Marlowe's cousin, ushering Ms. Shou up the steps to Abby's front door.

"Knock, knock. We're here," Belle said, opening the screen door.

"Hey, Belle," Abby said, hurrying over to hug her. "Hey, Ms. Shou." Abby kept her distance from the old woman.

"Abigail," Shou said curtly.

Shou Shou always had a way of making Abby feel like she didn't like her, but for some reason, Abby wasn't buying it. Shou Shou had been there when Abby told Marlowe about the day her mother died and saved Abby from dying, too. Right after she'd finished her story, Miss Shou leaned in close to Abby and whispered, *"Your angel ain't never far away from you, Abigail."* She smiled, her breath smelling like peppermint. *"She told me to tell you that."*

"How'd your appointment go, Auntie?" Marlowe asked.

"I'm dying," Shou blurted out indifferently.

"Anytime soon?" Marlowe asked.

"Not today. Probably not tomorrow."

Shou wore black shades bigger than her head, red lipstick and nail polish, and a floor-length, African-print sheath that swallowed her thin and frail body. She took three steps into Abby's home and stopped, raised her chin, and tilted and turned her head as if she could actually see something. An immediate chill ran down Abby's spine. Belle and Marlowe stood on either side of the old woman like bookends, calmly letting her do whatever it was she was doing.

Shou abruptly turned her attention to Abby. "You scared, Abigail?"

Abby nodded. "Yes, ma'am. I saw him a few nights ago."

Shou nodded introspectively. "'Cause he was probably desperate."

"Desperate for what?" she asked reluctantly.

"Not what, sugah. Who?"

"Ida Green," Abby said, even though Shou hadn't asked.

The old woman smiled. "That her name?"

"Yes, ma'am."

Shou took several more steps toward the hallway on the opposite side of the living room and then stopped.

"It's been a long road," Shou said solemnly, her voice sounding at least two octaves deeper. "One that he keeps walking every single day since he's been gone. He wears shiny shoes, polished to look like glass, creased slacks, and a pressed white shirt." Shou hung her head and turned to them with a slight smile on her lips. "Looks like a white man—light, light skin and eyes." She raised her head and chuckled. "Thick hair with soft waves, brushed back." Shou raised her head in the direction of the hallway. "What he see in me?" She paused and took a breath, then tilted her head slightly. "In the ground. Buried."

A tear ran down her cheek. Was it Shou talking? Or was it Ida? Abby froze, fascinated that at least one of her ghosts had a voice.

Shou dried her tears with the collar of her dress. "His love is obsessive," she said, sounding more like herself. "Maddening love that kind that don't stand to reason."

Abby looked at Marlowe and Belle, who stood there looking at their aunt like she spoke the language of ghosts on a daily basis.

"You were right, Marlowe." She nodded in Marlowe's direction. "It's not finished. It won't be until he gets what he wants, until he gets her, but she's not ready for him to have her yet, because he's not ready."

"Is he angry?" Abby found the courage to ask.

"Frustrated, Abigail. Weary. His hope is fading, but . . ."

Shou's *but* hung in the air like a lead weight.

"He's forgotten something. Something that she wants him to remember. Until he remembers it, he can't have her and he thinks he might have found somebody who can help him."

"Me?" Abby asked, placing her hand to her chest.

"Naw, not you, girl. Whoever that is that's got you chirping like a bird, though."

What? Abby wasn't chirping. She looked at Marlowe, who shrugged. Belle pressed her lips together to keep from laughing.

"Is he . . . could he hurt me if I stay here?"

"He's not interested in you, except that you sometimes remind him of her."

Abby thought carefully before asking the next question. "Can you tell him to stop scaring me?"

"Now you're being silly," she said dismissively.

"I'm not trying to be silly, Ms. Shou," Abby retorted. "He scared the hell out of me the other night."

"I'm sure there's some hell left in you, Abigail."

Abby rolled her eyes in frustration.

"Don't," Shou said, raising that walking stick in Abby's general direction. "Watch your respect, Abigail."

Again, Abby glanced at Marlowe and Belle. "Yes, ma'am." Abby sighed. "Can you just tell me if it's okay for me to be here?"

"It's your house, ain't it?"

"Ms. Shou," she beseeched her. "Please?"

Shou held out her hand, and Belle immediately appeared at her side and walked her over to where Abby stood. Marlowe grabbed hold of Abby's arm and pulled her to stand in front of Shou. The old woman raised her hand, and Belle helped her place it on Abby's cheek.

"He's not the man you need to be afraid of," she whispered and smiled. "Be brave, my sweet girl. Be strong, 'cause that man of yours is the biggest and scariest thing that will ever happen to you."

Abby swallowed.

Shou removed her hand and laughed. "Belle, I want me some of that fried catfish you brought me the other night."

Belle led her aunt to the door, followed by Marlowe. "Didn't that doctor tell you to lay off the fried food, Auntie?" Belle fussed.

"Like I give a damn what he said. I'm gonna live longer than him. I've already decided."

Abby shuddered at Shou's declaration that could've been interpreted any number of ways.

"Oh, catfish sounds so good," Marlowe agreed, disappearing outside with the rest of them.

Abby just stood there, dumbfounded and speechless.

Someone's Underground

"SORRY TO BE CALLING SO LATE, but it took me some time to convince him to call me back."

Robin sat up in bed and turned on the lamp on the nightstand. "It's all right," she said, rubbing sleep from her eyes.

"He's got it in his head that he's going to go down in a blaze of glory, a hail of bullets, war cry, and his ass being carried out in a body bag," Alex Richards explained in a dismal joking tone.

"He doesn't trust that you can get him off at the retrial?"

"He's an idiot," Alex huffed.

"Where is he?"

He sighed. "Tell me what you want with him, and maybe I'll tell you where to find him."

"It's personal, Alex."

"He's my client, Robin, and the last thing I need is for that idiot to say anything to anyone that might incriminate him."

"I'm not interested in incriminating him."

Alex was silent for a few moments. "You can trust me. Whatever you've got to say to Frank, you can say to me."

"And you should trust me," she said calmly, "and know that anything I've got to say to Frank Ross is very personal and that I have no intention of hurting this case, Alex. I have my reasons for wanting to talk to him, and that's all you need to know."

Laredo International Airport. Much to her relief, there was an actual airport in Laredo, Texas. Robin hadn't bothered to go back to sleep after hanging up from the call with Alex. He had texted Frank Ross's number to her, and she'd immediately called him and talked him into agreeing to meet with her the next afternoon.

Robin flew from Dallas to San Antonio and then changed planes to take a flight into Laredo. Her eyes burned from lack of sleep, and she felt like she was running on caffeine and fumes. Had it really come to this? Staring out of the window at nothing but clouds, she felt like a fool, like she was a robot just moving without thinking. Is this what it felt like to be desperate for a man? Not desperate to have him, because she had had him, and she'd lost him. But desperate to punish him and to make him suffer.

Jordan was supposed to have been the one. Robin felt it the moment she first laid eyes on him. He was back at work after being out for nearly two months recovering from the shooting when Robin was introduced to him for the first time after being hired on to the company. The striking figure of Jordan Gatewood took her breath away, and the way in which his eyes locked on to hers, told her that he was just as interested in her as she was him.

She loved him. Why else would she feel so shitty knowing that he wasn't hers anymore? She loved him in a way she'd never loved another man. Robin had been willing to put him first in her life, to bend over backward or sideways to do whatever it took to make him happy. For the first time in her life, she wasn't the priority. He was. And now she felt like such a fool. More than fool. She felt ridiculous.

The reasonable thing to do would be to just walk away, leave the company and maybe even Dallas, lick her wounds for a while, and start over someplace else. But she couldn't let it rest. He had taken her for granted and used her. He'd disposed of her when it suited him, like she was nothing and like she never meant a got-damn thing to him. Men like him were used to tossing other people aside when they'd soiled them up. He'd discarded Robin like a used napkin, and he had to see, to know that that was not acceptable. Not for her.

Of course, Robin could've been wasting her time with all of this. She could land in Laredo, meet Frank Ross, and come away absolutely empty with nothing to show for her efforts.

She deserved better. He had been right about that. Robin had been with men who'd have given their right arm to have her. But Jordan deserved something, too. He deserved to know that some-one else in this world didn't worship the ground he walked on. He needed to know that he stood on a slippery slope, and if he wasn't careful, Robin would be the one to push him off of it. Jor-dan Gatewood was a walking, talking secret. And men like him had the dirtiest kind.

Lonnie Adebayo probably knew what they were. How he'd managed to keep his relationship with the woman a secret, espe-cially during this trial, was nothing short of a miracle. Of course she was the reason behind him putting so much money into Frank Ross's defense. Nothing else made sense. Adebayo was his type, successful and beautiful. She was an award-winning photo-journalist before she died, traveling the world to cover newsworthy stories that won her accolades throughout the entire journalism industry. Robin suspected that the two of them had been lovers, which could've been the reason behind his wife's suicide. The devil was in the details, and Robin flew all the way to Laredo hoping that Frank Ross might know some of those details. And even if he didn't, Robin knew how to read people and read between the lines. She could more than fill in the blanks left open by Ross.

Frank Ross had been working on a good drunk and a death wish when she'd spoken to him. The mention of Jordan's name gave him reason to pause and was a sign to her that she was on the right track in following this trail to him. She took a cab to a seedy motel off Highway 35 and knocked on the door to room 107. She must've knocked for five minutes before he finally answered the door, shirtless, with faded and dirty jeans barely hanging on to his hips, barefoot, and smelling like a brewery. He didn't even bother to say hello. Frank looked at her, turned, and left the door open for her to follow him inside.

He was tall, as tall as Jordan, slightly heavier, darker. She thought she'd noticed other similarities, but Robin quickly pushed those notions aside.

The room was small and filthy, littered with food containers, empty beer and soda bottles, dingy socks, and a pair of beat-up leather boots.

"What'd you say your name was?" he asked gruffly, stretching out on top of the unmade bed, crossing one ankle over the other.

Robin gingerly took a seat across the room in an old wingback chair, being careful not to lean back in it.

"Robin Sinclair," she said.

The room reeked.

He stared long and hard at her before finally cutting to the chase. "What do you want?"

It was the most natural question to ask in a situation like this. Robin wasn't surprised by it, but she was surprised by how ill prepared she was to answer it. As an attorney, she had interviewed her share of people for various reasons under various circumstances. There was an art to asking questions in order to gain the most insight from the individual.

"Why is Jordan Gatewood paying your legal fees?"

She'd caught him off guard. That wasn't the question he was expecting.

"Do you know him?" Ross's steely gaze locked onto her.

It was her turn to be surprised. "Yes."

"Then why don't you ask him?"

His tone and mannerisms made it clear that he wasn't going to tell her.

"Did you kill Lonnie?"

He shook his head and smiled. Robin's heart jumped in her chest. No. It wasn't . . . no.

"I did not," he said clearly and with conviction.

"Do you know who did?"

He shook his head slowly. "No."

"Were she and Jordan lovers?"

Again, Ross gave her a long, lingering, and probing look. "What'd he do to you?"

"What makes you think he did anything to me?" she asked far too defensively.

He huffed. "Oh, he must've." Ross's gaze slowly traveled the length of her to her shoes and then back up to her eyes. "You look expensive like him." He squinted slightly. "Let me guess. Girlfriend? Correction," he said, raising his thick brows. "Ex-girlfriend."

Robin didn't give him the benefit of a response. Frank Ross was good. Obviously, spending all that time in the courtroom and around lawyers had taught him the art of deflection.

"You could've saved yourself a trip," he said unemotionally. "I've got nothing to say on Gatewood, and I'm sorry for whatever it was he did to you. A word of advice. Let it go and move on. He's not the one you want to spar with."

"Did he kill Lonnie?" Robin was startled by her own question.

It had come from a dark and desperate place. Far-reaching, but still, possible. She hadn't come all the way down here to walk away with nothing.

Frank studied her. "Lonnie Adebayo played a dangerous game with all the wrong people. I don't know who killed her. I just know that I didn't."

"Why is he paying your legal fees?"

"That lawyer of mine don't come cheap," he explained. "He's one of the best from what I hear. Best there is. If anybody can get me off, it's him."

"If you truly believe that, then why are you here instead of awaiting trial in Dallas?"

He sighed and closed his eyes. "Because I'm tired. For too long I've let myself be pulled into bullshit schemes of other people's, thinking that I'd find my pot of gold at the end of some dumbass rainbow. And all it did was land me here."

"I just want to know why he's paying for your lawyer."

"And I'm just telling you that you've wasted your time coming here. Whatever game you're playing, lady, against Gatewood, you're on your own. I got nothing for you."

He was right. She'd come all the way down here, and he had only answered a single question. He'd said that he hadn't killed Lonnie. It was the things he didn't say that made this trip worthwhile. Frank Ross and Jordan Gatewood were related. She didn't know how, but physically both men shared undeniable similarities: their smiles, the slopes of their foreheads, and even the same heavy brows. That would provide one explanation as to why Jordan was paying for his defense. But the media hadn't connected Jordan to Ross in any way. And Ross certainly wasn't going to own up to it. Jordan, of course, never would. Did it matter? The scandal was Ross's, not Jordan's, especially if he wasn't involved. A lump formed in her throat. He was involved.

He and Lonnie were lovers. Frank hadn't confirmed it, but he didn't deny it either. Somehow Frank Ross had gotten pulled into Jordan's mess, standing trial for a murder he said he didn't commit, defended by a lawyer paid for by Jordan. She knew that Alex Richards commanded a pretty penny for his services. Had Jordan bought Frank's silence by hiring Alex to keep him off death row? Because Ross was a family member? Because Ross knew that Jordan was somehow involved in Lonnie's death? Maybe both.

She knew more now than she did before she'd gotten on the plane to come to Laredo. Robin was smart enough to fill in some very convincing blanks. Her version of what happened could make life very uncomfortable for Jordan. The deal of a lifetime hung in the balance, and a scandal like the one reeling in her head could absolutely derail it. Or it could force him to have to confess to his sins in order to manipulate the truth to suit his needs.

If there was no happily ever after for her, then he sure as hell wouldn't get one either.

Before boarding the plane, Robin sent one last text to Liza's investigator.

I need her address.

Come with Me

DAVE MORRIS, JORDAN'S DIRECTOR of federal acquisitions, had put a meeting on the executive staff's calendars for nine Friday morning. The rumor was that the feds had finally awarded that contract and would be making the formal and public announcement next week. All the key players were in attendance—Jordan, Vince, and Mike. Robin was the only one missing. She hadn't turned in her resignation yet, but Jordan assumed that it was inevitable.

Gatewood Industries had a snowball's chance in hell of getting this contract. When he'd first discovered the opportunity, Jordan had weighed it heavily, mostly alone, going round and round in his head how he could make something like this work. It was an endeavor involving the creation of an entirely new division of GII, with a new facility, engineering, and operational staff. The division would be all R&D, offering a wholly different kind of challenge from what he was used to, and he looked forward to it.

"They contacted all the candidates late yesterday," Dave said with a heavy tone, looking at each one of them. "It did not come down to cost. They didn't award to the lowest bidder, which, as you know with government, is everything."

Heads dropped, sighs filled the room, and disappointment started to weigh heavily. It was as if everyone knew where this was going.

Jordan leaned back and nodded slowly. "It's our first shot," he began calmly. "And we made it a lot further than anyone expected us to this first go-round. There'll be other opportunities, gentlemen," he said confidently. "We'll just keep at it until something pans out."

"It's already panned out, Jordan," Dave said with a sly smile.

Jordan stared at him.

"We won the contract." Dave's voice cracked.

"You're shitting me," Jordan said in disbelief.

Dave shook his head. "I shit you not, boss!"

Dave laughed. Whoops and hollers filled the room. Some selective curse words flew overhead. Jordan pounded his fist on the table.

"Yes!"

Everyone stood up and started shaking hands across the table, everyone except for Jordan. This was bigger than anything he could've dreamed, but Jordan did dare to dream it, and it happened. Jordan was so caught up in his own disbelief that he didn't notice everyone standing around the table staring at him. He looked up and then slowly stood up, too, and grinned from ear to ear.

"I guess we're in the aerospace industry. We did it."

"You did it, Jordan," Vince, his COO, said, reaching out to shake his hand.

Everyone else in the room nodded and then applauded.

Jordan raised a hand to quiet them. "All right. All this man love is nauseating," he joked.

They all laughed.

"Now the real work begins." He looked at each of them. "We've got a new division to stand up and an engine to develop."

The day had been filled with meeting after meeting. Jordan hadn't made the announcement to the rest of the corporation, and he wouldn't until it was formally announced by the government. He'd had so many incredible and amazing accomplishments since he'd taken over the business after his father's death. The first decade had been a bitch. Jordan made too many mistakes, and he'd watched it gradually start to crumble away from him piece by piece, painstakingly destroying Julian's legacy. At the end of those first ten years, there was hardly anything left of it except for a company car, a dilapidated building, and a receptionist. That was an exaggeration, of course, but not by much.

For forty years, Gatewood Industries had been nothing but oil and gas. Winning this contract now ushered the business into a whole new realm of possibilities. The contract had been awarded to him under the guise of "best value," meaning the government believed that he could deliver the best product despite the fact that he couldn't deliver it as cheaply as the other candidates. But he would own up to that promise. Jordan's pride, his reputation, depended on it.

"Hey, handsome," Abby said, answering the phone.

It was just after seven in the evening when he called.

"I received some good news today, and I'd like to celebrate."

"Is it what I think it is?" she asked hesistantly.

"I need to see you."

Abby held the phone away, screamed, and then composed herself. "Well, okay, then."

He laughed. "I can pick you up, and we can go to the ranch."

"Nope," she said quickly.

Jordan was almost disappointed.

"I can meet you at the ranch," she added. "Say, by nine?"

"I'll see you at nine, sugah."

Shortly before nine, Jordan stood outside the door of his ranch home as Abby pulled up in her truck and climbed out wearing cutoff jean shorts, a Superman T-shirt, an oversized cardigan, and cowboy boots, carrying a bottle of champagne. She'd pulled her mane of curls into a puff on top of her head. Jordan smiled at the sight of her. Abby raised up off her toes to kiss him.

"Brought you something," she said, handing him the champagne bottle. "It's probably cheaper than you're used to but it's good."

Jordan slipped her overnight bag off her shoulder and onto his. "You brought me you," he said, ushering her inside. "That's all that matters."

Jordan wasted no time once inside, hoisting Abby up over his shoulder and carrying her upstairs to the bedroom.

The sex was hot and sticky. Abby was pliable, unhinged, and loose. She trusted him with her, and he honored that trust. Jordan wanted to make love all night. He moved slowly, deliberately, with long and even strokes, relishing the cream of her covering his shaft. Inhaling and committing her scent to memory so that he could take it with him when she wasn't with him. Full and bountiful breasts filled his palms, his mouth. She dug her nails into his arms and back, at times begging him to stop, then changing her mind and begging him not to.

Jordan was determined to make her his, his pussy, his woman. He would leave an indelible mark on her so deep, so profound that the thought of another man touching her would repulse her. Sweet Abby Rhodes, charming and funny, kind. Pretty woman. She had no idea of the effect she was having on him. Abby changed him, brought him back to life, gave him a new sense of desire and purpose that had nothing to do with Gatewood Industries or money or power.

"Jordan," she said breathlessly, grabbing handfuls of sheets as he pounded into her from behind. "Oh, Jordan, I'm coming. I'm coming, baby."

Yes! He licked his lips and grabbed hold of her small waist and pushed deep enough into her for her to cry out—in pain? Pleasure? Both.

He cried out, too. Abby's inner walls wrapped around his dick so perfectly that in this moment, they weren't two separate people.

"Oh! Oh, Jord—"

"Fuck—Abby!" he closed his eyes, reared back his head, and growled like an animal as he released.

"Ahhhh!"

This was spiritual and cosmic. He fucking exploded inside this woman, coming so hard that it took every bit of his strength to remain standing. And she came with him, pulsing against him, massaging him, and siphoning all his energy and will from him, until all he wanted was to be hers.

"Shit! Shit!" Jordan repeated, the room spinning and Abby convulsing underneath him.

He couldn't help himself. Jordan lowered himself on top of her, pinning her underneath him, passionately kissing her shoulders and the back of her neck. He slid off her just enough to keep from crushing her, but he wasn't going to let her go. No. He'd been searching for her his whole life. And he'd found her. And he was never letting go.

"I'm so happy," she said lazily, lying on top of him. "I mean, happy that you got that contract."

He kissed the top of her head. "I'm happy, too. And that contract is a bonus."

Keeping Us Afloat

"DAMMIT, JOE. YOU TOLD ME that this part of the yard was clear."

Abby was livid. The city engineer had surveyed the backyard of the Perry house for gas lines and anything else that might be hidden that could cause problems, ensuring Abby that her team was cleared to dig up ground to start grading the ground to install a new swimming pool. Ten minutes after breaking ground, one of her employees, Isaac, who was operating the excavator, hit a water main, and water rushed out and flooded the whole backyard.

"This ain't in the plans, Abby," Joe argued, turning the brim of his ball cap to the back of his head, shoving his computer tablet in her face.

The scene was complete and utter chaos with the residents shadowing Abby and Joe, cursing at them, Abby's crew trying to get that heavy equipment out of the yard before the ground became so saturated that it all started to sink. The water company crew showed up demanding that everybody get out of their way, including the panicked and angry Perrys.

"Who's gonna pay for this, Abby?" Dirk Perry kept asking. "We shouldn't have to pay for this."

"Jake and Carla," Lisa Perry said, calling out to her kids splashing around in the muddy yard. "Get over here! Now!"

"I wouldn't have opened up the ground without your okay, Joe," Abby angrily retorted. "You said we were clear to dig."

"And you know how these old houses are. People did shit all the time without going through the city for permitting."

"What are you accusing me of, Joe?" Dirk asked belligerently.

"I'm not accusing you of nothing," Joe shot back, then waved him off and turned back to Abby.

"I'm not paying for this," Dirk said over and over again as he walked back over to his wife. "We're not paying for this."

Abby was sick to her stomach. The customer wasn't always right, but in this case, he wasn't wrong. She was going to have to pay the cost on this one. She knew it, but she sure as hell didn't want to admit it out loud. Joe owed her, though. He owed her big, and he knew that, just by looking in her eyes.

"I'm sorry, Abby."

She shook her head, turned, and walked over to the Perrys. "Don't worry. We'll take care of it," she said dismally before heading back to the front of the house to her truck. Abby desperately needed a shower and a cup of tea.

Two hours later, Abby sat stretched out on the sofa in her living room, talking to Isaac, who had been quoted a cost of $600 from the city for repairs of that water main.

"So, we eatin' this one?" Isaac said in that unemotional drawl of his.

She sighed. "We are. How long before we can start digging again?"

"I give it a week or two as long as it don't rain." He chuckled, and even that was indifferent.

Abby's doorbell rang. "I've got to go, Isaac."

"Am I off the rest of the day?"

"You wish." She smiled. "Doug is over at Mrs. Phillip's house on Blake Street working on that porch. Why don't you go over and see if he needs help?"

"Yeah."

The woman standing at Abby's door looked like she'd stepped right out of the pages of a *Vogue* fashion shoot. She was stunning, towering over Abby by nearly a foot, wearing designer jeans, stiletto pumps, a silver silk blouse, and what looked like a Chanel jacket, dark gray. The only reason Abby had any clue about Chanel jackets was because Skye loved them and was saving up her money to buy an authentic one someday.

Bone straight, burgundy-colored hair, parted on one side, fell gracefully over her shoulders. And her makeup was impeccable, with perfectly arched and manicured brows, eye shadow so succinctly applied that it looked like it was just her skin, and a lip color that seemed to have been custom made for this woman.

"Can I help you?" Abby asked cautiously.

It was obvious that she wasn't from around here.

"Ms. Rhodes?" she asked, sounding as polished and pristine as she looked.

"Yes?"

"May I come in?"

"Who are you?" Abby asked, not that she was afraid of the tall, slender woman, but she didn't just let anybody come into her house.

"My name is Robin Sinclair," she said eloquently.

Hell, even her name was classy.

"We have a mutual friend in Jordan Gatewood."

And just like that, all kinds of alarms were set off inside Abby. She reluctantly pushed open the door and stepped back to allow the woman inside. Her perfume wafted through the air, permeating Abby's living room. She wanted to hate it, but didn't. A knot the size of a fist swelled in Abby's stomach as the woman turned in a slow circle, surveying the room until she finally stopped and stared at Abby.

For a moment, the two of them stood there without saying a word, each of them, no doubt, assessing the other in relation to Jordan. The woman was an amazon, tall, gorgeous, and classic, like him. She was the epitome of who and what a man like Jordan Gatewood represented.

"I think we both know where this conversation is going to go," Robin Sinclair eventually said, locking those dramatic eyes onto Abby's.

Abby made a mental note to maintain her composure and dignity at all costs. After the day she'd had, this was the last thing she needed.

"You're seeing Jordan?"

She raised her chin slightly and looked down her nose at Abby. "I've been seeing Jordan for the last seven months."

Her knees buckled, but she wasn't going to give this woman the benefit of seeing it. Abby braced herself. The declaration struck her across the face like a slap. And she'd said it like she'd intended for it to knock Abby over. The first thought to run across

Abby's mind was that the woman was lying. The second thought was, she wished she'd never answered the door.

"I get it," Ms. Sinclair casually continued. "Jordan swept you off your feet without even trying. He's good at that."

Abby's heart pounded so hard that she was surprised it didn't shake the house. Was this really happening? She took slow, deep breaths to calm herself. Rational thought was key here. Abby had to tap into that part of herself that looked at things from an objective and cogent viewpoint before letting her emotions get the best of her. One by one, the building blocks of logic started to fall into place.

"How did you find out about me?" she calmly asked.

Abby studied her for reaction, and for a moment, a brief one, the woman looked uncomfortable.

"He's been distant lately," she admitted. "Busier than usual—too busy for him and me." She glanced away. "Preoccupied and more aloof than usual. I had my suspicions."

She had him followed. That's the only thing that made sense. Abby continued to focus on keeping her emotions in check, even though inside she felt like a volcano about to erupt. Jordan had been convincingly forthright with Abby. It didn't make sense for her to take the word of some random woman over his.

"Have you told him that you know about me?"

Again, the woman's expression changed, just slightly, enough for Abby to wonder what this woman's motives truly were for coming here.

"I asked him if he was seeing someone else. Of course, he lied."

That statement struck a nerve with Abby. Jordan, as far as she knew, had lied to her once. When they'd first met, he'd told her that his last name was Tunson. Since then, though, he seemed to have been an open book with her.

"So, you came here to confront me about seeing Jordan, expecting what exactly?"

Was he really seeing this woman while he was seeing Abby? Or was she here trying to stir the pot? It took everything in Abby not to blow a gasket.

"I'm here because I love him. I'm here because I wanted you to know about me, about us." She let her gaze flow down Abby to her feet and then back up to her face again, with a slight sneer in her expression. "And you need to know that at best, you're a chew toy to a man like him," she said condescendingly.

"Oh, trust me. I'm no toy," Abby coolly shot back.

Expensive clothes weren't a substitute for class or dignity. Abby wasn't the one trolling another woman, trying to convince that woman that the man between them didn't give a rat's ass about her. Jordan had proved otherwise.

"You fuck a rich man and all of a sudden, you think highly of yourself," she said condescendingly.

"No. I've always thought rather highly of myself, rich dick or no dick."

Robin Sinclair laughed. "There you go, sweetie. You fight tooth and nail for your little dignity. But after I leave, I suggest you take a good long look at yourself and be honest, brutally honest. While he's creeping down here to be with you, I'm on his arm in Dallas out there for the world to see. I'm not a secret. This is a battle you can't win, Ms. Rhodes. You are not equipped to play this game on this field."

Bitches like her were so clichéd. Abby almost felt sorry for her, but she was too pissed that this cow had had the audacity to come to her house and crap on an already crappy day to make it even worse.

"You are absolutely pitiful," Abby said, shaking her head in dismay. The woman's expression darkened. "And a disgrace to

SEDUCING ABBY RHODES | 215

women everywhere, that you would lower yourself to this level over a man is baffling to me. If I believed that Jordan was seeing someone else, I'd leave him. I wouldn't degrade myself to another woman over any man. I don't give a damn how rich and fine he is. I've got my self-respect. What happened to yours?"

She clenched her jaws so tight that Abby feared that woman might break some teeth if she wasn't careful.

"You've been a good little side chick long enough, Abby. Jordan's probably dumbed down quite a bit to keep from overwhelming you, but trust me when I say that he will never fully allow you into his world because you do not fit."

"Dumbed down?" Did this heifer just call her dumb?

"Jordan Gatewood has sat at dinner tables with royalty, senators, governors, even a president, Abby. He's on a first-name basis with sheiks and celebrities. Where do you think someone like you would fit in?"

"What makes you think I need to fit in?" Abby took a bold step toward this absurdly tall woman. "I don't need Jordan Gatewood," she said angrily. "He makes the two-hour trip down here and back to see me, to sit in my little house and sleep my small bed, to see me while he's, according to you, leaving your ass sitting alone and lonely, pining away in Dallas, hiring private investigators to see what's going on down here." Yeah. That got her. "Are you sure I'm the side chick?"

Abby said it, but the truth was, nobody had better be his side chick.

She glared at Abby. "Trust me when I say that I have wrapped myself around Jordan more times than you can count. You're nothing to him. Instead of insulting me, you need consider the relationship that you think you have with him. I would not waste my time coming here if I wasn't trying to do you a favor."

"Doing *me* a favor?" Abby laughed.

This was some Jerry Springer shit unfolding right here in her living room. The only thing missing was the fight, and she was real close to punching this broad in the jaw.

"Do me a real favor and get the hell out of my house," she said as she turned, walked back to the front door, folded her arms across her chest, and motioned with her head.

Robin Sinclair took her sweet-ass time taking that first step. Any longer and Abby would've gotten behind her skinny ass and pushed.

She stopped in front of Abby at the door. "Don't let history repeat itself."

Abby looked stared back at her.

"I don't know if you realize that Jordan was married before. His wife, Claire, committed suicide."

Abby had read that on the Internet, so it wasn't news coming from this woman.

"You and I aren't the first two women to have a dispute over Jordan."

Abby unfolded her arms.

"Lonnie Adebayo," she said. "Look her up. Interesting woman. Murdered over a year ago, and they've found the killer. Two women." She smiled weakly. "Both dead. And he's the only common denominator. Wouldn't it be sad if we ended up being next?"

"Are you threatening me?" Abby asked, appalled.

"Not me," she stated simply. Robin pushed open the screen door to leave. "But Jordan's a beautiful monster, Ms. Rhodes." She stepped out onto the porch and never looked back. "Many women would likely attest to that."

Crazy Laughter

ROBIN SPED AWAY FROM THAT house, pissed that that bitch had the nerve to think so highly of herself. Her country ass was high on Jordan's dick. That's all it was. She had amnesia about who and what she truly was or, more fittingly, wasn't. And she wasn't anything more than an amusement to him. A basic form of entertainment that he'd get bored with quickly once the stickiness of her wore off, since it likely didn't wash off with soap and water.

She'd allowed herself to sink to new lows, wallowing in the filth of jealousy and into the trenches of the bullshit that looked and smelled like a pot of chitterlings simmering on the stove. Abby Rhodes was trash. Ghetto, backwoods trash who had the audacity to think that she could ever compete with a thoroughbred like Robin. Her kind had been the cooks and maids that Robin had grown up with. The black-ass mammies with big tits and hips, smelling like gotdamn corn bread all the time. How he'd managed to dig that one up was beyond Robin.

Hot, bitter tears blurred her vision as she drove. Without even thinking, she had her phone dial his cell phone number.

"Robin, I'm busy," he said curtly over the speaker of her car.

"I don't give a damn how busy you are," she practically yelled. "What the hell ever possessed you to fuck around with someone like her?"

"What are you talking about?"

"I'm talking about the little country mouse you've got tucked away in Blink fucking Texas, Jordan."

"Where are you?"

"Where are you?"

She laughed. "Where the hell do you think?" Robin wanted to scream at the top of her lungs she was so hurt and angry. "She's nothing, Jordan," she sobbed. "And you chose her over me?"

"What the hell did you do?"

"I had to see her for myself," she said, struggling to compose herself enough to talk without wailing like a banshee.

"You spoke to her?"

"Damn right I did. I had to let her know who the fuck she was dealing with," she said menacingly.

Jordan was no saint. He was a bad guy trying to pretend to be good, trying to make amends for his past mistakes, but underneath it all, he was still as tainted and seedy as they came.

"I've got to admit, you surprised me with this one. If you were going to leave me for anybody else—anybody else, Jordan—I could've eventually come to terms with it. But this? This grimy little ignorant bitch—"

The phone suddenly went dead, but she'd made her point. He'd sunk to a new kind of low in Robin's eyes. Robin had been dreaming of a wedding and children with this man, but now she knew better. She'd have been settling with a man like him, the same way Claire had settled while he was out fucking around with Lonnie Adebayo. Robin had no proof that he'd actually had an affair with the woman, but all it took was a little imagination and some speculation, and one could easily create the scenario to that particular episode of Jordan's sordid past.

Claire killed herself after finding out that Jordan was having the affair. Police reports had said that there was evidence that Ms. Adebayo had had sex recently before her death. Whether it was forced or not, they couldn't say, and they also hadn't found a DNA match to the sample they'd found. Maybe Jordan had killed her after he'd fucked her. Maybe the two of them had made love and she'd threatened to tell his wife about the affair. The details weren't important. What was important was the fact that Robin had enough of a story to ruin him.

Telling his little secondhand girlfriend about him was just the tip of the iceberg. In the grand scheme of things, it meant nothing, except to derail this temporary little brisk note of happiness he was enjoying during this pathetic fling. But there was so much more at stake. Jordan Gatewood had just been awarded a multibillion-dollar government contract. Imagine what the feds would do if they found out that he may have actually killed a woman and then hid his own involvement and pinned the murder on Frank Ross.

Robin's thoughts reeled over the media frenzy over the news, all nipping away at him like piranhas. Then, of course, the police would get involved. Frank Ross hadn't been acquitted, but if the DA's office was smart, before wasting time on a new trial, they'd look for new evidence. And they'd have to look at Jordan, if they hadn't already. A man like him held a whole lot of power in Dallas. She'd found a connection to Ms. Adebayo by doing a simple Internet search. Any policemen worth their weight in doughnuts could've just as easily have found it—and maybe they had.

Her phone suddenly rang, and it was Jordan, who started talking before she could even say hello.

"You get your shit and get the fuck out of my building," he demanded.

"Oh, I'll go," she assured him. "But I'm not through with you."

This time, it was Robin who hung up.

His rejection of her had soured in her stomach in a way that wasn't natural. He was the man of her dreams. Everything about him complemented her to perfection, from the way he looked, walked, and dressed to his status and wealth. Robin was made for him, and she knew it the moment she'd first laid eyes on him in person. No other man she'd dated impacted her the way he did. Jordan had a way of looking at her, touching her, that sent shock waves through her.

To know that he was sharing himself like that with another woman was bad enough, but with this woman, this common, ordinary nobody, was absolutely humiliating. What did it say about him, except that he was like his father? Julian Gatewood had died in this town, killed because he was having an affair, too. Shit. She suddenly laughed. Was Blink, Texas, the place where all Dallas millionaires came to find bed wenches?

He was too stupid to see what he'd had in front of him in Robin. Together, they were royalty. They were powerful and could've ruled the world. Or they could've settled down in that ranch house of his, had a few babies, and grown old together. He'd ruined it because of pussy. Men were too damn simple sometimes. And Jordan's simplicity was about to cost him everything.

Dreams of You and Me

HE DIDN'T HAVE TIME for this. Jordan had been in meetings all day and had a flight to D.C. at six thirty the next morning, but Abby wasn't answering her phone. He'd left several messages explaining that he'd see her as soon as he arrived back in town, but anxiety got the best of him, and the next thing he knew, Jordan had thrown an overnight bag in the passenger seat next to him in his Bugatti and had gotten on the freeway headed to Blink. It was just after seven in the evening when he arrived.

Jordan knocked several times. "Open the door, Abby," he said, staring at her truck parked in the driveway.

He'd expected Robin to be upset, but he never saw this coming. She'd taken this shit to a whole new level, and he could only imagine what kind of damage had been done to his relationship with Abby.

Jordan knocked again. "C'mon, honey. We need to talk about this."

"I thought you said you had a flight to catch in the morning," she said from the other side of the door.

He couldn't help smiling at the sweet sound of her voice.

"I do, but since you wouldn't talk to me over the phone . . ."

Jordan heard the click of the dead bolt, and Abby slowly opened the door. She looked like she'd been crying, but he knew she'd never admit it.

"You all right?" he asked, tilting his head to the side to get a better look at her.

She thought about it before finally answering, "I've been better."

"Can I come in?"

Abby, wearing one of those long, floral, slip-like dresses that women seemed so fond of, pressed her pretty lips together and reluctantly stepped aside to allow him in.

"It's been a pretty shitty day," she said, turning and walking over to the sofa. She sat down, tucking her legs underneath her. Jordan sat down next to her.

"I'm sorry," he said sincerely.

He wanted to pull her into his arms and hold her but thought better of it.

"Is it true?" she reluctantly asked. "Are you seeing her . . . too?"

"I was," he admitted. "I met her before I met you, but it wasn't serious with her."

"She seems to think it was," she said softly.

Jordan pondered that for a moment. As far as he had been concerned, he'd made it clear to Robin from the very beginning that he wasn't interested in a serious relationship with her or anyone else. Until Abby had come along, that was true.

"She wanted it to be serious, Abby. I didn't."

He didn't want this situation with Robin to be a deal breaker for him and Abby. It seemed ridiculous that it could be, but he could see those wheels turning behind her eyes. Abby's first instinct was to take care of Abby, to protect Abby from being hurt or misled. The last thing he wanted was for her to feel as if she needed to protect herself from him.

"I stopped seeing Robin nearly a month ago, Abby, at the fundraiser in San Francisco and only because we had committed to it months prior to the actual event," he explained as rationally as he could. "Before that, I had been spending all of my free time with you, and that was the night I realized that I needed to be clear with her and end our relationship."

It was absolutely honest, and it was absolutely important to him that she know it.

"You told her about us?"

He shook his head. "No. Honestly, at that time, I didn't know if there was an us, sugah. I think I was curious about where this could lead, if anywhere at all, but Robin was—"

"Catching feelings?" she asked.

Catching feelings. It was an amusing phrase. "Yes," he said with a smirk.

"So, she came here to be vindictive," Abby concluded. "How'd she know about me and where I live?"

Jordan thought for a moment. "That's a good question."

Robin must've hired someone to follow him, which pissed him off, but right now wasn't the time to deal with it.

"I don't know what she said to you, and I don't need to know, but I have been honest with you, Abby."

"Except for that time when you told me your last name was Tunson," she reminded him.

"Except for that time," he reluctantly agreed.

"But I understand why you did it."

"This isn't a game for me. I'm forty-nine years old, I'm incredibly busy, and I don't have the time or interest to play musical women."

"And rationally, I reached the same conclusion."

"Good. It's a rational conclusion."

"Who's Lonnie?"

The name struck him in the chest like a fist.

"How do you know that name?" he reluctantly asked.

"Robin."

Just how deep into his life had Robin truly gone? Lonnie was history, and not good history. She was his own personal, private ghost, one he dealt with daily and that he would wrestle with for the rest of his life. She was his penance, maybe even more than Claire was.

"She's someone I used to know," he said simply.

All of a sudden, he didn't like the look in her eyes.

"A long time ago, Abby."

"Were you seeing her while you were married, Jordan?"

Trepidation. Apprehension. Abby was filled with both. Honesty was all that he had in this moment. Jordan Gatewood, the great negotiator, manipulator, was backed into a corner. He could lie or he could tell the truth. If he wanted this relationship to last, to even grow with Abby, then he'd have to take a chance on truth.

"Yes," he admitted.

Abby's eyes immediately filled with tears and doubts about him.

"Is that why Claire killed herself?"

He looked away from her for the first time since he'd shown up at her door. "Claire killed herself because she loved me far more than she should've."

"And Lonnie was part of that reason?"

"She was."

Abby sighed and leaned away from him slightly, leaving too much space between the two of them. All sorts of retorts ran through his mind. *I was a different man back then, Abby. I was a cad and a fool. I was selfish.* All those statements were true, and they all sounded canned and clichéd. Jordan had no idea how to explain to her that he had changed from who he'd been back then. Words seemed insignificant. He needed time with her, time to show her who he was now, especially with her in his life.

"Sometimes I am so careful and so cautious about men that I end up being single most of the time. My best friend, Skye, tells me that I'm overprotective of myself. But it's only because being in love is everything to me," she tearfully explained. "I don't recover so well from a broken heart." Abby looked embarrassed. "I'm not as strong as I go out of my way to make people think I am. Unfortunately, I don't bounce back all that well."

Was she saying what he thought she was saying?

"You love me?" Jordan dared to ask.

Her hesitation said it all. Jordan went against his better judgment and pulled her into his arms, onto his lap, and held her so tight that he had to make a conscious effort not to squeeze the breath out of her.

Abby cupped his face in her hands and kissed him. "I don't ever cry this much. I think I'm PMSing." She laughed.

"I'm not here to hurt you, baby," he murmured between her kisses. "I love you, too, Abby, and I swear, I will be as careful with you as *you* are with you."

"No secrets," she said, staring into his eyes. "Not ever."

"None."

"I so want us to work, Jordan," Abby murmured sincerely. "I've never felt like this before and I don't know what I'd do if—"

He kissed her before she could finish.

Abby wrapped both arms around his neck and held him tightly as he slipped one arm between her legs and his, scooted to the edge of the sofa, stood up, and carried her into the bedroom.

Jordan was up and dressed by four the next morning, standing on the steps to Abby's house. She stood a step above him, leaning into him.

"I will call you," he promised, pressing his forehead to hers.

"Are you sure that you don't want to try to take a later flight?"

"I have a meeting at the Pentagon as soon as I land."

She smiled. "That sounds like something out of the movies."

He kissed her, slowly and passionately. Abby tasted so damn good. She was warm and soft, and just like that, he was under her spell again.

Jordan swayed slightly. "I really need to go."

She smiled. "Call me as soon as you get to the airport," she said, concerned. "Let me know you made it all right."

"I will."

She laughed. "No, you won't, because you're a big boy and don't need to be reporting in to nobody when you travel."

"I'll call anyway."

He kissed her one last time and then turned to leave, glancing over his shoulder to get a glimpse of her smile.

At that time of the morning, there was hardly any traffic on the road. Robin had done her damnedest to derail his relationship with Abby, but she'd failed. What the hell did she know about Lonnie, though? What did she think she knew? Any sympathy he'd once felt for Robin was gone. Any guilt he'd felt for possibly leading her on was a moot point. She was navigating dangerously close to forbidden territory in his life. He hadn't played dirty in a long time, but if she insisted on pushing this agenda of hers, Jordan would have no choice but to push back. God help her if he actually did.

Have to Sacrifice

THE LOOK ON SKYE'S face said it all. The two of them had met at Pristine's for tea, and after listening to Abby catching her up on the recent events of her life, Skye was beyond pissed.

She sat across the table from Abby with her arms folded, nostrils flaring, and squinty eyes that seemed to deepen in their shade of blue. "You have truly pushed the boundaries of our friendship to new lows, Abby Rhodes."

Of course Abby felt bad. The two of them had always shared their deepest secrets with the other since they were in grade school. "I'm sorry, Skye. It was a secret that started out being more for his sake than mine, and then it turned into this unbelievable thing that didn't seem real, not even to me."

"What did you think I was gonna do?" she challenged. "Blab it to the whole town that you were dating an oil barron?"

"No." Abby sighed. "But you'd have told David and he'd have blabbed it. It would've been a chain reaction, by no fault of your own, Skye. And the thing is, I never expected any of this. I mean, he's amazing but it's all happened so fast. All this time, I've been trying to come to terms with it myself. I didn't know how to tell you what was happening since I wasn't even sure."

Skye's long, drawn-out, overly dramatic silence was as impactful as a scream.

"Okay," Abby finally huffed, still looking angry, but trying to resign herself to the fact that the damage to their friendship had been done.

"Would it help if maybe I bought a few round of drinks the next time me and you go out?"

Skye rolled her eyes at Abby.

"Maybe throw in dinner, too." Abby smiled.

Skye cut her eyes at her and sort of smiled, too.

"And I'll get you a real nice Christmas present this year just to say I'm sorry for not being a better friend and telling you all my business."

"It's what we do," Skye responded as pitifully as she could muster.

"It is. And I promise to remember that going forward."

"So, obviously, you have a reason for revealing this bit of news to me now," Skye expertly concluded.

"I'm in love," she finally confessed after a dramatic pause of her own.

Skye's eyes widened. "You haven't been in love since college, Abby, and even then, I don't really think that's exactly what it was."

"It was love the best I knew it to be at the time. And besides, I've been with other men since college, Skye."

Skye turned introspective. "Do you even know what love is? I mean, I think we've had this conversation before, but I don't think you've ever been able to give me a clear-cut answer to what you believe love is."

"I'm thirty-seven, Skye. I think I should know by now."

"You should, Abby, but you and I both know how developmentally slow you are emotionally."

Abby was offended, and it must've shown on her face.

"I'm not saying this to hurt you, sweetie," she said apologetically. "But come on, Abby. I mean, while the rest of us were getting goo-goo eyed over boys, practicing kissing on the backs of our hands, and trying to master the delicate but menial process for putting on our stockings and balancing in our first pair of high heels, you were following your daddy around with a saw and a power drill, building tree houses."

"I was ten, Skye."

"You were fourteen, hiding those big, enviable boobs of yours behind oversized football jerseys."

"What's that got to do with anything?" she asked irritably.

"It's just an example of how, yes, at thirty-seven, most women know what love is, but with you, I wonder."

"Can I just finish telling you what's going on, Skye?" Abby snapped irritably. "Please. Can I finish?"

Skye leaned back and waited. Abby wasn't here to argue the definition of love, the scope of love, or whether or not she was really in love with the man. She felt what she felt, and that's all there was to it. And to her, what she felt for Jordan was love.

"A woman showed up at my door," she reluctantly began, "claiming to be in a relationship with Jordan."

Skye's whole defensive demeanor softened. "He's cheating on you?"

"He had been seeing her before me, and according to him, he broke it off when he felt that there might be something between me and him."

Skye took several moments to process what Abby had just told her. "You don't believe him?"

"I do."

"But?"

"But there were things that she said that have stuck with me. Things that bother me."

"Like what?"

"Jordan is a widower. His wife committed suicide because she found out that he was having an affair."

"Whoa!" Skye softly exclaimed. "Did you ask him about it?"

Abby nodded. "I did, and he pretty much admitted that it was true. But he also said that things were different in his life back then. He was different."

"You're wondering if he really was?"

"I'm wondering what I've gotten myself into, Skye," she said, exasperated. "You know me. I don't do drama. I run from it like it's a wild animal chasing me down to try to eat me."

"But do you trust him, Abby? Do you think he really cares for you the way you care for him?"

Abby thought about it. All this time, well, before Robin Sinclair had brought her tight, stuck-up ass to Abby's house, everything unfolding between her and Jordan had felt authentic and organic, genuine. The conversation with Robin had tainted it somehow, and all of a sudden, Abby had doubts and questions that had never crossed her mind before.

"You know me," Abby said, smiling. "I am not insecure by any means. I have always known my worth, Skye, maybe to a fault and to my detriment, which is why my vibrator has been my one and only for so long."

"Vibrators, Abby," Skye said laughing, emphasizing the *s*. "Plural."

Abby laughed, too. "If I were going to put a man like that with a woman, it wouldn't be with me. I'm not saying that because I don't think I'm cute enough or smart enough. But I'm not big-city like him or her. Jordan looks and smells cosmopolitan, even when he's been riding horses and herding cattle all day. She looked like she spent her Sunday afternoons at Neiman Marcus traipsing around with a personal stylist and sipping expensive champagne."

"What's your point?"

"My point is, what are his intentions with me?"

"So, you think he's playing some kind of game?"

"I don't think that. I just wonder if he's not caught in something that isn't more of a fantasy than real life."

"But you're not worried that he's going to cheat on you like he did his wife? You're not worried that he might be running some game on you just for the hell of it?"

Why would she purposefully plant seeds of negative thoughts like that in Abby's head? She already had plenty.

"I'm worried that I'm in over my head," she finally admitted. "That I have no business in this relationship and that I really can't deal with the kind of drama that comes with the territory of being with someone like him."

Skye smirked. "You're scared?"

"I am," Abby said softly.

"Scared that it might not work out, or that it might and then what?"

Abby nodded.

"Scared that you think you might know who he really is, but then again, what if what you think you know turns out to be wrong, and what if he ends up being nothing like you thought?"

"Exactly!"

Skye suddenly burst out laughing. "Then I guess you really are in love, Abby, because that's exactly how it feels, girl."

Abby stared at Skye as if she were speaking Latin.

"Of course you're scared and overwhelmed. You have no idea what you're getting yourself into, and it's terrifying and exciting, and you're miserable and elated, and you're a whole bunch of other shit that makes your head feel like it's going to explode."

"You say that like it's a good thing."

"It sucks, Abby. But it's like a bear trap, and once it's got you, that's it. There's nothing left but to wait and see. There's no telling how it's going to end or if. Chances are, there'll be some pain and disappointment involved on some level. If you're lucky, you'll get to laugh more than you cry. You'll love him more times than you hate him. Hopefully, there'll be times when you miss him when he's gone, and there'll be fewer times when you'll roll your eyes because he came home early from work and your ass really doesn't want to be bothered.

"Love is a verb," she said with conviction. "It requires work and action and more work. You wake up every day and make the conscious effort to *do* love. Not be in it. It's clinging to the pretty parts, like when he calls you *baby*, kisses you for no reason, makes love to you like you're all he wants in the world. It's forgiveness, patience, and acceptance and pushing beyond the crappy parts. The things he does to make you mad, that irritate you, and make you wonder what you ever saw in him in the first place."

Abby frowned.

"Why do you love him?"

Abby had never really asked herself that question before. Was it because he was handsome? Wealthy? Or did she love him despite those things?

After some careful consideration, she finally came up with her answer. "Because he makes me feel like it's okay to be the girl."

Skye smiled.

"I can be soft around him. And I don't have to prove how tough

I am, and how strong I am. It's okay to let him open doors for me, and call me sugar without me getting defensive and accusing him of being sexist. And he trusted me with a football pass. He trusted me with it when nobody else would."

Skye laughed again and raised her teacup in a toast. "Welcome to being a grown woman, Abby. Finally."

To Give Away

"HELLO, MS. SINCLAIR," JORDAN'S ASSISTANT, Phyl, said, standing up to leave as the hostess ushered Robin to Jordan's favorite table in the back of the restaurant, overlooking the lake.

Robin smiled politely as she sat down and waited for Jennifer to leave.

"I'll get started on that report as soon as I get back to the office," she said to Jordan. "Do you need me to reschedule the meeting with Mr. Braeden from Hawk's Refinery this afternoon?"

"No," he said curtly. "I'll see you back at the office."

Jennifer damn near curtsied before leaving.

The Statesmen was one of the premier steak houses in Texas. He'd called, asking to talk to her, but Robin was no fool. She'd pissed off one of the most powerful men in the state. She'd agreed to meet with him, but only in public. Robin might never know for sure if Jordan was actually the one who'd murdered Lonnie Adebayo, but she wasn't about to take any chances.

"Thank you for coming," he said without bothering to look up from the steak he was cutting into. "You'll forgive me for not waiting. I have another meeting soon."

A server immediately appeared at the table. "Can I start you off with something to drink?" she politely offered.

"Martini," Robin said. "Dirty."

Jordan waited to begin his conversation until the server returned with her drink. Robin turned down food. The sight of him turned her stomach too much to eat. He, on the other hand, had no problems wolfing down that steak as if it were the last piece of red meat on the planet.

"For me, this was never personal, Robin," Jordan said, wiping his mouth with his napkin, dropping it on top of his half-eaten steak, and finally pushing the plate away from him. He leaned back casually in his chair. "Never."

It was a simple statement, but the depth of the true meaning behind it was clear. This, their relationship, was never personal to him and she'd never meant a damn thing to the man.

"I'm beyond getting my feelings hurt by you, Jordan, so stop with the subtleties."

"Then let me speak plainly. I let my position be known to you from the very beginning of this relationship, and yet you chose to make your own assumptions about where you wanted it to lead."

"What happened to 'I never intended to hurt you, Robin'? Where's that sensitive guy who was truly sorry for ever leading me to believe that he wanted something more than just to fuck?"

"You're the one who wanted to do away with subtleties," he said coolly. "You are no longer a part of my personal life, Robin, and therefore, what I do in private and who I choose to do it with are none of your business."

"But I've chosen to make it my business, Jordan."

"You've chosen to leave your dignity on my doorstep? Is that what I'm hearing? A woman like you who has men scratching at her door, begging for a few moments of her time, would rather grovel the feet of a man who has moved on? Seriously?"

"Groveling?" She swallowed. "Is that what you think I'm doing? As if I would ever even consider taking you back after what you've done to me?"

"You're humiliating yourself, Robin. And even now, I still believe that you deserve better than to turn into what you are becoming."

"Oh, I am so much better than you, especially after seeing how willing you are to go slumming in the backwoods of Texas for some dumb country ho."

He sighed, as if unbothered by her insult of his little girlfriend, but it had to have resonated, especially if the woman meant anything to him at all.

"That little stunt of yours was to punish me. Was that your intention?"

Robin thought about it and then responded. "It was to punish her."

"She didn't know about you and me."

"It doesn't matter," Robin said, feeling emotionally drained and numb all of a sudden. "I know you, Jordan. I know how debonair and sensual and elegant you are. You're charming and attentive, making sure that a woman feels like she's the only woman in the world for you. Even if it's not true."

Jordan stared at her.

"I wanted her to know the real you and what you are capable of. I wanted to break her heart first, before you had a chance to."

"But you didn't," he said calmly. "You failed."

"I planted a seed. Trust me. You might think that you've mended what I've broken, but it's still cracked. She has her doubts, and she always will because of what I said."

There. A faint glimmer of satisfaction filled her chest. Robin had made her point in that steely facade of his. Finally. And now she was ready to drive it home.

"Who is Frank Ross to you?" she asked.

Jordan's expression darkened, a sign that she was sailing into dangerous waters.

"I see a resemblance, subtle but distinct," she said, studying him. "Doesn't matter. He's family, and you're doing everything you can to see to it that he doesn't go to prison over the murder of Lonnie Adebayo."

Jordan stiffened at the mention of the woman's name. "I have no idea what it is you think that you know, but I'm certain that it's incorrect."

"Is it?" she calmly asked. "Or is it enough to turn the DA's attention away from Ross and to look at you?"

He gradually relaxed. "I have nothing to do Lonnie Adebayo's murder if that's what you're hinting at," he said confidently.

"Maybe not directly," she surmised. "Indirectly, perhaps? In any event, news like that would certainly affect this new government contract award. Wouldn't it? It could affect Gatewood Industries' stock prices. Certainly, the scandal would no doubt be, at minimum, embarrassing and bad for business. And then there's the issue of little Ms. Rhodes."

A muscle ticked in his jaw as Jordan clenched, holding in his anger.

"Do you really think a wholesome little thing like that would stand by your side, trust in the love that you two have found in each other, maintain her loyalty to you, knowing full well that you may have very well murdered a woman?"

"You're planning to what? Take your theory to the media? To the police? Good luck with that."

"I don't need luck. I know how the system works, Jordan. God knows I spent many years navigating it and manipulating it to my advantage before becoming a corporate attorney. I swear, I should've been a gardener." She laughed. "Again, it goes back to planting seeds, the right ones in the right places at the right times yield the sweetest fruit."

Robin suddenly had all the power now, and both of them knew it. He might have believed that he'd crushed her, but truly, he'd only made her stronger, reminded her of who and what she really was at the core. Robin was a warrior. She'd fought huge and impossible legal battles and had come out the winner time and time again. She was a master manipulator, like he was. She was a magician.

"As for what my plans are," she said, pausing to take a sip of a very delicious martini, "I haven't decided yet."

"You have nothing but a theory, Robin, and before coming for me, the DA will need more than that."

"But the media won't. The feds won't. Ms. Rhodes won't."

Robin had the advantage. Jordan was like a bug in her hands, and all she had to do to destroy him was clap them together. His life was hers now. She needed to figure out what her next move would be.

She studied his handsome features. "It's too bad things had to turn out this way, Jordan," she said sincerely. "You had the woman for you right under your nose the whole time. I'd have done anything for you."

"Now, you'll just do anything to me. Is that it?"

Robin took a long sip of her martini. "Thanks for the drink," she said, standing to leave.

Robin waited until he finally stood up, too, and she smiled.

"I'll be in touch, Jordan. I promise."

She walked out of that restaurant feeling better than she had in weeks. Robin had reclaimed herself, her dignity, and her status. She was not some broken, rejected, discarded lover of a man who was too ignorant to recognize the value of a woman like her. Robin Sinclair was in control again, and Jordan Gatewood was a bug cringing helplessly underneath the toe of her shoe, wondering if she'd let him continue to survive or see him ruined.

No River Too Wide

THE PENTHOUSE ATOP GATEWOOD Industries' corporate offices had always been a very personal sanctuary for Jordan. Even Claire had only been here a handful of times, claiming that the place seemed sterile and cold. Deep down, he'd always suspected that her description spoke better of their relationship than of this place.

The first thing Abby did when she walked into the place from the private elevator was to slip out of her shoes so as not to scuff the polished wooden floors. The thought had never occurred to him that his shoes might be a bad idea. She padded barefoot, staring up at the thirty-foot ceilings with a look of awe and disbelief in her eyes. As she walked, Abby turned slowly, noticing every detail, every piece of art and furniture. For the first time since he'd had it built, he cared what another person thought of this place.

Abby made her way past the living room and through the kitchen, stopping long enough to study the millwork of the custom cabinets and the fixtures. She made her way over to the floor-to-ceiling folding glass doors leading to the outside deck and saltwater pool. Abby marveled at the cedar underfoot and walked over to the outside railing and took in the view of the city.

Her mouth moved as she continued exploring, but whatever she was saying, she was saying it to herself. At best, Jordan could make out words like *wow* or *whoa*. Abby came back inside and lightly glided her fingers on the mahogany stair rail as she made her way up the stairs. Jordan quietly followed her. She gasped at the sight of his bedroom.

Abby stopped in the doorway. "That bed is bigger than my whole house," she murmured.

Of course she was exaggerating, but perhaps not by much, he smiled, amused. Abby made her way into Jordan's bathroom, a simple design of dark wood and soapstone, with an open shower with multiple showerheads, and next to that was his sauna. Abby walked over to the closed door on the other side of the room.

"Closet?" she asked, turning to him.

He shook his head. "The other bathroom."

He'd gotten it built with Claire in mind. The other bathroom was meant for her.

"My goodness," she said as she entered.

Of course, it wasn't as masculine as his, but still, it was a simple design, with lighter cabinets and Italian marble. Eventually, she did manage to get to both closets. One, of course, was empty.

Abby stood inside Jordan's room with her mouth open. "It's all so beautiful, Jordan. Like living on top of the world. Literally."

"Not quite," he said quietly. "But close."

They had dinner, made love, showered, and ended up back in bed with Abby facing and straddling him, wearing one of his shirts. He was enjoying every second of having her here, but the conversation he'd had a day ago with Robin was never far from the surface of his thoughts. Because of that conversation and its implications, Jordan was starting to feel as if he were on borrowed time with Abby.

She had pulled her hair back and braided it, showing off those eyes and cheekbones.

"So, do you have a speech written?"

Jordan had told Abby about his upcoming press conference about the contract he'd just won from the government.

He smiled. "Not yet, but I'm working on it."

Her smile lit up her face. "Are you nervous?"

Jordan shook his head. "No. It's just business as usual, Abby."

"For you, it's business as usual. I'd be so nervous I'd break out in hives."

"I take it you're not big on public speaking."

She shook her head. "I got kicked out of speech class in tenth grade."

"You were that bad?"

"My attitude was." She shrugged. "But it didn't matter. My speeches weren't any better."

Jordan wondered if Abby was aware of how much she had been toying with his hand. She seemed comfortable here with him. That revelation was a small victory for Jordan. Abby in Dallas. She'd made it clear that she was a small-town girl at heart and always would be.

"What are you thinking?" she smiled, leaning in close and planting a small peck on his lips.

"I'm thinking about how much I'm enjoying you being here."

"This place is more like you than the ranch house," she said. "That place, although very beautiful, doesn't seem finished. It's like it's just convenient, a place for you to sleep when you're there. But this penthouse . . . it's all you. This is where I feel you're most at home."

"You're right," he admitted. "How comfortable are you in this place?"

"I'm comfortable with you," she said without hesitating. "But I'm kind of afraid that I might break something."

He laughed. "Then we would just have to replace it."

We? Jordan hadn't meant to say that, but he didn't regret it. Abby didn't seem to catch that slip, but the idea of her spending more time here was one he didn't mind entertaining.

"What happens when you get this new division up and running, Jordan?"

"What do you mean?"

"You're going to be busier than usual."

He nodded introspectively. "More than likely. Yes."

She looked disappointed. "It'll be harder for us to spend time together. I mean, even though we only live two hours apart, it's still kind of a long-distance relationship."

"We will make it work, Abby," he said confidently.

God, he wanted it to work. Despite Robin's threats and time and distance constraints, Jordan desperately needed for this relationship to work, now more than ever because now there was a threat looming over it, one that he wasn't sure he could stop.

"Whatever happened with Robin?" Abby asked hesitantly. "Have you heard from her?"

Jordan paused. His first inclination was to lie, but that was a habit he wanted to avoid in this relationship. But there were things that he felt Abby was best left not knowing.

"I've spoken to her," he reluctantly admitted. "She knows now to keep her distance from you."

"It's not like I'm scared of her. She's taller than I am, but she's skinny, so I know I could take her if it came down to it. Besides, she'd be too busy worrying about scruffing up her makeup to get down and dirty. I've got older brothers, so I know how to fight," she said proudly.

Abby was serious, which he found amusing.

"It's just that she's reality television drama, and that's the part I have a problem with."

"I understand. I do too."

"I mean, I get it. You broke her heart so she's pissed," she concluded. "But there's no need to get messy. Know what I mean?"

"I know exactly what you mean."

"I just really don't want her to raise such a fuss that we end up in the tabloids or something."

He laughed.

"I'm serious, Jordan. You're a celebrity."

"I'm a businessman, Abby."

"Who happens to be a celebrity. You're a major person, and your life is wide open for everybody to see."

"Not all of it."

"And I'd like to keep it that way."

"You mean, our relationship?"

Abby nodded. "I don't want to be chased down by the paparazzi."

"You're ashamed of me?" he asked teasingly.

Abby's eyes grew wide. "Heavens, no! Of course not. How could you think that?"

Jordan cocked a brow. "That's what it sounds like."

In dramatic fashion, Abby wrapped both arms around him and held him tightly. "You know that's not what I mean, Jordan." She kissed his cheek, then his nose, forehead, and lips. "It's just that

I'm afraid that if a reporter asks me something, I could say the wrong thing. I'm not always tactful."

He laughed. "You are . . ." Jordan sighed. "My goodness, Abby." Jordan stared longingly into her eyes. "You have saved my life, baby. I don't think you realize just how much."

She stared expressionlessly at him. "Does that mean the press will never know about us?"

"No," he said in all seriousness. "The moment the press finds out about you, they will hunt you down like a pack of wild dogs."

Abby suddenly looked very worried. And she waited for him to deliver the punch line, to laugh or joke his way out of this. But Jordan didn't. He couldn't because it wasn't a joke.

"But I'll manage it," he whispered, kissing her sweetly. "I will take care of you, if you get out of my way and let me."

She thought about it for a few moments and then swallowed. "Promise?"

"With my whole heart, sugah."

Jordan meant it. If by some miracle, this beautiful woman could become a permanent part of his life, he would take such good care of her. He'd be the kind of man to her that he had failed to be to Claire. He would give her his undivided attention and make sure that she knew how much she meant to him.

She took a deep breath and thought for a moment. "They say that television adds ten pounds to people. If the media does find out about us, we might end up on TV. Think I should lose a few pounds?"

"Don't you dare," he said kissing the tip of her nose.

My Heart Came to Life

FROM THE OUTSIDE, THIS placed looked like an old, abandoned warehouse. Inside, it was a dark maze of long hallways, concrete floors and walls, and thick metal doors. Jordan walked like he knew exactly where he was going, though, holding Abby by the hand and walking confidently as he pulled her behind him. This place reminded her of something out of *The Maltese Falcon*.

Finally, they made their way to the end of one long corridor, and Jordan tapped on the door using a hammer hanging on the wall next to it. The door opened, and Abby was hit with a burst of cool air and music so loud that the bass from it would've knocked her on her ass if Jordan hadn't been standing in front of her. A tall, dark man with a brilliant white smile held the door open and ushered them inside.

Structurally, this place was a phenomenon to somebody like Abby. The expansive room had ceilings at least sixty feet high. There had to have been a few hundred people in that room, with spaces blacked out where windows should've been. Abby marveled at how something like this was actually designed and hidden so deeply into what amounted to a dump from the outside.

It took being in a place like this to witness the meaning of what it was to be a Jordan Gatewood. This was the second time he'd taken her out dancing, but that was a public nightclub. This one was private. As soon as he walked into that room, all eyes fell on him—them. People cleared a path for him, and someone immediately ushered the two of them to loft seating up a flight of stairs, enclosed behind a glass wall with a glass door to keep out most of the noise when it was closed. A bottle of some brand of vodka she couldn't even pronounce appeared as if by magic, chilled and already being poured.

"Can we get you anything else, Mr. Gatewood?" the gorgeous server asked.

He shook his head. "No, this will do for now."

While Abby was beyond impressed by the impeccable service the two of them were being provided, Jordan acted as if this sort of thing was expected. From their vantage point, Abby could see everything, including all the people staring and pointing at the two of them. He, on the other hand, seemed absolutely oblivious to it. Jordan sat down on the elegant sofa and pulled her down next to him, then leaned over and kissed her softly and smiled.

"Would you like to dance?" he asked so abruptly and so out of character that Abby couldn't help but laugh.

"I'd love to dance."

Dancing for Jordan consisted of planting his feet and swaying that beautiful, muscular body of his from side to side, with Abby spinning and gyrating around him like a top. They laughed, drank, danced, and made out like teenagers perched high away from everyone else. And Abby forgot that he was overwhelming and that his life was too damn big for her. She forgot what her life had been like before he'd come into it. And the only thing that made sense now was that he would never leave it.

"I want to grow old with you," she remembered saying, draping herself over him like a blanket. "I never thought I'd ever say that and mean it."

Abby was so damn drunk, but it was good drunk.

"You say something like that to me, I'm holding you to it, dahlin'. I told you that you have saved my life, and I meant it. I am hoping that you will keep saving it."

"I don't know what I've done," she said humbly. "I think it's the other way around. I think you saved me," she confessed.

"You are gorgeous," he said warmly. "And funny and unique. Sweet. Sexy. You talk funny," he said jokingly, "but your smile lights up my world, honey. So, yes. I appreciate the hell out of you."

Hours later, Jordan slept soundly next to her. Abby had passed out for a bit, but then suddenly, she woke up and couldn't go back to sleep. She eased out of bed, slipped into one of his shirts, and quietly crept to the door, down the hall, and then down the stairs. Abby would be heading back to Blink in the morning, but this weekend, she'd felt like a princess, wined and dined by this magnificent man who had fallen in love with her. Abby had to keep reminding herself that all of this was real, but for that to be the case, there had to have been a higher power at work here.

She belonged with him. It was something she just knew, felt it deep down inside, and once she'd come to terms with it and got out of her own way, let go of those silly doubts and insecurities, there was no denying that the two of them were meant to meet and they were meant to be together. It was the logistics that gave her pause. Abby lived in Blink. She had a business and a home and family in Blink, Texas. And Jordan's world was here in Dallas. Never in a million years had she ever contemplated what it might be like to live in a place like this.

He'd promised her that they'd make it work, though, and Abby trusted him. She trusted him with all of her, and she loved him more than she imagined she'd ever loved any man. The thought of leaving him tomorrow made her want to cry. She'd grown accustomed to falling asleep next to him and waking up with him.

"Abby," he called softly to her from the top of the stairs.

"I'm here."

"Come back to bed, baby," he said.

Abby turned on the balls of her feet and hurried up the stairs to get to him, standing naked and holding out his hand and waiting for her. Inside the bedroom, Abby slipped off his shirt and slid back into bed, curling up next to him. Robin Sinclair had tried to do a number on Abby. And it had damn near worked. Every now and then, since talking to that woman, doubts would rise up in Abby about how a man like him could possibly truly care about someone like Abby, who wouldn't even register on his radar in a big city like this, swimming with the Robin Sinclairs of the world.

Fate had brought Abby and Jordan together and introduced them in her house that day. All the stars had to have been aligned, and every element in the stratosphere had to have been in place to have put the two of them together, and that's exactly what happened. Even in Abby's logical-thinking, reason-worshiping mind, she had finally come to accept that yes, there were such things as ghosts, and yes, she and Jordan Gatewood were soul mates.

Gone Inside

LOATHING HIM WASN'T ENOUGH. Despising him for what he'd done to her couldn't change the feelings she still had for him. Robin's desperate need for Jordan was turning her into a madwoman, crazed with twisted thoughts of punishing him and getting him back.

"I guess you're still not taking me seriously," Robin said unemotionally over the phone, staring at the picture sent to her by Liza's detective, of Jordan hugged up with Abby Rhodes.

"You need to lose my number, Robin," he responded bitingly.

She recognized the club they were in. It was one of the most exclusive clubs in Dallas called A Little Piece of Heaven. You needed a special pass to get into a place like that, and Jordan had dragged country trash inside it.

"No. I need to see you, Jordan," she said, summoning him.

"I don't have time for this. I don't have time for you."

"What part of I can ruin you with a single phone call to the press don't you understand?" she said intensely. "I need to see you. Maybe I need to truly drive my point home to you in person."

She abruptly hung up and continued studying the photographs e-mailed to her. Jordan had a thing about kissing this woman. He couldn't keep his mouth off her for some reason, which stabbed at Robin's heart. He'd always acted as if kissing were a vile act. Jordan always told Robin that he had a thing about it. It turned him off. But apparently only when it came to kissing Robin.

She hated him for how he'd made her feel. Inadequate. Undesirable. Ugly. Angry. Bitter. Insecure. The toll all these emotions were taking on her was immeasurable, transforming her into someone whose face she hardly even recognized when she looked into the mirror. No man had ever had this effect on her. No man had ever given her such an overwhelming sense of self-loathing. This was the truth that Robin curled up next to every single night since she'd found out about this other woman. And every single day, she wrestled with just getting out of bed in the morning and struggling to make it through the day without breaking down in fits of self-pity or rage.

"Is he in?" she asked defiantly, marching past his assistant's desk.

"Yes, but he's on a call," the woman said, rushing over.

Robin ignored her, walked into Jordan's office, and immediately shut the door behind her.

"I'll have to call you back," he said before hanging up on whomever he was on the phone with.

"Now is not the place and time for this," he said, bolting to his feet.

In the hour since she'd first called him, Robin had run the gamut of emotions and stood before him now, utterly drained of the energy to fight.

"Sit down, Jordan," she told him.

"I need for you to leave," he demanded.

The tone of his voice, the disdain in his eyes cut into her like hot steel. Robin straddled the fence between love and hatred for him, and it tormented her so badly that she couldn't just leave.

"I need to make some things clear to you, Jordan," she said gravely.

Jesus! Couldn't he see what was happening here? Did he truly not understand the depths to which she was willing to go with him?

"This has got to end," he said, calming himself. The reasonable and rational Jordan gradually appeared in the place of the angry bull sinking into his chair behind that desk. "You've got to get past this, Robin. It's not worth it. You are an exceptional woman. This . . . this is beneath you."

Robin listened carefully to the things he said, and they hit home. She nodded slowly in agreement. "Yes," she whispered.

The longer she held his gaze to hers, the more he started to look as if he cared. There was sincerity in his eyes, a warmth and genuine concern for her. "I am so sorry for what I have done. I'm sorry for having misled you. I had no right to do that. And I take full responsibility, Robin. I do."

Jordan Gatewood was such an impressive man. He had a way of luring you in and making you feel as if you were the most important person in his life. And you believed him. But Robin knew all his tricks, and she had made up her mind never to fall for them again.

"You're afraid," she tenderly offered.

He appeared to be taken aback by her comment.

She smiled. "You're afraid that I'll tell everyone what I know about you and Lonnie Adebayo."

"There's nothing to know," he said convincingly.

"I don't believe that," she murmured more to herself than to him.

Robin had reached her own conclusions about Jordan and Adebayo. She'd drawn lines and connected the dots to the only scenario that made any sense. Jordan had been caught in an affair with the woman. His wife, Claire, had discovered his secret, confronted him about it, and killed herself because of it. At some point, Jordan had had an altercation with Adebayo, and he'd either murdered her himself, or he'd hired someone to do it. Frank Ross? Maybe. It would explain why he was paying for the man's defense, especially if Ross had planned on coming clean about the whole scheme and risking a scandal for Jordan.

"Speculation, Robin. You managed to get your hands on a few dangling particles of information and stitched them together to fabricate some story that you can't even prove. Even if you were to go to the police with what you think you know, a team of decent lawyers could unravel your story before it even went to trial."

Robin's eyes filled with tears. "Ah, but it wouldn't even need to go to trial to ruin you, Jordan," she said, gloating. Looking at the sudden change in his expression, she almost felt sorry for him. But not quite. "You truly underestimate me, but that's okay."

"You'd ruin all these months of hard work, yours included, over a relationship?" he asked in disbelief. "Really?"

Robin nodded and swiped her hand across her cheeks to dry her tears. "Yeah. That pretty much sums it up."

"That's madness, Robin."

"I agree. But that's the effect you have on me, Mr. Gatewood. It's maddening." Robin took a daring step closer to Jordan. "You're right. I've got my speculation, my circumstantial evidence, hearsay. I know that you and Lonnie had an affair, but of course, there's no proof. Yet."

He did his damnedest not to flinch.

"I'm pretty sure that Claire found out about it and killed herself over it. Lonnie wasn't the first, but your wife was sick of your shit. And suicide was the only way she knew to escape you."

He lowered his head. "You have no idea," he muttered. "I'm not going to let you hold me hostage over some bullshit theories."

"A few billion dollars isn't worth being my hostage, Jordan?" She smirked. "Staying out of prison isn't worth being my hostage? Losing every damn thing you own isn't worth being my hostage?"

She let her questions marinate with him for a few moments.

"They still have that DNA sample that they found inside Lonnie the night she died," she continued. "Never matched it to anyone, not even Frank Ross." Robin sighed. "But then, I imagine they probably just never got around to finding the right person to compare it against. This is the point where you ask me what it is that I want."

It was likely that Jordan had never met his match before. He was used to winning, always. Not this time, though. She knew it, and from the look in his eyes, so did he. He would give her anything she wanted. Robin held him in the palm of her hand, ready and able to close her fist around him and squeeze him until there was nothing left.

He had stripped her of her dignity, peeled away her self-esteem until she was raw and exposed. Robin would never recover from this, from him and how he'd left her reeling in this unfamiliar territory of despair.

"There is no happily ever after for either one of us, Jordan," she said sorrowfully. "People like us, like you and me, we don't get to be happy. Not really. Oh, we have all the trappings of success and happiness—money, cars, and homes, fancy friends, and our parties. We look so damn good on the outside, but inside, we're rotten apples. It's a trade-off."

"What do you want from me?" he finally asked.

"I want you," she finally admitted.

Robin swallowed what little pride she had left to say those words to him, and she meant them.

Jordan looked at her like she had lost her mind. "You've got to be kidding me."

"No," she said softly. "I want to be Mrs. Jordan Gatewood. And I want you to show me off to the world, to be proud to have me as your wife, and to devote yourself to me for the rest of our lives together."

In lieu of everything that he could lose by Robin making one simple phone call to the press, Jordan had no choice but to make peace with her.

"This is insane, Robin. You want a man who doesn't want you."

She cringed at his words. "Don't. Don't ever say that to me again," she warned. "You want me . . . to keep my mouth shut, Jordan. You want me to keep your secret. You want me, and you will show the world that you do, or I swear I will destroy you."

Oh yes! Finally. Finally, he understood. Robin could see it in his eyes, a reflection of resignation and defeat. He was no longer in a position to dismiss her. He no longer held the power in this relationship. She did.

"If you ever see her again, I'll know it," she threatened. "If anything happens to me, a letter will be sent to *The Dallas Morning News* with all the dirty details of what I know, and I know so much more than you realize."

Robin had just secured her future and put her life back on track. She slowly walked around his desk and stopped beside him, embraced his face with her hands, turned it to her, and kissed him.

Holding Myself Close

"I LEFT HIM A MESSAGE earlier today, but he hasn't called me back," Abby said to Skye over the phone. "I figured he's been pretty busy with all this press conference stuff."

She sat down on the sofa with a bowl of freshly popped popcorn and a glass of white wine.

"So, do you call him *bae*?" Skye asked.

Abby laughed. "No. Once you meet him, you'll understand why. Jordan is no bae, Skye. He's more like a *honey* or a *darling. Sweetheart*."

She picked up the remote and turned to CNN. This announcement was so much bigger than just local Texas news. This was national news.

"Channel thirty-four," Abby told her.

"Got it."

"Okay, I'll let you go. I don't want to miss a word he says."

She and Skye hung up, and Abby waited another ten minutes before the press conference started. She gasped at the sight of him, wearing that dark gray suit and navy-blue tie. Abby started smiling. He looked so handsome, so distinguished. Jordan didn't look like he was even a bit nervous, but Abby was sitting there on the sofa in her robe and slippers actually trembling like she was the one about to make that announcement.

"I'm so proud of you," she whispered lovingly.

To think that this was her man. She squirmed, laughed out loud, and then felt silly about it as her stomach fluttered with the sensation of butterflies.

"It's a great day for Gatewood Industries," he casually began, looking out at the press snapping pictures of him. "We took a chance, a pretty big one, in competing for this very high-level, high-visibility contract with the Department of Defense. Compared to most of our competitors, we were the little guy, and we went in to this thing knowing that we'd probably lose."

Jordan paused, seeming to reflect on what he would say next.

"My father broke barriers in the oil and gas industry. He had a vision for what could be and fought tooth and nail to get it knowing that odds were against him, that society as a whole was against him. But still, he pushed forward until he saw his dream realized."

A lump swelled in Abby's throat as Jordan spoke about his father.

"After he died, I inherited more than just the responsibility of running his company. I had to continue his legacy and continue to embrace his vision of taking Gatewood Industries to the next level, beyond oil and gas. And with this endeavor, we're taking it to outer space." He smiled, and cameras flashed like crazy.

Abby's heart beat so fast in her chest, and she couldn't stop smiling. He was the most amazing person she'd ever known.

"Gatewood Industries has competed for and won one of the largest contracts in the history of the federal government. Partnering with the US Air Force and NASA, we will begin developing rocket engines powerful and efficient enough to carry men and women to Mars and beyond. With some of the greatest scientists and engineers in the world, we will begin to take space exploration to exciting new levels."

She watched with tears in her eyes as Jordan finished his speech and then answered questions from the press like he had been doing it his whole life. After he finished speaking, some military guy came up to the podium. Skye called immediately.

"Oh, my gosh, Abby," she said, excited. "That's him? That's your Jordan?"

Abby nodded. "Yes," she said as if she couldn't believe it either.

"I am so jealous!" she yelled. "He's so fine, girl! He's like royalty if we had royalty in this country."

"Exactly. That's exactly what he's like."

"When's he coming back here? Because I want to meet him."

Abby smiled, warmly. "I'll make sure you do."

By the time they finished gushing over Jordan, the general was wrapping up his speech, and he and Jordan reached out to the front row of the audience and began shaking hands.

"Let me let you go," Abby said quickly. "I'll call you back."

She couldn't call him right now, of course, but she'd give him a few hours and then try him again, if he didn't call her first. Abby took a sip of wine, and that's when she saw her coming up to the side of the stage and reaching for Jordan. It was Robin Sinclair, smiling up at him and taking hold of his arm as he stepped down. It didn't make sense at first. Why would she be there? Jordan stepped down next to her, looked at her, and paused. Robin pulled his face to hers and kissed him on the lips. Jordan jerked back, slightly, and returned an awkward smile to the woman.

Abby's phone immediately started to ring, but she didn't answer it. Robin looped her arm in Jordan's, and the two of them disappeared from the screen together. Abby sat frozen, confused by what she'd just seen. She didn't know how long she sat like that before finally picking up her phone and dialing his number.

"Jordan. Call me, please. I-I saw the press conference." She paused. "Call me. Okay?"

Abby spent the better part of the night trying to make sense of what she'd seen. Jordan had made it clear that there was nothing between the two of them anymore. Abby had no reason not to believe him. It was strange seeing the two of them together like that. It wasn't natural. In her gut, she knew that something wasn't right. Robin was desperate for him. And maybe she'd used the media to her advantage, knowing that he wouldn't reject her in front of generals and television cameras.

Skye kept calling, and eventually, Abby answered.

"What happened?" Skye asked. "Who was that?"

Abby had no idea what to say. "I-I'm not—," she said, finally beginning to give way to tears.

If she'd told Skye that it was the woman who'd stopped by her house a few weeks ago, it would open up a whole other conversation that Abby wasn't prepared to have right now.

"Have you spoken to him?"

Abby shook her head, and the tears started falling. "No. Not yet."

"I'm sure there's a reasonable explanation, Abby."

"Oh, I'm sure there is." She swallowed and dried her eyes. "He'll clear it up when I talk to him. But, I'll call you tomorrow, Skye," Abby said, hanging up.

Jordan had been so busy lately, that that had to have been the reason why he hadn't returned any of her calls. When Robin came to her house, it took every ounce of Abby's resolve not to give in to doubts about him. For the first time, Abby wanted to be the kind of woman that didn't run at the first sign of trouble. She wanted to be a rock for him and for herself, because love required commitment. And if she wanted forever with him—or with anybody, for that matter—Abby was going to have to learn to stand fast.

It took hours for her to fall asleep. She kept expecting to hear the phone ring, but it didn't. He loved her. He'd convinced her of that. Why would he go through all that trouble to do that if he didn't mean it? He'd said himself that he didn't have time for games. No. Something was wrong. Or at least, it wasn't right. She needed to speak to him. That's all. Abby rolled over and tried not to cry. She tried so hard. But in the end . . .

Got 'Til It's Gone

_____

ABBY HAD LEFT SEVERAL messages over the course of the last few days, and Jordan hadn't returned any of them. Lonnie Adebayo would have her redemption, one way or another. He had loved her in his own way. In his own terrible and selfish way. Her death hung over his head like the dark cloud of Claire's. So, was it any wonder that he was still suffering the consequences of the role he'd played in both their lives?

He stood at the window of his office looking out at the city, marveling how he could be on top of the world and at the same time underneath it. Abby Rhodes had been the sweetest slice of something he could never have. Peace. Robin was right. People like him didn't get happily ever afters. Karma wouldn't allow it.

Lonnie had been a casualty in a long line of casualties in Jordan's life. Whether she would ever know it or accept it, Abby was spared. Jordan wasn't wallowing in self-pity. He was a self-made man, and he'd made himself all sorts of drama unlike anything Abby could ever possibly understand. She was not fit for his world. Deep down, he'd always known it, but he'd hoped that somehow, some way, he could've buffered her from the truth of the kind of man he was at the core. Hell, he'd almost had himself convinced that he had changed. Jordan hadn't changed, though. He'd just gotten caught up in the delicious fantasy of Ms. Rhodes.

"Jordan?"

Robin, on the other hand, was a perfect fit for this life.

He turned to her standing in the doorway, looking flawless and unruffled as if the events of the last month had never transpired. Robin's long hair was swept up off her shoulders. Her fitted charcoal-gray skirt and crisp white blouse were complemented nicely by navy-blue pumps.

"What time will you be picking me up tonight?" she asked sweetly.

In the last week, they'd fallen into their roles effortlessly. "Seven?"

She smiled. "Seven's perfect," she said, turning and walking away.

What Robin knew, or thought that she knew, could derail him completely. If she went to the press, Jordan could end up being more than humiliated. Gatewood Industries could have that new contract snatched out from under it, before the ink even dried. And too many people had worked too long and hard for this victory to have to suffer the loss because of his mistakes. He could end up standing trial for murder. He could end up in prison.

They were attending a reception tonight in his honor at the governor's mansion. All his so-called friends and most devoted enemies would be there, congratulating him and smiling in his face, while talking about him like a dog when they thought he wasn't paying attention. Robin understood this game. She knew it well, and she would have his back like a pit bull.

This wasn't even about love. It was a merger, an arrangement for the both them. Jordan could keep his freedom and his government contract, his good name. And Robin would have her man. This was a business deal.

It was just after six. Jordan adjusted his tie in the mirror, then stepped back to take a look at the results. His phone rang. Jordan knew exactly who it was.

"This is Jordan," he said to answer the system wired throughout his penthouse.

"It's Abby," she said sweetly.

The sound of her voice broke his heart.

She waited for him to say something, anything, but he didn't.

"What's . . . I don't understand, Jordan."

"I know, Abby."

"Will you please tell me what's happening?"

There was no easy way to say it. Jordan would dismiss the formality of kindness, because no matter how he broke the news, it would hurt her.

"We can't see each other anymore, Abby."

Jordan felt as if he'd been stabbed in the chest, but he couldn't let her hear his pain.

"What happened? W-why?"

Jordan owed her some sort of explanation. Even if it was a lie. She needed an answer, one that hopefully she could eventually live with.

"I made a mistake with you," he began.

"No. No, you didn't."

"Yes, Abby. We are from two very different worlds."

"But we've known that. From the beginning, we've never let that get in the way of us. It doesn't matter."

"It matters," he said sternly. "Robin and I talked, and we've resolved our issues."

"Issues? But you said you loved me."

He could tell that she was crying, and it tore him up inside. "I care about you."

"No. That's not what you said. You said that you loved me."

"Don't make this harder than it is."

"I don't think you have any idea how hard this is."

He knew all too well. "I never meant to hurt you."

"How come I'm starting to get the feeling that you say that to all the girls, Jordan?" she asked sarcastically.

It was a dig, a sweet and polite dig, and he appreciated her for it.

"I will miss you."

"Is it really that simple for you? You can't just do this to people. You can't pull someone close to you, promise yourself to them, just to push them away when you're finished," she said, crying. "Is that what you said to her? To Robin?" she sobbed. "So, she wasn't lying to me after all?"

"No." He took a deep breath. "She wasn't."

"You're not fair, Jordan. You don't play fair at all."

"You're right. I don't. But trust me when I tell you that this is for the best."

"Not for me it isn't."

"I wouldn't be doing it if I didn't believe it, Abby."

"Then you must know something I don't."

"I absolutely do," he said remorsefully.

Abby took a deep breath. "I hate that we ever met."

Hearing the pain in her voice when she said that felt like a punch in the chest.

"It was probably the worst thing to ever happen to me."

"It likely was, Abby."

"Right," she said sadly. "Be happy, Jordan. And good-bye."

Jordan was hollow inside, empty again, the way he'd been before he'd met her. It was the most natural feeling in the world. In the back of his mind since he'd started seeing Abby, Jordan somehow knew that it would eventually come to an end between them. It was inevitable, and now that it had happened, he was back to his old self again, and a part of him felt relieved.

Robin was in her element, ever the graceful and social beauty. She was mesmerizing in a slinky purple gown, cut low in the back, clinging to her beautiful curves. All eyes were on the two of them. Jordan played his role even better than she'd expected.

"First, the deal of the century," one man touted to Jordan, then eyeing Robin like she was a filet mignon. "Are wedding bells next?"

She blushed, turned to him, and smiled. "I'm crossing my fingers."

Jordan warmly kissed her forehead. She tried not to look surprised by the gesture.

These people were her tribe. She played them all like instruments, saying the right things, laughing on cue, placing a tender touch on an arm, expertly tempering warm embraces. Together, they were the perfect couple. Enough people said it until even Jordan was starting to buy into it.

"If I didn't know better," she whispered to him at the bar, "I'd almost think that you were enjoying being with me."

"But certainly, you know better," he said casually.

She mimicked an exaggerated cringe. "There's the Jordan Gatewood I know and love."

"You still believe that you love me?" he asked, genuinely interested. "After everything that's happened between us?"

Robin's expression turned serious. "I know I do. And I know that in time, you could love me, too."

"But what if I never do, Robin?" he asked sincerely.

Robin looked away from him, trying to hide the hurt in her eyes. He placed his hand underneath her chin and turned her face to his.

She shrugged. "I'll either get used to it or learn to accept the lie that I tell myself."

Jordan raised her hand to his lips and tenderly kissed it, then looked up into her eyes again.

"You're not going to see her again? It's over?"

He slowly nodded. "It's over."

She turned her head slightly to one side and eyed him suspiciously. "How do I know you're telling me the truth?"

Jordan knew that his next words would be brutal, but Robin was a big girl. She could handle it.

"Because I love her, Robin. And ending it with her will save her from us."

Robin glared angrily at him. "You're an asshole."

He smiled. "But I'm your asshole. Isn't that all that matters?"

Robin had revealed the true nature of herself to Jordan. It was only a matter of time before she truly understood the fullness of what she'd fought for and won. She thought she knew him. But she'd only just scratched the surface. The real Jordan Gatewood had a soul as black as oil. And he was nobody's puppet.

Alone with My Fears

ABBY STOOD NEXT TO REALTOR Luther Michaels, surveying the outside of the property.

"How many units did you say it has?" she asked.

"Nine. Four two-bedroom apartments, and the rest are one-bedroom units."

Abby had never taken on a project of this magnitude before, and this thing needed a whole lot of work. It was a three-story apartment complex, brick, but with some serious foundation issues as indicated by the sizes of cracks through the exterior.

"I know it needs some major work, Abby, but they're practically giving it away."

"Is it safe to go inside?"

"Sure," he said, leading the way to the main entrance.

She'd never considered property in Clark City before, but this was a deal that piqued her curiosity. The price was right, and looking at the place, Abby could probably even talk them down from what they were asking and get the place for damn near free.

"Are any tenants in here now?" she asked, surprised by what sounded like a television show coming from one of the floors upstairs.

"Three. They've been given until the end of next month to move, though."

Clark City was almost twice as big as Blink, and once she finished renovating this place, Abby could easily find renters. Taking on a project this big could take months, maybe even close to a year, but she had time. And she needed something like this to keep busy. Keeping busy, that was the key.

"Is anybody in here?" she asked, stopping at one of the doors.

"I don't think so," Luther said, trying the doorknob, turning it as he pushed it open. "This is one of the one-bedrooms, I believe."

Single-paned windows. Dirty carpet.

"What kind of floors are underneath here?"

"I'm guessing concrete maybe."

Of course, the kitchen and bathroom were outdated. Abby walked into the bedroom and then over to the window on the opposite side of the room and stared out at a wide-open field behind the building.

"Whose property is that?"

"It comes with the building. There's a lake just beyond those trees." He pointed. "Pretty good size."

"I'd like to make an offer," she finally said.

She needed this. Abby had been in that house too long, and it was time to go.

"Sure," he said eagerly. "They're asking two thirty-five. It's a great deal, Abby. Sitting on about five acres. What do you want to offer?"

There were moments when Abby evaporated into clouds of numbness where she had to remind herself to snap out of it. This was one of those moments.

"One seventy-five." She turned to him. "Let's start there."

It had been a month since Abby had last spoken to Jordan. It'd only been about a week since she'd finally stopped crying over him every time she thought about him, which was pretty much constantly.

She sat in Skye's living room, sipping on wine and waiting for Skye to play some music.

"It gets a little easier every day," Skye said, turning to Abby. "Right?"

"I suppose," she said, sounding pretty unconvincing.

"Wanna listen to Adele?"

"Do you wanna sit and watch me slit my wrists?" Abby asked, slightly appalled. "Put on something upbeat."

Skye smiled, and suddenly, Macy Gray's song "Kissed It" flowed from Skye's Bose speakers.

"How's that?" She smiled, sitting down next to Abby.

"Perfect," Abby said, raising her glass to toast with Skye.

"At least you're getting out of that house for more than just work."

"Yeah. I'm actually thinking about moving, though."

Of course Skye wasn't expecting that. "But you love that house, Abby."

"I need a different house, Skye."

"Memories?"

"Yeah, and not all of them mine," she said introspectively. "There's an apartment building in Clark City that I put an offer on."

"Clark City? Why there?"

"It's a great deal. Got nine units, and based on market value, I could easily make five to eight hundred a month on each one. That's good money."

"So, if you move out of your place, are you planning on living in one of those apartments?"

"Thinking about it."

"Do you think it'll help?"

Abby didn't answer right away. "This is what my life was like before Jordan. It was just me, renovating property, working, sitting here having wine with you." She smiled.

"Teaching belly dancing to the rest of us," Skye reminded her.

"Exactly. In the few months that I knew him, I didn't realize how much it had all changed, how I'd changed. Things are just getting back to normal." She shrugged. "That's all."

"Normal didn't mean you were necessarily happy, though, Abby," Skye murmured.

"I thought I was," Abby reluctantly admitted. "It took being with him to show me that I wasn't. I was just settled into a routine that didn't ripple the waters much. At least, not in a way that I couldn't handle."

"Are you going to cry?"

Abby sighed. "No," she said firmly. "Crying's overrated."

"But you don't hate him?"

"I most certainly do," Abby admitted. "I hate him with a passion, and I never want to see him again. But I don't regret him. I did, but not anymore. Being with him taught me some things."

"What'd you learn, sweetie?"

"I learned that it's okay to be careful, but not too careful. I've missed out on so many opportunities in life by being too careful. It's okay to be spontaneous, to pack a bag and take a trip. It's okay to have a one-night stand if I want to, as long as I use precautions of course."

"Of course." Skye nodded and shrugged.

"Maybe I'll meet someone one day who'll be the man of my dreams, for real, or maybe I won't, but how would I know if I never give anybody a chance? And if I never meet him, I'll still be okay."

"Do you want to get married, Abby?"

Abby thought about it. "Yes."

Skye laughed. "I've asked you that question a hundred times, and that's the first time you've actually given me a straight answer and not some algebraic, engineering, physicist formula that had nothing to do with nothing."

Abby laughed, too. "Yes. I want to be married, and before my eggs dry up, I'd like to have at least one baby."

Skye's eyes widened. "A kid?"

Skye had two; both of them were mercifully at her mother's house for the weekend.

Abby nodded. "Crazy, huh?"

Skye stared warmly at her. "No. Not crazy at all."

"But I'm going to have to hurry, Skye. I'm thirty-seven."

"Girl, please. Janet Jackson's fifty. You've got plenty of time."

"Yeah, but I ain't got Janet Jackson's money, so my fifty will a whole lot different from her fifty."

Skye grinned. "I've got faith in you."

Fortunately, Skye fed her before Abby left her house. She needed food to soak up all that wine sitting in her belly. It was after ten by the time Abby made it home, showered, and sat on the side of the bed.

The floor was freezing! Why was it so cold? She looked down and saw that her feet were bare. The furnace must've gone out. She huffed in frustration and saw her breath. Abby walked over to the wall where the thermostat should've been, but it wasn't there. Abby paused in confusion.

"What the hell happened to the—"

The sounds of crickets outside the window caught her attention, and she walked over to look out. It was pitch-black outside. No stars or moon. She realized all of a sudden that she'd misplaced something. She'd put it away for safekeeping and had forgotten where she'd put it.

"I need to find it," she said out loud, starting to search the room with an obsession that defied logic. She opened and closed drawers and doors, searching frantically for this thing she'd lost. And the funny thing was, she couldn't even remember what it was.

"It's important," she said earnestly. "So important."

Her heart pounded as panic began to set in. Lord! Where could she have put it? How could she have misplaced something so valuable, so precious? Her memory was fading. More and more, she was starting to forget things, simple things like faces and names.

"Time's running out," she whispered.

She knew that it was. Time was so short, and soon it would be gone and . . . and she needed to find it before it was too late. In frantic haste and without realizing why, she headed for a door, and suddenly, she was outside. Was it here? The darkness was suffocating and thick. She tried to catch her breath but couldn't. It was here. Out here. It had to be. But where? Oh, Jesus! Where?

Buried.

"What?"

The dirt under her feet started to soften, like mud, but warm.

Buried. Deep.

She looked down at her feet, but of course, she couldn't see them. It was too dark, and the ground was starting to swallow her.

Abby suddenly opened her eyes.

"Oh, God. Oh, God," she said over and over again, blinking and bracing herself, trying to get her bearings. It took several moments for her to grasp where she was. Abby choked back panic and fear and confusion. The sun was just starting to come up, and after a few moments, she realized that she was standing outside in her backyard.

Ever After

"I MUST SAY," OLIVIA Gatewood said admiringly as Robin entered the room and sat down, "your pictures do not do you justice, dear." She smiled and clasped her elegant hands together.

"I must say the same about you, Mrs. Gatewood." Robin smiled.

Jordan's mother was stunning. Her silver-streaked hair was cut short and flawlessly styled. She was draped in a multicolored silk chemise that brought out the golden glow of her beautiful complexion.

Robin had been summoned.

"Thank you for agreeing to visit," Mrs. Gatewood said as the server set a tray down between them with two delicate teacups and saucers and a small porcelain pot. "Do you take sugar and milk with your tea?"

"No, ma'am."

The invitation had come quite unexpectedly. The only thing that made sense was that Jordan had told his mother about her. In the past month, Jordan had been more attentive and committed to making this relationship work than he had been in all the months of their relationship previously, and no one was more surprised than Robin.

The server poured the tea and waited patiently as Olivia surveyed the presentation and then dismissed her with a polite "Thank you. That'll be all for now."

She picked up her saucer and cup, carefully brought the warm liquid to her lips, tasted it, and then sighed.

"I suppose that you were taken aback by my invitation?"

Robin smiled. "A bit, Mrs. Gatewood, but pleased by it."

She laughed. "Please. Call me Olivia," she insisted warmly.

Robin had grown up around women like this. She remembered being a small child and watching her grandmother entertain her friends over tea poured in porcelain cups with lumps of sugar dissolving in them.

"Yes, Olivia," she responded.

Olivia carefully placed her drink down on the table and casually leaned back, crossing one lean leg over the other. "I will get straight to the point, Robin," she said, squinting her lovely eyes slightly to express the seriousness of her intent. "When I found out that my son had been spending time with a woman consistently for more than a few weeks, my curiosity was piqued," she said playfully. Olivia laughed.

Robin laughed softly, too. "I certainly understand."

Robin took a sip of the tea. It had a lovely floral scent and flavor to it. "Jasmine?"

Olivia nodded. "My favorite. I've seen pictures of the two of you in the papers and on that tablet computer he bought me. The two of you make a lovely couple."

Robin marveled at this polite and engaging woman. A year ago, Olivia Gatewood had put two bullets in her son's back, and

Jordan had nearly died. The papers had said she'd had a psychotic episode. But Robin would never know it from sitting here with her now.

"Thank you, Olivia," she said, genuinely touched.

The woman's expression softened. "Ever since the death of his wife, he's been lost and lonely."

Robin nodded her acknowledgment.

"I've hoped that he would meet someone, maybe fall in love and give me some grandbabies." She smiled.

Robin, surprisingly, blushed.

"Like any mother, I want more than anything to see my children happy."

"Of course," Robin agreed.

"Is he happy with you?"

Robin was caught off guard by the question and the abrupt but subtle change in the woman's demeanor.

"I believe he is. Yes."

Happy wasn't quite the right word to use for Jordan's current state of being with Robin. He was resigned to this relationship. But that was none of Olivia's business.

Olivia's stern gaze pressed hard on Robin. "How come I'm not convinced?"

Robin's expression must have spoken volumes.

"Yes, dear. Let's stop being polite," Olivia said casually. "I know my son even better than he knows himself, though he never sees fit to give me the credit I deserve."

Robin's own defenses were suddenly on high alert. "So, you asked me here because you screen all your son's love interests?"

Olivia laughed. "If I believed he loved you, you likely wouldn't be here."

Robin quickly weighed her options. She could sit here and go at it with a senior citizen, or she could leave. She picked up her purse to go.

"Not yet," Olivia said sternly. "I'm not finished."

"Maybe I am," Robin retorted angrily.

"And I thought you were different," she said curtly. "The problem with Claire—lovely, sweet Claire—was that she had no backbone to speak of. She was a jellyfish, one that my son trampled on regularly, and yet she stayed, she loved, she sacrificed for him until she was empty. I was just about to give you some credit for having a spine, beautiful Robin."

It was true. Olivia Gatewood was insane.

"Of course I can see the disdain he feels for you behind his eyes, even when he's smiling. You don't see it because you choose not to," she said smugly. "Perhaps you believe that he can grow to love you over time, that he will forget how you trapped him into this relationship."

"What makes you think that I had to trap him?" she said defensively.

Olivia looked as if Robin had just insulted her. "I know the look all too well, Robin," she said, sounding surprisingly solemn. "It was the same look in his father's eyes when he thought I wasn't paying attention."

Robin felt as if this woman had kicked her in the stomach.

"I'm not so old, girl. And despite what everyone wants to believe, I am not so crazy. Jordan emulates his father in ways he doesn't even realize. He's idolized him without meaning to. He worships him, and sometimes, I swear, they share a soul."

"Why did you ask me to come here?" Robin asked, clenching her teeth.

Olivia casually picked up her teacup again and took another patient sip. "If you're going to play this game, you'll need to be diligent. Allow him his frivolities and toys. Courage is key, Robin. Remind him to respect your position in his life," she warned. "But know that the more you tighten the leash, the harder he'll buck against you."

"You're talking about affairs? You're telling me to let him have affairs?"

"I'm telling you that he will have them. I'm telling you that if he doesn't love you now, he never will."

"Excuse me for asking, Olivia," she challenged, "but wasn't your husband killed in the house of his mistress?"

If Olivia Gatewood wanted to play dirty, then Robin would get down in the mud with her.

Surprisingly, Olivia's demeanor softened. "You believe that I'm the last person you should be listening to about relationships."

"I do."

Olivia sighed. "Hindsight is the best teacher, Robin. And I have more lessons behind me than I do ahead of me. You are certainly a lovely woman who apparently is determined to be with my Jordan. And I certainly hope that it pans out, for his sake."

Robin stared at her like she actually was crazy. "What exactly are you saying, Olivia?"

"Contrary to what he believes, I don't want to see him dead. And trust me, neither do you."

Robin needed to get the hell away from this woman.

"I don't know what you have on him, but whatever it is, I would suggest that you make sure that all your demons are hidden well."

"I have no demons," Robin said bitingly.

Olivia smiled. "No, dear. Of course you don't."

Ordinary Pain

"ONCE AGAIN, YOU HAVE OUTDONE YOURSELF."

Jordan and Robin had just finished having dinner at Lamont's, one of the best, if not the best, seafood restaurants in Texas. He led the way out onto the enclosed patio afterward, where they were immediately met by one of the servers.

"Two cognacs," Jordan ordered. "Please."

Robin purred like a cat, then sat down luxuriously on the tufted velvet sofa, crossed her legs, and twirled a strand of her hair around her finger.

"It's been a lovely evening, Jordan," she continued. "You've been your usual attentive, engaging, and generous self."

Jordan took his drink from the server and took a sip as he stared out the window. "Thank you," he said to Robin.

"So, after this, you'll take me back to my place, walk me to the door, and kiss me good night, I suppose."

Jordan didn't bother to respond. She knew the drill.

"Don't you ever want to make love to me, Jordan?"

It wasn't as if he hadn't been expecting this topic to come up in conversation. Still, he wasn't interested in discussing it. Jordan took another sip of his drink and turned slowly. Robin was a vision of beauty slinked across that sofa.

"You've got a noose around my neck, sweetheart," he said with a slight smile. "It's not so easy to get it up under that kind of pressure."

"For another man," she said seductively, "I'd have to agree." Robin stood up, made her way over to him, and pressed against him until he leaned back against the window. "But for you"—she ran her finger across his lower lip—"let's just say, I think it'd take a lot more than a noose to keep you down."

Jordan couldn't help but to stare at her in disbelief. "I am giving you the performance of a lifetime, Robin. You wanted the world to see you on the arm of your knight in shining armor, and I am showing you off like the queen you are. Surely, you understand that patience is needed here. Baby steps. You don't rush something that you want to last forever."

Robin took a hesitant step back, then turned and went back to the sofa, sat down, and sipped on her cognac. She had him where she thought she wanted him, but maybe she was starting to see that Jordan wasn't exactly the prize she thought he was. And she certainly wasn't the prize he'd hoped for.

"Do you still think about her?" she begrudgingly asked.

"Yes."

She looked at him. "The least you can do is lie about it."

"There's no place for lies between you and me, Robin," he said dismissively. "We're building this relationship on trust," he said sarcastically.

"That being said, I would love to know what it was that you saw in her?"

Robin's jealously shadowed her lovely face.

Jordan thought and chose his words carefully before finally responding. Abby soothed that beast in him that Robin had awakened and that he'd hoped he'd long since buried. Jordan could let his guard down with her because she bore him no ill will. She had no agenda other than to love him, and she wasn't the enemy. She was like Claire in that regards, only instead of taking those qualities for granted the way he'd done with his wife, Jordan had a second chance to embrace and relish them.

He glanced at Robin and realized that she was studying him. "She had nice jugs." He shrugged.

Robin didn't seem to find his answer funny. But no matter. What Jordan saw in Abby was none of Robin's damn business. Neither was the fact that he missed the hell out of Abby. Jordan had made a deal with this devil, that he'd stay away from the woman he loved for the rest of his life, but with each passing day, he knew that it was fast becoming an impossible promise to keep.

"I met your mother earlier today," she said, clearing her throat and effectively changing the subject.

"So I was told."

She looked surprised that he knew.

"Does she screen all your women?" she asked sarcastically.

"She does the best she can."

"Still a momma's boy even after she tried to kill you?"

"Sure. Why not?"

"What if I were to tell you that I don't think your mother is crazy? What if I were to say that I think she knew exactly what she was doing when she shot you?"

"I'd say that you are a very astute woman and as brilliant as you are beautiful."

"And yet, she'll never see a day inside a courtroom for attempted murder. You Gatewoods are experts at skirting the law. Aren't you?"

"You don't know the half of it," he said casually.

"But I know enough." She tilted her chin slightly. "Don't I?" Jordan stared at her.

"I want marriage, Jordan. I want a ring and an engagement. I want a big wedding with all our family and friends in attendance." Robin paused and waited for him to . . . what? To protest? To draw a line in the sand? "I want to honeymoon in Bali, and I want children."

"I want those things, too. Just not with you," he said.

The three drinks he'd had tonight were finally starting to catch up with him, thankfully. That icy stare of hers would've chilled another man to the bone. Jordan had cognac to warm his.

His insult registered a bull's-eye with his date.

"You need to tread lightly, Jordan," she warned.

Robin was pissed. Robin's feelings were hurt, but he didn't give a damn. Jordan was sick of playing this role for her. Robin had crawled into the hornet's nest, and if she insisted on pushing this agenda, then she'd have to contend with the stings.

"You came for me," he responded maliciously. "Maybe you need to truly understand what that means."

"Are you calling my bluff? Do you think that I won't follow through on my threat to expose you?"

He studied her. "I'm wondering how far that threat of yours will get before it blows up in your face, Robin."

She had her theories, her speculations of Jordan's involvement in Lonnie's death. Jordan had a team of the best attorneys at his disposal, acquaintances in all the right places, including the media and the Dallas Police Department, who could turn her little story into a fairytale with one phone call.

She stood up and walked over to him. "Is marrying me so distasteful that you'd take the chance and risk everything just to be with your little country mouse? Do you really think she'd take you back now?"

"I'd take the chance just to be away from you."

Robin turned, walked back over to the table, picked up her glass, and took another sip of the caramel-colored liquid. Slowly, she turned to him. "We should start having children right away," she continued with tears glistening in the rims of her eyes. "I don't want a big wedding," she said with resolve. "Something small. Intimate."

"What part of it's not going to happen don't you understand?"

She rushed over to him and stopped. Her hand came out of nowhere and landed hard against the side of his face. "You selfish sonofabitch!"

Jordan glared at her. "I'm the sonofabitch that you wanted."

"Was she supposed to have been your savior, Jordan? That sweet little thing, innocent and naïve about the kind of man you really are?" She leaned in close enough for him to feel the warmth of her breath against his face. "Did she even know the kind of evil that you're truly capable of?" Robin leaned back and laughed. She stared quizzically at him, as if seeing him for the first time. "I think I get it," she said introspectively. "You showed her the Jordan that you wanted to be. Mr. Clean Slate and Second Chance. You nearly died but didn't, and now life has taken on new meaning, and you finally get the chance to reinvent yourself, to redeem yourself. Abby Rhodes was a means to an end. A prop. You were brand new with her. Is that it?"

She stepped back, walked back over to the table, and picked up her glass. "Cheers, Jordan," she said, raising it in a toast. "Cheers to having the audacity to believe that you are the good guy, the man of her pathetic, little dreams. Cheers for believing that you *almost* had everything you dreamed of."

She'd done it again. Robin had managed to find that nerve he believed he'd thoroughly tucked away and never have to tap into again. Jordan had demons, plenty of them. And, yes, there were things about him that Abby could never know.

"But I'm who you deserve," she admitted bitterly. "You and I are two peas in a pod," Robin continued. "The sooner you realize that, the sooner you'll open up and allow yourself to accept it."

Jordan's phone rang. It was Phyl, and he put her on speaker, for Robin's benefit, of course.

"Yes?" he answered, pulling it from the inside pocket on his sport coat.

"Hey, Mr. G." Phyl sighed. "Sorry to be calling so late, but I finally managed to finish that report you asked for. I just wanted you to know it's your in-box."

"Thank you, Phyl. Get some rest."

"Yep. G'night."

He hung up.

Two peas in a pod. That they were. Only Robin had a way of resting on her laurels that Jordan never could manage to do. One-upmanship. He'd always been too competitive for his own good, and he'd always been too stubborn to lie down in defeat, even when it was clearly obvious that he had lost. But he was a fighter. Fighting was what he did and would always do until he took his last breath.

Water

"FOR THE LAST TWO NIGHTS, I've been staying at the hotel," Abby explained, sitting on Marlowe's couch in her living room. "I don't sleepwalk, Marlowe," she said earnestly. "I never have in my life, but I woke up outside in the backyard in my panties and T-shirt, and I had no idea how I'd gotten there."

"Do you remember dreaming?"

Abby shrugged. "I remember bits and pieces of a dream, I suppose," she said, feeling frustrated. "You know how dreams are. When you first wake up, you remember just about all of it, but over time, it fades. I remember a feeling, though."

"What?"

"Rushed? Like I had to hurry up and do something. But I can't remember what it was."

Marlowe stared at her for a long time.

"How many times do I have to tell you not to do that? You creep me out when you do that."

"I know," she said indifferently. "Where's Jordan?"

Abby was caught off guard by the question. She hadn't mentioned him to Marlowe at all. "In Dallas."

"What's wrong, Abby?"

"I just told you what's wrong," she said, agitated. "I walked in
my sleep, Marlowe. That's what's wrong, and I need to know if it
had something to do with the ghosts in that house."

"I'm sure it did. But what else is wrong?"

"Nothing," Abby said, shaking her head.

Marlowe turned her head slightly to one side and squinted,
convicting Abby with a look. She might as well have put a gun to
Abby's head.

"We broke up," she reluctantly admitted. "H-he was seeing
someone else."

Marlowe would not stop staring at Abby.

"Maybe coming here was a bad idea," Abby eventually said.

"It was the woman," Marlowe said. "She's the one who had you
up walking in your sleep."

"Why?"

"I told you when you first bought the house, Abby, that something's not finished there. My guess is she wants you to hurry and
finish it."

"How? What? I don't even know what *it* is, Marlowe."

"Me either. But it's selfish of you to leave that house."

Abby was stunned to hear her say that. "She scared the hell
out of me. How do you expect me to stay there with her taking
over my body like that?"

"I don't think she plans on hurting you."

"Oh, you don't *think*," Abby shot back angrily. "I don't think
you know for sure what she plans on doing to me."

"It could have something to do with Jordan being gone."

"I can't help it that he's gone," Abby said, fighting back tears. "But he's not coming back. So, I don't know . . . those ghosts are just going to have to do whatever ghosts do under the circumstances."

Marlowe had the nerve to look disappointed.

"So, since you're basically saying that there's nothing that can be done?" Abby asked. "I need to sell the house, Marlowe."

"Sell it?" Marlowe asked, stunned. "I thought you loved it."

"I'm over it. I need to move on. I'm looking at other properties. Non-haunted properties that are much better investments than that house. They can't follow me. Right? I mean, these ghosts are tethered to this house. Isn't that true?"

"So, you're just going to leave them hanging?"

They were ghosts for crying out loud and certainly weren't her responsibility. "They were *hanging* before I moved in."

"So, you're just going to let them scare the shit out of somebody else?"

"What do you expect me to do?"

"Same thing they expect you to do. Finish this."

"I'm scared to death. Can't you and Shou Shou go in there and do some kind of exorcism or something?"

"We don't do things like that," she said, looking and sounding absolutely insulted.

"Well, I'm sorry," Abby said defensively. "I didn't know."

"You need to get Jordan back to the house," Marlowe blurted out.

"Would you stop saying his name?"

"This isn't over."

"It is for me. I'm selling this house, and I'm moving on." Abby stood up to leave.

"You're putting too much faith into a broken heart, Abby," Marlowe said as Abby started to open the door to leave.

Abby stopped. "No, Marlowe. I put too much faith in him."

Twenty minutes later, Abby pulled her car into the driveway at the house and made it all the way to the front door before she realized that she'd meant to drive back to the hotel. She hadn't meant to come here. But still, she put her key into the lock, opened the door, and stepped inside. A rush of warm air enveloped her like a hug, and sorrow filled her chest. She was so lonely, so empty inside without him. Tears flooded her eyes and began to stream down her cheeks. She hadn't cried in over a week. Abby had worked so hard to ignore the ache he'd left behind, but all of a sudden, she couldn't ignore it anymore.

She walked over to the sofa and stretched out facedown on it and sobbed into one of the throw pillows like a child. He had awakened something dormant and buried so deep inside her that she didn't even know it was there. Abby had dared to open herself up to him, dared herself to step outside the box she'd lived in her whole life, and loved him. Now she had to get back to who she had been before she'd met him, only Abby didn't seem to remember the way. She'd been happy before Jordan had come into her life, but she couldn't seem to find that place again despite the fact that she knew what it looked and felt like.

I cried.

She looked up from the pillow, peering into every space of that room. "Ida?" she asked cautiously.

Abby sat up and wiped away her tears. Daylight filtered through the house, so it wasn't as scary as it was at night. Abby sat there for a moment, still weighed down in sorrow, but then she started to wonder if it was just her sorrow she felt, or Ida's, too.

Marlowe expected for Abby to reconcile whatever it was that was keeping these ghosts stuck here. Some things made sense. Julian Gatewood and Ida Green loved each other, passionately. Marlowe kept telling Abby that something wasn't finished, but Abby had no idea what that something could be or how to finish it. Even if she did, though, so what? Two ghosts go skipping off into the afterlife together, happily ever after. And she'd still be stuck here trying to mend a wound that might never heal.

She'd had no idea that she was so fragile. Abby had always been tough and resilient. Nothing ever got and kept her down for long, but this, this was new, and she was left raw from it.

Find it.

"Find what, Ida?" Abby began to sob again. "I don't know what you want." Abby bolted to her feet. "I don't know what the fuck you want."

She needed to get out of this place and out of her own head and out of her own misery. Abby spun around to face the door and nearly jumped out of her skin at the sight of the image standing between her and that door. It was Jordan.

"I want you," he said, stepping closer to her. "I have never stopped wanting you, Abby."

Jordan wrapped his arm around her waist and pulled her against his chest. Was she dreaming again? Abby inhaled Jordan's scent and closed her eyes, and he lowered his lips to hers and swept his delicious tongue through her mouth.

Wake up, Abby! You need to wake up.

Jordan lifted her off the ground and sat her on his lap as he sat on the couch. "I tried to stay away," he said, breathless between kisses.

Yes. He should've stayed away, but Abby held him tightly. She kissed him passionately.

"I couldn't," he whispered.

She cried because he felt good in her arms. She cried because she'd missed him so very much, and because she needed him more than . . . more than . . .

Die Without You

"I'M SICK OF THIS SHIT," Jordan grunted, angrily mashing the gas pedal, taking his silver Maserati to ridiculous speeds.

He slammed on the brakes and turned the wheel until the car came to an abrupt stop in the middle of the road, facing the car behind him.

Jordan climbed out of his car and started marching toward the other driver while that car was still rolling. By the time the driver managed to stop, Jordan was next to the window on the driver's side. Another car, a black sedan, pulled up behind the two of them and stopped. Jordan angrily pulled the door open.

"Whoa! Whoa! Whoa!" the driver exclaimed, raising his hands in surrender. "What the fuck's wrong with you, man?"

"You're what the fuck's wrong with me, motha fucka!"

The other man apprehensively stepped out of his car. "What?" he asked nervously. "Did I cut you off or something? Was I following too close? What?"

Jordan loomed over the dude who couldn't have been more than five eight, a buck fifty on a good day. "Yes," he said emphati-

cally. "*You were too damn close, and you have been for too damn long.*"

This was Robin's little bluebird that had been perched on her shoulder, watching Jordan's every move for the last month, at least.

"*I'm sorry. There's no reason to get all bent outta shape over my bad driving. I probably wasn't paying attention.*"

"*But I was. You turn your ass back around. You stay the fuck away from me, and you find another way to earn your money.*"

"*I was just—*"

"*I am well aware of what you were just—*" *He pushed the dude back against the car.* "*You tell her that I'm none of your gotdamn business anymore,*" *he warned.*

In the sedan stopped behind the two of them, a man climbed out of the passenger side and came over to the two of them. "*I'll drive,*" *he said to the man who had been following Jordan. He grinned.* "*You can ride shotgun.*"

Nothing else needed to be said. The threat was implied by Jordan, and it was thick and undeniable. The man following him made his way around to the passenger side of the car, while Jordan started back toward his.

Jordan had been away from her for far too long. And the notion that he could ever possibly stay away from Abby was absolutely ridiculous. Jordan lost himself inside this woman, and as he blanketed her with himself, stroked slowly in and out of her, inhaled and savored the flavor of her, he understood that this connection to Abby was spiritual, ethereal, and eternal. She was always his.

"I need for you to tell me what's happened, Jordan," Abby said softly, her head resting on his chest. "You have to tell me the truth."

The truth? The truth was a tangle of barbed wire that would only push her farther away from him, and that's the last thing he wanted.

"I'm working through some things, Abby."

Abby raised up and looked into his eyes. "That's not good enough. What things?"

Of course she deserved answers, but Abby had no idea of the depth of her question. This was about more than Jordan and this other woman. His answer would reveal the darkest parts of himself, those parts he'd hoped had been buried, that he'd somehow been redeemed from, but two women were dead because of him. There would never be redemption from that, and he was selfish and a fool to ever think that there could be.

"Jordan, please. What are we doing here? Where is this relationship going? I can't . . . I won't be your Ida Green. I won't sit here in this house waiting on you to show up when it suits you. I'm not going to make myself convenient like that for you."

"I wouldn't expect you to."

"Then what is going on with you and Robin Sinclair? Are you still seeing her? Did you ever stop?"

"I'm in love with you, Abby. Not her."

"I'm old enough to know that sometimes love isn't enough, Jordan," she said sadly.

Jordan raised his hand and swept hair back from the side of her face. Abby rolled over to the side of the bed and pulled the blanket up to cover her chest.

"I don't want Robin, Abby. I made that clear to her and to you," he reluctantly began to explain.

"Then why are you with her?"

"Because of what she thinks she knows about me. And because she's willing to use this theory of hers to ruin absolutely everything I've worked practically my whole life to achieve."

Abby turned to face him. "I'm listening."

Jordan took a deep breath and internally weighed just how much of his past he could share with her. "My wife killed herself because I was having an affair, one of many."

It was subtle, but Abby's expression started to change as she stared into his eyes.

"One particular woman, the last one, was Lonnie Adebayo. She was an established photojournalist who had covered stories all around the world."

There were so many details, so many extraneous circumstances to this story that Jordan absolutely did not want her to know about. His relationship with Lonnie had been passionate and tumultuous, dark and dangerous. Jordan had sunk to his deepest, most demented levels of his personality to the point that he'd even scared himself. He absolutely would not share those details with Abby.

"Claire wanted me to end the relationship."

"Did you?" she asked wearily.

"It ended for a time, but not completely."

"Claire found out?"

He nodded. "Lonnie Adebayo was murdered." He swallowed the bile building in his throat from the memory of that night. "I was at a hotel with her. Claire found out, showed up, and . . . she shot her."

Abby rolled over onto her back and stared up at the ceiling.

"I pulled some strings and made sure that Claire and I were never implicated."

Abby looked at him as if she were seeing him for the first time.

And Jordan immediately knew in this moment that he'd said more than he should've.

"A man named Frank Ross stood trial for Lonnie's murder."

"Why would they think he did it?"

"He knew Lonnie. The two of them were working on a scheme to—"

"To what, Jordan?"

"Frank Ross is my half brother. At the time, no one knew that I wasn't a Gatewood by blood. At the time, it seemed important to keep that fact a secret."

"Did you make the police believe that Frank had killed Lonnie?"

"The police put together their own case against Frank, but"—he paused—"I never came forward with the truth, Abby."

Listening to himself tell her these things, Jordan felt as if he were reading from some cheap pulp fiction novel. It all seemed too fucking surreal and far-fetched to have actually happened, but it was real, and it was his life. And he was an asshole.

"Immediately after Lonnie was killed, I sent Claire to Europe. That's not what she needed. She needed me. But because of me, two women are dead."

"Robin found all this out?" she asked softly.

"Robin thinks that I killed Lonnie. And I guess I did," he admitted. "Not directly, but shit, Abby. I might as well have pulled that trigger. She's threatened to take this theory of hers to the police, to the press, to anybody who'll listen."

"But Claire is the one who shot Lonnie."

"And I destroyed Claire. I owe her, Abby. I owe her the legacy of her name, of her gentle nature. If it came to it, and I had to own up to Lonnie's murder to save Claire's reputation, then I'd have to do that. Because ultimately, I am to blame."

Abby was quiet for the next half hour. She'd even turned her back to him as he dressed to leave. Jordan had come here on impulse. His need for her had outweighed reason, and maybe in the back of his mind, he believed that by seeing Abby again, by touching her and loving her, that somehow this would all magically resolve itself. Nothing could change the past, and nothing would ever relieve Jordan of the burden of Claire's and Lonnie's deaths.

If things went Robin's way, his penance was set. Robin would get her big, fancy wedding, her life as a Gatewood. And Jordan would always love a woman he could never have. Sitting on the side of the bed, thinking about it, it seemed to be a fair and equitable resolution. But one that he'd regret for the rest of his life.

"The idea of not having you in my life doesn't bode well for me, Abby," he said, dismally. "What we have comes along once in a lifetime, if you're lucky. And maybe I haven't earned the right to have you, to spend my life with you, but dammit, if I still don't want it."

Abby slowly rolled over on her back and pushed up in bed, leaning back against the headboard.

"But you don't want to lose everything you've worked for either," she softly reminded him. "If the police think that you killed that woman, then you could go to prison."

Jordan rocked his head slowly in a nod. Losing a contract was one thing. Life in prison was something else entirely. "I've got more skeletons in my closet than I can count," he said, hanging his head. "It was only a matter of time before somebody came along and yanked on one of them."

"We've all got skeletons. What happened back then, it just—"

We've all got skeletons. Jordan latched on to that statement like a fish on a hook. He turned and looked at her. "We all do have skeletons," he said in a revelation.

Jordan had been playing this thing all wrong. He'd been waiting for Robin to make a mistake, to mess up, giving him an out from this arrangement. He'd been looking through her past, trying to find one mistake that he could use as leverage. Jordan had come up empty, time and time again, but what if he hadn't been looking far enough or deep enough?

Before leaving, he kissed her softly on the shoulder, and whispered, "I love you. Never question that. Never doubt it."

Jordan had to leave, but he'd come back. Would she be here when he did?

Soul on Ice

ABBY LAY IN BED LONG after Jordan had left. How in the world had she ever gotten herself tangled up with a man like him? These last few months, Abby didn't even recognize herself, giving into whims and fancy that normally she'd have shirked off as being ridiculous and left them right where they were, without giving them another thought. Haunted houses and seductive strangers had made her lose sight of the very practical nature that she'd always been so proud of, that she'd always nurtured and clung to as if her life depended on it, because in reality, it had.

She climbed out of bed, walked over to the bedroom window, and stood looking out at the massive tree in her backyard. Being in this house had robbed her of her spirit. Being with Jordan had cost her her pragmatic stronghold over her life. Abby had prided herself on being able to read people, on her ability to tell within a five-minute conversation if that person was someone she should get to know or avoid. She'd missed the signs with Jordan. Probably because she was more caught up in how he looked and the things he'd said. Abby let her loneliness get the best of her, and when someone like him, tall, handsome, and charismatic, paid attention to her, she lost her damn mind and ultimately, her heart.

The question now was, how could she find her way back to herself? It was over between them. Abby had dodged a bullet, because Jordan Gatewood was not the man she'd thought he was. Maybe he wanted to be. She didn't doubt that he was trying to turn over a new leaf. A near-death experience had certainly impacted him, and people deserved second chances. But he was drowning in guilt and responsibility for situations so devastating that Abby couldn't even wrap her mind around them. Women loved Jordan, literally to death. She didn't want to be one of those women.

Abby's ringing phone snapped her out of the fog she was lost in. She found the phone in the living room on the kitchen counter.

"Hello?" she asked, not recognizing the number.

"Marlowe gave me your number." It was Ms. Shou.

Abby was of course shocked. "Hey, Ms. Shou. What can I do for you?"

A long pause and then a deep sigh came through the phone. "You need to finish what you started," she said definitively.

Abby rolled her eyes in frustration.

"Roll 'em again," Shou snapped. "I dare you."

"I'm not doing this," Abby angrily retorted, not fully understanding what she meant by "this," but she was not listening to some old woman about finishing anything.

"Then who gon' do it?"

"What are you talking about?"

"You know what I'm talkin' 'bout. I'm talkin' 'bout all of it. Walkin' round thinkin' you better. Actin' like you so high and mighty and perfect."

Anger swelled in Abby's chest. "What the hell are you talking about, Shou Shou?"

"That's *Ms.* Shou Shou to you, girl! You watch yo' respect."

Abby was so mad that she'd actually cussed at that old woman.

"Dark follows him. Always has, Abigail. Always will. But he ran from it to chase the light."

What was she talking about? Who?

"That man of yours, girl! That's who I'm talkin' 'bout."

"Auntie." Abby heard Marlowe's voice in the background. "You're scaring her."

"Good," she shot back. "Her little ass need to be scared. She chose you, Abigail. Picked you out of everybody to help lead him back to his light. And you will not abandon her," she said, her voice cracking. "Because she's tired, and he's losing his way."

A chill rushed over Abby's naked body. "You mean Ida Green and Julian?"

"They connected."

Oh, this was crazy. Abby's whole world had crumbled around her, and this old lady was fixated on ghosts that had nothing to do with Abby.

"I know that you don't understand, Abigail," Ms. Shou said, softening her tone. "Not yet you don't. But you will."

Without realizing it, Abby slowly began to sink until she knelt on the floor. "I need to go. You don't know . . ."

"I know some things, sweet girl. I can't tell you how, because I don't understand it. But your pain pierced my heart, Abigail. Your sorrow brings tears to my eyes. He is not who you think he is. Sometimes, he worse. Sometimes, he better. But he is true."

Jordan. She was talking about Jordan. Or Julian? Abby was so confused.

"You don't understand," Shou said sympathetically.

Abby shook her head. "No," she whispered softly.

"But you will. Finish this, Abigail."

Abby trembled. "I'm afraid, Ms. Shou."

"With good reason. Be of good courage, Abby. He requires it. Be brave. You'll need to be."

Abby was numb, inside and out.

"Abby?" Marlowe said over the phone.

Abby swallowed. "Hey, Marlowe."

"Between the devil and the deep blue sea," she murmured. "I've been there, honey. Sometimes, I'm still there. But trust your heart this time and not your head."

They had no idea what they were asking her to do. Abby's good sense told her to get the hell up, get dressed, run out of that house, and never look back. And never, ever speak to Jordan Gatewood again. If she wanted to save herself, that's what she had to do.

Abby sighed. "I'm cold, Marlowe. I'm sitting naked on my living room floor, and I need to get some clothes on."

Marlowe laughed. "I'm not going to ask you why you're sitting naked on your living room floor, but you go and get dressed, Abby."

"What happens if I don't finish this?" Abby asked.

Marlowe was silent for several beats before responding. "Well, then, I guess you go on as you always have, Abby." She signed. "But do you really want to?"

Wasn't that what she wanted? That was all she wanted.

"And Ida and Julian?"

Marlowe was silent for a moment. "I get the feeling that she won't wait forever. Or that he'll lose his way. You and Jordan are beacons. If the two of you find your way, I think they were hoping that they'd find theirs."

Tears streamed down Abby's cheeks. Was she crying for her

and Jordan or Ida and Julian? Both? "I need to go and get some clothes on, Marlowe." She stood up. "I'll call you back."

"Soon, Abby. Okay?"

Abby hung up without saying good-bye.

None of this made any sense. It was like the whole world was going crazy all of a sudden, and there was nothing she could do to stop it. And somehow, she'd gotten swept up into all this and desperately wanted her life to get back to normal.

Whatever Ida Green and Julian Gatewood failed to reconcile before they died was their problem and not hers. Ms. Shou and Marlowe could believe what they wanted, but Abby chose to believe that she was still in charge of her own life, and nothing or no one was going to take that from her.

Ten minutes later, she sat in her car in the driveway, staring at her house. Living in this place had certainly proven to have been a wild ride for someone like Abby, who had always walked a very straight and narrow path of her own creation. Daring to believe in ghosts had always been the aspect of her personality that didn't quite fit the mold she'd created for herself. It had order. It lacked chaos. And it was safe.

Magic was real. And after moving here, she'd allowed herself the privilege of getting caught up in it. Maybe that's why she fell so easily and so hard for Jordan, because he was absolutely make-believe, a fantasy that couldn't possibly be real. Today, he'd revealed things about himself that she'd rather he had just kept secret. Now that she knew them, though, Abby would never be able to forget them, and she'd never be able to separate him from them. And for some reason, that mattered.

The Troubles

JORDAN AND HIS ASSISTANT, Phyl, and his small army of engineers were on his private jet, a $42 million Bombardier Global 8000, headed to Washington, D.C. This was to be the first meeting between his team and government officials for the rocket engine and fuel initiative scope of work for a more detailed discussion on Jordan's plan of action and the expectations of the feds.

"Are you all right, boss?" Phyl, sitting across from him, asked.

Jordan had been staring out the window for the last half hour. He looked at her. "Yes. Why?"

The striking, tall redhead peered back at him with her emerald-green eyes. "Have you had a chance to look over that report I sent to you a few weeks ago?"

"Yes. Yes, I did."

"Was it helpful?"

Jordan shrugged. He'd asked Phyl to pull Robin's background investigation report done for all new hires at Gatewood Industries. Jordan hadn't hired her directly, so he'd never seen it, but in reviewing it, there was nothing about her background that raised any red flags.

"Nothing pertinent."

It had been a week since he'd seen Abby, confessed to Abby. Jordan had resigned himself to the fact that the damage to their relationship was more than likely irreparable. The truth about Lonnie and Claire was more than he'd ever wanted her to know about his past. Jordan was not the man of Abby's dreams. He'd wanted to be, but he'd trespassed on too many lives to be that gleaming hero in her eyes.

"If you told me exactly what it is you're looking for," Phyl continued, "maybe I could target my search to something more specific."

Phyl's tone and expression offered the suggestion that she suspected something but didn't feel at liberty to fully state her suspicions. She'd only been working for him for a year, but in that time, Phyl had proven to be efficient and trustworthy with the day-to-day issues. But this was much more personal.

"I'm looking for leverage," he stated simply. "Things aren't as they seem between Ms. Sinclair and me," he admitted. "But it's difficult for me to move on."

Jordan would not go into detail with Phyl. And he could see from the look on her face that it wasn't necessary. He may very well have lost Abby in all of this, but that didn't mean that Jordan had to sell his whole soul.

Phyl nodded. "Got it," Phyl said confidently. "I'll see what I can find."

Jordan was an icon and Phyl had become his biggest fan. He'd have thought that she was silly if she'd ever told him that, but it was true. Phyl marveled at the reverence he got just by walking into a room. He was never much of a conversationalist, but the respect that he had for Phyl played out in unexpected ways, subtle but sincere.

The two of them had learned to communicate without even speaking. She knew when he was having a bad day, or when she needed to keep the sarcasm to a minimum. And she understood that even though he might not have laughed at her jokes, it didn't mean that he didn't find them funny. Phyl was great at reading people, and from the beginning, she had him pegged. He was no nonsense, mysterious, and private but also genuine. And he trusted her. Phyl had made it a point never to let him down. The two of them had chemistry, he'd told her once. Of course being Jordan, he never elaborated on what he'd meant by that, and being Phyl, she didn't ask him to. It was a compliment, and she took it for what it was worth.

Perfect people didn't exist and *perfect* Robin Sinclair had always given Phyl the willies. On the surface, the woman was flawless. Not only was she one of the most gorgeous to grace God's green earth, but she had lived an exemplary life for every one of her forty years. Robin had practically grown up a princess. She'd had nannies and housekeepers, attended the best private schools. Daddy was the CEO of a pharmaceutical company before he retired, ten years ago. Mommy was a socialite and philanthropist who donated and helped raise money for all the downtrodden in Robin's hometown of Seattle. Ms. Sinclair was valedictorian and prom queen at her high school, then went off to Stanford to become the lawyer extraordinaire that she was today.

Phyl couldn't put her finger on it, but there was something not quite kosher with this woman. It could've been the way that she stalked Jordan. If she couldn't get him to take her call or respond to her text, she'd hit up Phyl to find out where he was. She had it bad for him, which Phyl could understand. If Phyl wasn't a lesbian, she'd probably have it bad for him, too. As exceptional as Ms. Sinclair seemed on the surface, Phyl had seen that crack in her facade when Robin had invited Phyl for drinks so that she could get the 411 on why Jordan had been missing in action.

She was a natural problem solver. In fact, Phyl had been considering joining the police academy and studying biochemistry in college just so that she could eventually become a forensics specialist, but she decided against it when she realized that real-life CSI detectives wore uniforms and didn't dress as cute as the actors on the television show.

She'd freelanced as a personal assistant for a few years when she got a call from a headhunter looking for someone to fill a position working for a CEO at an oil and gas company in Dallas. Phyl lived in Denver at the time. She interviewed over the phone with Jordan's office assistant, Jennifer, and the next thing she knew, she was being flown to Dallas to speak with Mr. Gatewood himself. She walked away from that interview feeling like she'd made a complete and utter fool of herself. A few days later, she got the call that he wanted to hire her.

"Thanks for agreeing to meet with me," Phyl said to the woman sitting down across from her at the table in the coffee shop. "I know it was short notice, but I'm only going to be town for a few days."

The polished woman smiled politely. "When you mentioned Robin's name, I had to admit that I was curious."

Blaine Stevens had actually worked with Robin during her short stint as a criminal attorney in Jersey. She was teaching federal criminal rights law at Howard University and had been for the last seven years. A black woman with a very stylish and enviable pixie cut, large-framed fashionable glasses, full lips with the perfect shade of red lipstick, she was very attractive. Phyl's type? A little too conservative for Phyl, but cute.

"How do you know Robin?" Blaine asked casually.

"We work for the same corporation," Phyl broadly offered.

In reality, Phyl didn't work directly for Gatewood Industries. She worked independently for Jordan.

"Gatewood Industries in Texas," Phyl continued.

"She's a corporate attorney now?" Blaine asked.

"Yes."

"Interesting," Blaine said introspectively.

"Why is that?" Phyl probed.

Blaine was pensive in her demeanor. "She never showed any interest in the corporate world. That's all."

Phyl was going to have to tread carefully with this one. Blaine was here because she was curious, not necessarily because she wanted to give up any potentially damaging information about Robin Sinclair.

"What is it that you want to know about Robin that you can't ask her directly?"

Lawyers. They had a way of asking questions that left the door open for self-incrimination. Phyl had thought about becoming one until she realized how much reading and writing was involved. The thought of all those words gave her a headache.

"What can you tell me about the Langston Riley case?"

Blaine's expression changed. She tensed for a moment and then took a deep breath to try to calm whatever alarm inside her Phyl's question had set off.

"I haven't heard that name in years," she said pensively.

The trick to getting people to give you the information you

needed was to get them to trust you, or to make them think that you knew something about them that they didn't want anybody to know. It was an age-old tactic used in every investigative television show that Phyl had ever watched and studied. Shit. Who said that television wasn't educational?

"The two of you worked that case together. A criminal case," Phyl added. "It was the only one that either of you lost."

Blaine smiled ever so slightly. Phyl had hoped that the woman had been out of the courtroom for far so long that she'd forgotten how to play this game.

"That was almost ten years ago," Blaine said. "It was the biggest case either of us had ever worked on."

"Mr. Riley was your client," Phyl said earnestly.

The woman paused. "We both defended him," she reluctantly admitted.

"Two defense attorneys. That's impressive. Why two?"

Blaine's lips tightened. "What exactly do you want to know?"

Langston Riley was nobody special. He ran a small distribution company in Newark and was indicted and stood trial for trafficking heroin.

"First of all, why'd he need two attorneys? I mean, how could he afford that?"

The woman turned her head slightly to the side. "Tell me again what this is about?"

"It's about Robin," Phyl said quickly.

Blaine put down her cup of tea and slipped the strap of her purse over her shoulder. "Then you should talk to her about it directly."

"The two of you together couldn't get him off, even after it was later implied that it was his business partner, Clark Rollins, who may have had personal connections with known drug dealers."

That stopped her ass from leaving. Blaine slowly sat back down, staring awed at Phyl.

"Both of you graduated from Stanford Law. You'd never lost a case before him or after. The evidence against this man was circumstantial at best. How could he have possibly been found guilty?"

It wasn't as if Phyl had actually read trial transcripts. She'd pretty much just done some Internet searches and managed to find a few news articles on the trial. Basically, she was bullshitting most of what this woman thought that Phyl knew. It was all in the attitude. Phyl had mastered the art of looking and sounding like she knew exactly what the hell she was talking about when in fact, she might have only had 50 percent of the story. Almost immediately, she knew that she must've hit a major nerve, because prim-and-proper, tight-ass Blaine Stevens's eyes suddenly glazed over.

Blaine stared at her with a smirk on her lips. "You watch a lot of law shows on television?"

Phyl felt her face flush red. "Why would you say that?"

"You remind me of the DA on *Law & Order.* I watch a lot of law shows."

Phyl reluctantly shrugged. "Well, yeah."

The woman's expression turned serious. "Tell me what it is you think happened with that case?"

Phyl had no idea what to think. She was following a lead. Robin Sinclair had been a criminal lawyer since graduating law school and this was the only case she had ever lost. Phyl had found it curious that a defendant who barely got any coverage at all, needed two exceptional lawyers to defend him, and yet, they still lost the case.

After Phyl explained all of this to her, Blaine sat and stared back at her. "I never expected Karma to come back looking like you." Phyl braced herself.

"We were friends once," Blaine began to explain. "Fiercely competitive in school and during our internship, but, we enjoyed the sparring. We made each other better."

Phyl was practically holding her breath, hoping that this woman would tell her something about Robin that she hadn't been able to find out on her own.

"I couldn't live with myself after what happened," she reluctantly admitted. "I certainly couldn't bring myself to keep defending people."

"What happened, Blaine?" Phyl probed.

Sadness washed over the woman's face and then her features hardened. "I don't know what she's done. I don't care to know. But you keep my name out of this. I'll deny everything if you don't and it'll be your word against mine."

Phyl was raised Catholic. And confession was everything to a Catholic. Phyl wasn't a priest, but Blaine didn't seem to care.

"He died in prison," Blaine said sorrowfully. "That wasn't supposed to happen."

Answer Me

FIGHTING WAS WHAT HE DID. Being a fighter was what he was. A black man with balls big enough to jump into a white man's game, and they hated him. But he was a fighter. Dammit to hell to anybody who tried to tell him what he could or couldn't be, what he could or couldn't have.

How long had he been marching? That cold, slate-gray sky pressed down on him the same way it always did. The road under his feet, muddied and thick, tried to pull him under like quicksand, but he wasn't having it. He'd taken a wrong turn somewhere, which sometimes happened, but never enough to derail him for good. Nah. Up ahead. There it was. Home. Small and insignificant on the outside, but inside was his life. He kept coming back only to find it empty, but it didn't matter. Everything he needed was inside that place. His next breath was inside that tiny house, and he'd keep on coming back until he caught it.

All he could ever remember was reaching for the handle on the door, but he could never remember pushing it open. He just appeared, like magic, inside that house. Standing there in the room, something was different.

A hollow.

No voices.

No shadows.

Or whispers.

Ida! he called out. Her name, soundless.

He closed his eyes and listened. Waited. Nothing.

Opening his eyes, he was suddenly overcome with confusion.

Where was he? These walls looked strange to him. No life. No breath. No heartbeat. Not hers. He turned in a slow circle, searching for the way out. He had to leave this place, but he couldn't remember how. Trapped! Silent and violent panic began to erupt inside him.

He was lost. Disoriented. No, fear! A man like him was never afraid, but suddenly he was—he was angry for having wasted too much time. Wandering and searching for what he couldn't have. Searching . . . searching . . . searching! Memories dangling in his face, out of reach, scented with hints of what he desired the most. Looking good! Looking too damn good to turn away from. His palms itched to touch. To deny him was sinful! He knew what he wanted, and he had come so close!

Fuck!

His lips said the word, but the sound of it erupted only inside him, like an explosion. Where had his light gone? And who had hidden his path? He'd walked it. Walked it, yes, he did, following the trail of footsteps, leading him to his destiny like bread crumbs. And now it was gone? He was a prisoner in this tomb of gray walls and cold floors. And the one thing that he'd wanted most, that he'd needed most in his mind, body, and soul . . . was gone.

The thought began to crush him, pushed down on him like lead weights until he could barely stand. He'd fought and he'd lost? Had he lost? Her.

A Woman of Means

"THE RUMOR MILL IS CHURNING, my good friend," Robin's friend Liza Atkinson said lazily, wrapped in a towel and sitting across from Robin in the steam room at their favorite spa.

"Which rumor are you talking about, Liza?" Robin stretched her long legs out on the bench.

"The one circling about Mr. Gatewood's new estimated net worth now that the ink is dry on those government contracts."

Of course Robin had heard the rumors. She simply smiled.

"It's being estimated that his personal net worth is about to rise to more than $4 billion."

Robin pondered for a moment. "More like $4.7 billion," she said casually.

"Making him the wealthiest black man in the country," Liza concluded.

It was true. Literally overnight, Jordan's financial status had catapulted him to a new echelon of wealth. It was just a matter of time before it was officially announced to the rest of the world.

"Tell me that I'm going to be invited to a wedding soon," Liza teased.

Robin had been pondering the possibilities. "I'm thinking of a destination wedding. Europe, maybe?"

"Italy's always nice. Or Barcelona. I love Spain."

Jordan hadn't even given her a ring yet, but something like that was just a technicality. Robin had resigned herself to the fact that her relationship with this man, her life with this man, was not going to follow a path of normalcy. He was proud and stubborn and would put up resistance every step of the way, at least for a time. This wasn't how she'd dreamed it would be with the man she spent the rest of her life with, but things changed. People changed. She held on to hope that he would, too.

"Maybe Barcelona," Robin agreed.

"Then again, Greece is beautiful," Liza offered with a chuckle.

Liza didn't know the details of how Robin had reeled Jordan in, and she didn't need to, but she knew that Robin had played a powerful hand in persuading him to come back to her and to be the attentive lover she'd always wanted him to be. He still hadn't made love to her, though. Robin missed being intimate with him. Jordan was a beautiful lover, patient and accommodating, thorough.

"What is it?" Liza asked, reading the expression on Robin's face.

Robin hadn't wanted to openly discuss her thoughts on the matter, but keeping her concerns to herself was becoming more and more difficult.

"He still loves her," Robin admitted. "I'm not sure that he'll ever stop."

Liza shrugged. "He's not seeing her. Right?"

"No. He's not."

"Then it doesn't matter, Robin. He might love her for the rest of his life, but it doesn't mean shit if they're not together. I'm a firm believer that time takes care of everything. In time, she'll fade from his immediate memory, you'll push out a few adorable babies, and life will go on."

"She was no one special." Melancholy washed over her. "There was nothing exceptional about the woman."

And yet, he'd given her his whole heart. Of course it bothered Robin. It always would.

"To you, no, she is not special or exceptional, but who knows what men see in certain women? It's not going to do you any good to dwell on it. I mean, maybe she reminds him of someone. Maybe she told him a joke that made him laugh or she gave goddess-caliber blow jobs, Robin. It doesn't matter. You have him. She doesn't. What you need to focus on now is making him see that he's with the woman he's meant to be with. That you are the better choice for his life, his career, his image."

The spa visit had done wonders for Robin. She went home, slipped into her favorite silk pajamas, poured herself a glass of wine, sat on her sofa, and started flipping through the pages of half a dozen bridal magazines she'd bought on the way home. Robin stopped at a photograph of a bride and groom, newly married, standing on a white sand beach, facing the ocean, holding hands, and staring out at the water.

Liza had mentioned babies, and yes, Robin desperately wanted children. His children. It was time for the two of them to get busy building their new lives together. Jordan was resistant for now, but what choice did he truly have but to move forward with her? Abigail Rhodes was out of his life now. He was a big boy, and it was time for him to get over it. Robin picked up her phone and dialed his number. Jordan was on the East Coast in D.C., but she didn't want to wait for him to get back to Dallas to have this conversation.

"Yes?" he said abruptly when he answered.

Robin refused to let her feelings be hurt and decided to get straight to the point. "I want a ring, Jordan." Robin held his dirty little secret in the palm of her hand, and she was going to use it to her advantage every single chance she got for as long as she had to. "A beautiful diamond that very clearly expresses your level of commitment to me, your fiancée."

"Do you want me to pick up a loaf of bread and a gallon of milk, too, on my way home from the office, dear?" he asked sarcastically.

"I shouldn't have to threaten you to marry me, Jordan."

"No, you shouldn't, Robin."

Humiliation washed over her, but Robin was pushing a bigger agenda that required her to sacrifice her ego. "Fuck your disrespect, Jordan," she snapped. "I'm not the one stepping over the bodies of dead women. I will not have you ruin what I have always dreamed would be a happy day for me. You don't love me. I get it. But fake it, gotdammit!"

Robin took several deep breaths to calm herself while Jordan remained quiet on the other end. "Don't force me to do what I don't want to do," she said sadly. "Despite what you want to believe, I do care for you. I always have."

"You'll forgive me if I find that hard to believe considering the circumstances. You're playing an ugly game, Robin. And yes. I do resent you for it."

"But it's the nature of the beast, Jordan. Our beasts are more savage than most. Truthfully, I have loved you from the moment we met, and I won't apologize for that."

Jordan spoke after a long pause. "I wouldn't call this love."

She dried her eyes. "But in this case, I do. The most desperate kind. And if I have to call my bluff to prove it to you, I can. I have."

He hesitated before finally speaking. "What the hell does that mean?"

She sighed deeply. "Detective Bobby Randolph worked the Lonnie Adebayo murder case."

Again, Jordan was silent.

"He remembers speaking to you several times about Lonnie's murder." Robin swallowed.

Jordan hadn't been taking her seriously. And Robin desperately wanted to announce their engagement.

"We'll talk when I get home," he finally said.

"We will," she assured him.

Robin didn't want the next twenty years with him to be a wrestling match. The last thing she wanted to do was to ruin the man she loved, and she did absolutely love him. But would he ever love her in return? The better question was, could she live with knowing that he never would?

I'll Take You There

JORDAN HAD BEEN BACK in town from his trip to D.C. for two days when he called Robin and told her that he was on his way over to see her.

Detective Randolph. The only reason that man had backed off from suspecting that Jordan had murdered Lonnie was because Jordan had called in a favor with the police commissioner. Jordan had called her bluff, and she'd delivered. If either Robin or Bobby Randolph decided to take their suspicions to the media . . .

"I'll leave the door unlocked," she said seductively over the phone. "Let yourself in."

Soft music and lighting in her posh apartment had been staged to set the mood. Jordan immediately made his way over to the bar and filled two glasses with ice and bourbon. He took a deep breath, turned up his glass, and finished it in one gulp, then immediately filled it again, swirling the ice this time to give the liquid a chance to cool.

Robin appeared in the hallway, barefoot, wearing a simple,

sheer white and flowing sheath, with her hair parted down the middle, flowing long and luxuriously past her shoulders. She wore no makeup and looked like something out of a dream. Just not his. Anything he'd once found beautiful about her had soured in his stomach a long time ago.

"Can you tell that I've missed you?" she asked softly, standing an arm's length away from him.

Robin took a step closer, pressed her elegant hands against his chest as she leaned in, and kissed him softly.

Robin took her drink from his hand. "Believe it or not, I am happy to see you, Jordan," she said sincerely, gazing up at him with hypnotic hazel eyes.

Perplexed, he stared at her. "After all the things that I have said to you, hurtful and inconsiderate things, Robin, you are still determined to go through with this?"

She stared back. Jordan was taken aback by what looked like sympathy filling her eyes. Confusion filled him. Did she feel sorry for him?

Robin pressed a warm hand to his cheek. "It's not how I dreamed it would be. But it's something I'm coming to terms with."

"Because you love me?"

Sadness filled her eyes. "I need you," she whispered. "Love? Yes. I want to possess you. To keep you, even at the expense of losing myself." Robin laughed bitterly. "They say love makes you crazy. I guess it does."

It seemed strange to him that he should be the kind of man that women sacrificed so much of themselves for. Claire had sacrificed her happiness and any hopes of ever finding it outside of what she believed of their marriage. Jordan believed that Claire held on to that hope, searching for him, wishing and praying for it until she was finally emptied of every other emotion. She died void because of him. A sacrifice far too noble for a man like him.

Lonnie had sacrificed peace for Jordan and the chance to get even with him for hurting her the way he did. In his anger for what he felt was betrayal, Jordan tortured her, physically brutalized her, stripping her of her dignity, pride. God! He still ached deep in his core for what he'd done to her in a rage of madness and revenge. He had never hurt a woman like that before, and he would die before ever doing it again. But she died because of him, still at war with him. He owed Lonnie his soul.

Robin took a sip of her drink, took hold of Jordan's hand, and led him over to the sofa, where the two of them sat down close to each other.

"You'll spend the night?" she asked demurely.

He raised her hand to his lips, and kissed it.

Robin sank deeper into her seat next to him, pressed closer to him, and moaned. "This feels right, Jordan. I know you're angry with me for probing into matters that you'd rather keep private. I know that you don't want to have to keep reliving the past, and I promise you that I will not continue to remind you of those dark and painful memories," she said earnestly. Robin kissed him and stroked her fingers softly against his low-cut beard. "This doesn't have to be ugly. It can be like it was before. Don't you remember? We were so good together." She blinked away tears. "You still love someone else." She swallowed. "I'll respect that. But you could love me, too. I know you can."

Jordan stared perplexed at Robin. "You can accept that I'm in love with another woman?"

Robin took a deep breath and gave his question some thought before responding. "What choice do I have? But I'm convinced that in time your feelings for her will fade."

"And if they don't?"

He didn't mean for the question to be offensive. It was a genuine query.

"I'm here," she said pensively. "She's not."

"That's enough for you?" he asked sincerely. "Just to be here in my life and not my heart?"

Robin's eyes were filled with pain in reaction to his question.

"I don't mean to hurt you, Robin, I'm just—"

"But that's what you do, Jordan," she said abruptly. "You hurt me."

"And you let me. Why?"

She seemed to be surprised by what he'd just said. But it was a legitimate statement and question.

"Claire loved me even though I hurt her time and time again. I never understood why. I'd like to know."

Robin quickly gathered her thoughts. "It's because of who you are."

"An asshole? Selfish? Inconsiderate?" He shook his head and shrugged. "Who do you think I am?"

She stared at him with a glazed look in her eyes. "You're beautiful, Jordan. Handsome, strong, and . . . you're Jordan Gatewood," she said as if those two words together were indicative of some kind of wizard. "You're everything."

She had given him absolutely nothing. Robin hadn't said one gotdamn thing to him that explained this blind sense of so-called love she felt for him. It wasn't a man that she loved. It was an image, a persona—status. She didn't love him. She loved a concept, and it was time to end this.

"Langston Riley," he said and paused, looking back at her, gauging her for her reaction, which was instantaneous.

A stunned, helpless expression shadowed her pretty face, and recognition filled her eyes as the realization set in that Jordan was about to crush her. But in anger. Not in an act of revenge.

"I understand why you did it," he said carefully and empathetically.

Robin slowly backed away from him.

"You love your father. And he required a sacrifice. You gave him that," he explained evenly, unemotionally.

Robin shook her head slightly. "Wh-what are you talking about?" she asked, forcing back the fear in her voice.

The specifics were ugly. Jordan had spent the last two days combing through every sordid detail that Phyl had found on that case and on Robin's past. Daddy, Montgomery Sinclair, was a rich CEO of a pharmaceutical company named MonClair Pharmaceuticals. They had developed and sold heart medication that ended up costing him a fortune in lawsuits to the point of nearly bankrupting him.

"I'm talking about drug trafficking, Robin. I'm talking about how your father could afford his fancy houses, private boarding schools, his car collection."

Color washed from her beautiful, golden complexion. "You don't know what you're talking about," she said, her voice shaking. She was trembling as she stood up and moved away from him, taking a seat in the chair on the other side of the coffee table.

"Langston Riley was a distributor of your father's legitimate medication. That's all he was."

She wouldn't look at him. Robin gripped the arms of the chair so tight her knuckles turned white. "We did the best we could," she weakly protested. "We tried to save him. But the evidence . . ."

"Circumstantial at best," he murmured.

"They found crates of that shit in his warehouse," she snapped angrily, making eye contact again, defying him to argue the obvious.

"Who put it there?"

Unexpectedly, tears streamed down her cheeks. "How the hell should I know? There was an investigation. They had a search warrant, and they found five hundred kilos of heroin hidden in a secured room in the back of one of his warehouses, Jordan! There was nothing we could do. The evidence spoke for itself."

She was right. Detectives searched all Riley's warehouses and found heroin hidden in a secret and secured room in the back of one of them.

"Clark Rollins, Riley's business partner, swears to this day that your father paid him to put that shit in that warehouse."

Robin wiped the tears from her cheeks and laughed. "Clark Rollins was a fucking junkie," she retorted. "If he's all you've got, then I feel sorry for you, Jordan. There's not a cop in Jersey who'll take his word over my father's."

He nodded. "The same probably goes for Blaine Stevens, I'm assuming," he said casually. "They won't believe her either?"

Robin angry stare bored a hole in him. "She'd be incriminating herself." Robin paused, waiting for Jordan to offer another alternative. "So, is this how this is going to go? Tit for tat? I dig up something on you, and you, in turn, dig up something on me? Is this what you want? A wife for a sparring partner?"

"I don't want you for my wife," he said maliciously.

"You're a fucking bastard," she snarled angrily at him.

Robin glared at him with such hatred, Jordan could almost feel it. Before he realized what was happening, Robin was on top of him, pounding on him with her fists. Jordan grabbed her by her wrists and pushed her down onto the sofa next to him.

"This would be us, Robin," he blurted out bitingly. "You want a lifetime with me? Then this is what you'd get."

"Mother fucker!" She sobbed, struggling against his grasp.

"That's exactly what I am," he declared, relishing in that fact. "Your father, Montgomery Sinclair, has a bull's-eye on his back. And for now, no one knows his involvement."

"Let me go!" she demanded, still squirming, sliding off the sofa onto her knees on the floor in front of him. But Jordan wasn't finished.

"Langston Riley was not a drug trafficker, but he was no saint. He trafficked guns, Robin. He had ties to organized crime, who lost access to millions of dollars when he went out of business. Shipments went missing, and they waited for Riley's trial to end before going to him to find out where their shit was."

She stared wide eyed at him. "H-how do you know this? How the hell could you possibly know?"

Adrenaline rushed through his veins. "You've got skeletons, Robin. Some of them talk. For the right price, they did."

All color washed from her face.

"No one will believe it," she retorted. "Especially after I turn you in to the police, Jordan. Your fucking name will be smeared like mud by the media."

"One phone call," he said, holding up a finger. "One. And Montgomery Sinclair will become a person of interest, Robin," he threatened. "But not to the police."

She stared at him in disbelief. "It's been a decade. Nobody will give a shit about guns after ten years."

"Guns? No. Millions of dollars to be made from the sale of those guns, money that was lost because of those guns, yes. Somebody gives a shit. Trust me."

Greed made monsters of men.

"Only Langston knew where the guns were hidden," Langston's *ex-business partner Rollins had told him. "He thought that he'd get off. That he'd be found not guilty, so he never told where they were. He thought the fact that he was the only one who knew where they were would keep him safe. Alive. He was murdered in prison almost as soon as he got there. Took the secret of where he'd hidden them, with him."*

"Your father cost the wrong people too much money, Robin. One call from you and, yes, you can ruin my life. One call from me, and your father won't have one."

Robin didn't move. "My father has nothing to do with you and me, Jordan."

"This is who I am, Robin. I am the man that you want to spend a lifetime with. You play dirty. I play dirtier."

"I could still send you to prison," she said, lacking the same conviction she'd once had in the threat.

"And I could send your father to hell. You choose."

He left without waiting for her to answer. Montgomery Sinclair was sixty-three years old, living happily ever after since retiring early, ten years ago. Jordan had no idea if that old man had any knowledge of any guns. But to be sure that Robin didn't call his bluff, he made sure to tie up any lasting loose ends.

Lab assistant Lois Anderson needed the money. She needed a lot of money. A single mom raising three kids on her own, trying to stay one step ahead of an abusive ex-husband, yes. She needed the money. She tore open the package of the dry DNA sample from case number LA-5438654 and burned it in a glass jar and shoved the ashes down into the bottom of the trash can right before she left the office. Evidence got lost sometimes. This was just one of those times.

I'm Drowning

TWO BELLY DANCING CLASSES and a protein shake later, Abby was at the house packing up the last of her belongings.

Skye had called to say that one of her kids was sick, so she wouldn't be able to help pack.

"All this rain is probably what's got him sick, Skye," Abby said, wrapping some glass figurines in newspaper before stuffing them into boxes. "Poor baby. Give him a kiss for me and make sure he keeps hydrated."

"Hey, did you ever find out how that vase got broken?" Skye asked.

Abby had come into the house a few days ago, and glass was shattered all over the living room floor. Her guess was that one of the ghosts had done it, but because she really wasn't in the mood to explain this whole haunting thing to Skye from the beginning, she decided to play it off.

"No. I probably left it sitting too close to the edge of the table. That's all."

After hanging up with Skye, Abby walked over to the large

window in her office, which used to be the second bedroom in this house, and stared out at the yard on the side of the house. It had been raining nonstop in northeast Texas for over a week now. Streets and homes were flooding like crazy, the ground was turning into swamps, and everything was just a mess. Fortunately, this place had been spared any major damage from water. Abby had just gotten an offer on it and was eager to get it sold. It was a lot easier to sell a house that wasn't underwater than one that was.

She'd recently closed on the apartment complex in Clark City. For now, Abby would be living back at the hotel until she finally got one of the apartments livable enough for her to move into it. The place needed so much work, but when it was all said and done, it was going to be a great investment. All that work would keep her good and busy for at least six months to a year. Being busy was therapy for Abby.

She hadn't called Jordan, and he hadn't called her. Both of them were smart enough to realize that moving on was for the best. Abby worked hard not to judge him. He'd done some monstrous things in his life, but did those things make him a monster? She kept telling herself that what he was or wasn't had nothing to do with her. The only version of Jordan that she knew was the one she'd fallen in love with. Still, sometimes love wasn't enough. Sometimes you couldn't outrun your demons. Sometimes the only thing you could do was to move on. And that's what she was doing. As hard as it was most days to act like she wasn't hurting as much as she really was, Abby had no choice but to pack up and move on.

Abby turned around to go back to packing when she caught movement in her peripheral vision. She looked up into the hallway, and nothing was there. Intuition told her, though, that either Ida or Julian was probably trying to get her attention, which she didn't want to give them, so Abby decided to leave everything and come back to packing another day. She walked out of her office and turned right toward the living room when she suddenly stopped. She stepped into the living room and felt as if she'd stepped into the frozen tundra.

Buried! Buried deep.

The whisper came from behind her.

"No," she murmured to herself, more determined than ever to get out of that house. "Not today."

Abby started walking again, when suddenly, she heard what sounded like a gunshot, followed by a loud, shrieking scream. She covered her ears with her hands and was suddenly struck by a wave of nausea and vertigo. Abby stumbled over to the sofa and sat down before she fell. Shadowed figures materialized in front of her, vague and blurred. Abby watched in disbelief like she was watching a movie play out.

A woman, no. Two. Two women yelling at each other. Out of the corner of her eye, she saw another woman. A girl? Crying? Abby felt like she'd been pulled out of her own body. This wasn't real. She had to keep telling herself that this wasn't real. Her breath caught in her chest. A man, tall, with light skin and light hair. She squinted to try to see his face, but she couldn't see it. She couldn't make out any of their faces clearly. Without understanding why, Abby raised her arm and swiped her hand through the air to clear the shadows from view. But she couldn't touch them. She jumped at the abrupt and piercing sound filling the air. The man clutched his chest and dropped to his knees.

Hurry up.

That chilling whisper filled the room again and drew Abby's attention to it. She saw a woman in the hallway, vague and shadowed like the others. But she was separate from them.

Buried.

The place where her mouth should've been was a dark and hollow space. She raised her arm and motioned toward Abby's office. Abby struggled to get to her feet, glancing back as she moved through the living room to the place where she'd seen those people, but they were gone. She looked back for the woman in the hallway, and she was gone, too. Abby continued to her office and found that torn picture of Ida Green on the floor. She bent to pick it up and held it. Without thinking, she walked back over to the window, looked up, and saw that woman that she'd seen in the hallway, the one in the picture that she held in her hand, standing outside in the rain underneath the huge tree in the backyard.

Buried deep. Without recalling leaving the house, Abby suddenly found herself outside in the rain. Panic filled Abby's chest as she crouched in the mud underneath the tree, tearing up the soggy ground with her hands. The urgency was real, and it was hers. She had no idea what she was looking for or why. But the burning need to find this . . . whatever it was . . . was all consuming. Abby cried desperately as she dug, moving from one spot to another when she couldn't find what she was searching for.

"Oh, God!" she cried, her hands and clothes covered in mud. "It's here! I know it is!"

Abby was overcome with so much emotion, sadness and pain, desperation. She dug as if her very life depended on it. It was as if she were watching herself from a distance, consumed by the madness of finding what was buried deep here in this ground. Abby wanted to stop and to run to her truck and drive off. She wanted to get as far away from this house as possible and never look back, never come back.

"Hurry!" she heard herself say. "Before it's too late!" She was losing him. Abby stopped immediately at the thought. *Losing him,* she mouthed to herself. Losing . . . losing . . . her heart filled with grief and despair. She'd lost him once. She'd been fighting for him ever since. She'd lost him once. "Hurry," she said helplessly, continuing to dig. And just when she thought she'd never find it, just when she'd given up hope that it was no longer here, Abby's fingernails scraped against the top of what felt like metal.

Her heart raced even faster as she pulled handfuls of mud from the hole. Abby's eyes widened at the sight of the dark box she'd finally found.

"Yes," she said breathlessly as she dug faster, scraping her fingertips around the edges and corner of the box to gouge deeper into the dirt around it enough to finally pull it up from the ground. "Yes!" she said, falling back exhausted and clutching the precious box to her chest. Abby sobbed in the rain like a baby, filled with joy and sorrow that she'd finally found what had been buried deep for all these years.

You Get What You Give

HER FATHER WASN'T A DRUG dealer. He was a businessman. Langston Riley wasn't an innocent man. He just wasn't guilty of the crime he was convicted of.

"We're really going to miss you around here," Dave Morris, her boss, said somberly, standing in the doorway of her office.

Robin continued packing her things. "Well, my job is done, Dave," she said, smiling. "Time to move on to bigger and better things."

He smiled in return. "If you ever need recommendations or a reference, I'll do a singing telegram on your behalf if you think it'd help."

"Thanks," she said sincerely. "I appreciate that."

"So, what are you plans?"

She shrugged. "Immediate plans include Saint Croix. After that?" She shrugged. "I'm thinking about teaching or maybe starting my own practice or both."

"You'll be great no matter what you decide," he said before hugging her and finally leaving.

Robin stared out of the window of her high-rise apartment, watching the rain fall. Gradually, the numbness she'd felt was starting to dissipate. A slow, boiling rage still burned within her. This whole ordeal with Jordan had awakened demons inside her that she never knew were there. Whether she'd ever be able to lay them to rest again, was a question she couldn't answer. Would she get over him? Was she over him? And what was wrong with her that she'd let her desire for him push her to crazed levels like that?

She hadn't seen or spoken to Jordan since he'd dropped the bombshell about Langston Riley nearly a week ago. After getting over the initial shock of what he had told her, Robin couldn't help accepting the fact that karma didn't give a damn who you were. If you owed, then it came for you. Until the other night, she thought she'd managed to escape it. He knew how to get down and dirty, though. Of course, she wasn't surprised. Any man who could cover up murder had to be diabolical, and Jordan certainly was.

What she had on him could destroy him, his empire, his life. Robin could call his bluff and snatch his freedom from him and all his luxuries with a simple phone call, and the thought had crossed her mind several times to do just that. But then Jordan could break her heart more than he already had. She adored her parents and had always been Daddy's little girl.

She'd found out about the drug trafficking by accident. Robin had a reporter friend who'd gotten wind of the feds closing in on a massive drug ring that led back to Newark. She'd mentioned that they were looking at some pharmaceutical company that they suspected might be involved somehow. Her father had tried to keep his financial woes from her, but Robin wasn't stupid. Mon-Clair Pharmaceuticals had been floundering under the weight of lawsuits for years. She put two and two together, then confronted her father on the golf course of his country club of all places.

"I need to know the truth, Daddy," she demanded from him. "I need to know what you're involved in."

"No," he said sternly. "You need to stay out of it. My business is not your business, Robin. I've told you that before."

"It is my business when the feds are sniffing around, trying to build a case around you. This is serious, Daddy. If they find out that you're connected to this drug ring in any way, you could go to prison, and Mom would lose everything. Do you want that?"

Of course he didn't. It took some prodding and honest and open talk between them for Robin to understand just how deeply he was involved. He'd stopped selling the heart drug he'd become known for.

"You know people, who know people, who know those people," he explained gravely over drinks after they cut their golf game short. "I needed to settle those lawsuits, baby girl. The business was dying a long, slow, painful death, and I needed to get out from under it. This was the quickest, easiest way to do it. And no one's batted an eye. The suits have been settled, and I've kept the business running as usual. I've even got detailed records of acquisitions and sales."

"Fabricated," she muttered, emotionless.

"But you'd never know it from looking at them."

For the first time in her life, she saw shame in her father's eyes.

"We have to do something if we want to divert the interest from MonClair, Daddy," she explained. "And we have to do it quick."

Langston Riley was just a middleman. He had been distributing empty boxes to fake addresses for MonClair for well over a year. It was Robin's idea to plant the drugs in his warehouse. And it was Robin who'd made the call, anonymously, to the police. Blaine Stevens, her friend and cocounsel, was paid enough money to live on for the rest of her life to keep her mouth shut. Two months after Langston began serving his sentence, he was murdered by another inmate. Shortly after that, Robin's father retired.

Jordan Gatewood had proven one hell of a point. That he was absolutely not capable of loving Robin and that he was determined, at all costs, not to marry her. It was difficult to ignore the pain of that realization. Robin's ego, of course, had gotten the best of her, and she'd made a complete and utter fool of herself over that man. She'd dirtied herself with him and diminished herself over him. She was almost another Claire. Robin couldn't help wondering if she might've found herself with a gun to her head in a few years of being Mrs. Jordan Gatewood. Or his.

Her father's life was on the line. That was enough of a threat for Robin to dismiss her own selfish desires for revenge against Jordan. Still, in the back of her mind, she couldn't help but wonder if he'd taken liberties with the details of the story he'd told her about gun traffickers the way she'd taken liberties with filling in the blanks surrounding Lonnie Adebayo's murder. Robin smiled slightly at the thought.

When I See You

STARTING UP A BRAND-NEW division had occupied Jordan's time from sunup until he closed his eyes to sleep at night, and even then, he dreamed about all the work that needed to be done. Jordan was being pulled in a hundred different directions, but he relished it. This endeavor was an uncharted chapter for Gatewood Industries, and no one was more excited about it than he was.

He was being touted now as America's newest billionaire and the richest black man in the country. Jordan hadn't had time to check his net worth lately, and honestly, he really didn't give a damn. Money was never the drive behind his work ethic. It was a by-product, but he'd been driven to be the best his whole life. It was his nature. If Jordan had been fated to collect garbage as a career, he'd have worked his ass off to be the best garbage collector in the business.

"Jennifer," he said to his executive assistant as he passed her on the way to his office after leaving another meeting. "Call down and get me a sandwich, will you?"

"Yes, sir. Turkey and cheese?"

"That's fine."

Jordan had half an hour to check e-mails and wolf down lunch before heading to his next meeting. He'd just powered up his laptop when his cell phone rang.

"Abby?" he asked, stunned.

Jordan hadn't spoken to her in months, and after leaving several messages for her and not having any of them returned, and making a trip to the house in Blink, only to find that she'd moved, he had come to accept the fact that he would never speak to her or see her again.

"Hey," she said sweetly. He released a quiet sigh at the sound of that one word. "Is this a bad time?"

"No. No." There was no bad time for her. His heart raced.

After a brief pause, Abby finally asked him, "How've you been?"

There were about a million different answers to that question, but he opted for the simplest. "Busy. How've you been?"

Jennifer showed up in his office with his sandwich, but Jordan wasn't hungry all of a sudden.

"Same. Um, I was wondering if you might have some time to meet soon?"

She wanted to see him? Jordan's heart felt like it had jumped up into his throat. "Sure, Abby. I'm . . . is everything all right?" he asked, skeptical.

There was something in her tone that left him feeling slightly unsettled.

"It's fine, Jordan. I just, um, came across something that I thought you might like to see. It's about your father."

It was hard for him not to give in to feeling a little disappointed. He'd hoped she'd wanted to see him about him, them.

"I think it'll clear up some questions you might have had. Maybe even give you some closure," she said sympathetically.

But would it give him closure from her?

"I know you're busy," she continued. "I wouldn't ask if I didn't think it was important."

Jordan sighed. "I can make some time Saturday morning."

"That'll be fine. Say around ten? Or is that too early?"

"Ten's fine, Abby."

She'd cut her hair.

Abby nervously ran her hand across the short crop of hair she had left. It was practically cut down to the scalp.

"It's kinda drastic," she humbly explained. "But I sorta like it."

Surprisingly, he liked it, too. Abby's beautiful eyes, high cheekbones, and lovely lips seemed even more impactful without all that hair to hide behind. She wore a denim jacket over a simple knit dress that stopped midway on her thighs, and brown cowboy boots.

"You look beautiful," he said sincerely.

She smiled.

The house was practically empty. All that was left was Abby's small dining table and one chair. She left him standing in the living room while she disappeared into the room she'd used as her office and came out a few moments later carrying a rusted lockbox. Abby motioned for Jordan to sit down in the chair at the table. And then she reluctantly took the only seat left—his lap. Jordan felt as if he'd died and gone to heaven having her this close to him again. He relished the weight of her, the scent of her, and her touch.

"I found this buried in the backyard," she softly began to explain. Abby slowly raised the lid. "Ida Green buried it before she died, Jordan."

Jordan leaned forward to get a closer look at its contents. On top was a small, brown spiral notebook. Abby pulled it out first and then flipped it open.

"She didn't really journal in the true sense of the word," she explained. "But I think that sometimes her emotions got the best of her, and she had to write them down just to try to make sense of them."

Abby flipped through a few pages, stopped at a particular one, and cleared her throat. "'I don't like doing this,'" she read. "'And I told him, but he won't listen.'" She glanced quickly at Jordan. "'I told him to let me go. Reminded him that he had a wife. But then he said that she wouldn't let him go.'"

Jordan sat motionless as Abby read, probably sounding a lot like Ida would've sounded if she were alive to say these words.

She flipped through several more pages, and started to read again. "'I'm not moving closer to Dallas. Blink is my home, and I'm staying right here. He thinks it's because I'm scared of big cities. I'm not scared. I just don't like them. Besides, if he insists on us being together, then he has to accept the fact that when he comes here, he's not rich and important like he is when he's home. He's just Julian. And that's all.'" She turned the page. "'And I'm just Ida. That's all I've ever been or wanted to be. When he's here, everything is simple and easy. That's the way I like it. I told him that. He said he understood.'"

Just Julian. All this time, Jordan and probably a whole lot of other people thought Julian Gatewood had been keeping Ida Green on the side like some pet. But maybe she'd kept him, Jordan concluded. It was starting to make sense. Julian Gatewood was a warrior in Dallas. But he had to leave his armor at the door when he walked into her house. He loved her enough to make himself small enough to fit inside this place, to fit inside the confines of her life.

Abby continued to one more passage. "'He came in mad today. Mad because she won't let him do what he feels needs to be done with the boy.'" She glanced at Jordan. "'She coddles him too much, according to Julian. She won't let Julian raise him as his son, because she thinks he's too hard on him. But he says that he has to be. The boy will run his business, and he has to be ready. I don't know what that means. Julian's firm. He thinks everybody else ought to be like him, steadfast. That's what he calls it. Oh, and disciplined. I just look at him and smile when he says it, because he knows all that kind of talk don't faze me. He usually changes the subject and pulls me onto his lap or something, and I run my fingers through his hair and he closes his eyes and moans. And then I kiss him. And he holds me so tight sometimes I can't even breathe, but I don't mind. I would marry him if I could. But I'd stay in this house. He comes here to rest. So, that's why I stay.'"

Abby took a deep breath and then finally closed the notebook and set it on the table next to the open box. "Maybe he wanted to be there for you, Jordan," she said softly. "He just didn't know how."

Jordan sat in silence, trying to put everything he'd just heard into context. Ida Green was filling in blanks about his father's life here in Blink and their relationship. Hearing those words was so surreal, but they painted a clearer picture of the man his father was and of the love he obviously felt for this woman.

Abby reached into the box again and pulled out a torn photograph. "Is that him?"

Jordan nodded. It was Julian Gatewood, thirty years ago. His eyes bright and shining, his smile broad. He wore his signature white button-down, monogrammed on his left cuff. Abby reached inside the box and pulled out the torn picture of Ida and held it up next to the one Jordan held. The two pieces fit perfectly, and a chill ran up his spine. She pulled two gold rings from that box, tied together with a thin, red ribbon, and then she pulled out a note card.

"It's from him to her," she said, unfolding it. Abby swallowed. "It says . . ." Her voice cracked, and for the first time, he realized that she had been crying. "'Home is not a place, Ida.'" Abby paused. "'Home is you.' Signed, JG." Her voice trailed off, and Abby turned and wrapped her arms around Jordan. "This is what he needed to remember, Jordan," she whispered in his ear. "He had forgotten, and he'd lost his way in this house, and she stayed to try to lead him home."

Jordan held Abby so tightly he feared he might break her. Jordan had been lost, too. His whole life he'd been looking for home. And in his death, his father had told him where to find it.

"I won't live my life without you, Abby," he said, raising her chin so that he could look into her eyes. "I can't do it," he declared with more conviction than he'd ever felt for anything in his life. "We were meant to be. I have no doubts about that. You belong with me."

She smiled and nodded and whispered, "I know."

Abby wrapped her arms around him, and Jordan closed his eyes and sighed. Yes. He understood the meaning behind the note his father had written to Ida. *Home.* Wherever Abby was, that's where Jordan needed to be.

He slowly opened his eyes and stared down the corridor leading to the bedroom in time to see his father looking over his shoulder back at Jordan, as Ida held his hand and led him inside the room. They faded away like mist.

Still

HE COULD NEVER GET enough of the pillow-soft lips of Ida
Green. Julian moaned as he savored the flavor of this beautiful
woman, his woman, his life, his heart and soul.

"I think that I will spend forever with you, Ida Green." Julian
rolled onto the bed next to her and tenderly pulled her into his
arms.

Ida rested her head on his chest. "That's a long time, Julian
Gatewood."

He sighed. "Not long enough, sugah. Not even close."